DARK TITAN
JOURNEY

SANCTIONED CATASTROPHE

THOMAS A. WATSON

A PERMUTED PRESS BOOK

ISBN: 978-1-68261-165-4
ISBN (eBook): 978-1-61868-734-0

Dark Titan Journey:
Sanctioned Catastrophe
Dark Titan Book One

Edited by Monique Happy Editorial Services
www.moniquehappy.com

Cover Art by Christian Bentulan

Permuted Press, LLC
permutedpress.com

Published in the United States of America

Please visit Thomas A. Watson's Author Page on Facebook

CHAPTER 1

Struggling out of deep sleep, Nathan thought he heard an alarm. As his brain slowly came back online, he heard a very annoying 'ting-aling-aling.' Slowly cracking his eyes and looking over at the hotel nightstand, he saw the light going off on the phone as it rang. Dragging his body over to the side of the bed, Nathan fumbled with the receiver, pulling it to his face. Looking at the clock on the nightstand he saw it was 4:11 a.m.

Before the receiver was even to his mouth, Nathan blurted out, "The damn building better be on fire."

"Dude, what are you still doing there? You told me you were leaving!" a male voice shouted.

Nathan sat up, blinking sleep out of his eyes as his brain notified him that it was not operational yet and needed more time. "Tim?" he asked into the phone.

"Yeah, it's me."

Looking back at the clock to confirm he saw the right time, Nathan asked, "You do know what time it is here right?" He glanced over as the blanket moved on the other side of the bed.

"Yeah, it's just after one a.m. here, but back to the question: I thought you were leaving," Tim said.

Letting out a yawn, Nathan stretched out. "I'm leaving today, Tim, but I got in contact with the man who owns the gun store and he's going to meet me there at six a.m."

"You have enough shit now, just leave, Nathan. If you don't have it, one of the others do, and if they don't, we don't need it," Tim snapped.

"Dude, you're worse than a wife," Nathan popped off.

"Something is wrong, Nathan, and you're too far away from home," Tim told him.

"Tim, I talked to the owner of the store yesterday after I talked to you. I really want to see what he has. It's one of the biggest gun stores in the south," Nathan replied, wanting Tim to understand.

Tim let out a sigh. "How long do you think it will take you there?" he asked.

The bed shook as the blankets moved again on the other side of the bed. "It shouldn't take long, Tim," Nathan told him.

"I know you when you get in any mega store, but a gun store? You could be there all day. You really need to head back home," Tim replied, almost whining.

"What has got you so riled up?" Nathan asked, pulling the blankets off the other side of the bed to reveal his German Shepherd, Ares. Ares lifted his head up, looked at him, then laid back down.

"I didn't want to say much on the cellphone yesterday, but we're seeing weird shit on the web. The government has called an alert for all forces for this weekend, even those overseas," Tim told him.

Nathan reached over and rubbed Ares' head. "Oh damn, the world is ending now," he replied sarcastically.

Tim groaned. "I really don't like talking to you when you first wake up. You're worse than Sherry."

"Don't you even compare me to your wife," Nathan shot back.

Laughing at that, Tim said, "Hey she's worried as well, and if you don't start heading home I'm going to let her hound you."

"They've been running alerts for a long time, Tim, so no need to get your panties in a wad," Nathan said as he pulled the pillow out from under Ares' head. Letting out a moan, Ares put his paws over his muzzle.

"Not all branches. The Reserve, DHS, FBI, BATFE and all the other alphabet soup agencies. Those stationed overseas are to move toward a disembarkation point for the exercise. The White House said they want to know how long it would take to move these forces," Tim replied.

Hearing the panic in Tim's voice, Nathan started laughing. "Your tinfoil hat is on too tight," he replied.

"Hey, Rusty is calling an alert for the group!" Tim barked.

"Tim, Rusty wanted to call an alert for the group when Twinkies weren't on the market anymore. He was certain it was a plot," Nathan replied.

"Hey, he likes his Twinkies," Tim answered.

"It's just an exercise," Nathan said as Ares sat up, looking at him. With the look on Ares' face, Nathan knew Ares wanted to go back to sleep.

"Nathan, there's more. The Nuclear Regulatory Commission ordered all nuclear power plants to start the turn-off phase and have it completed by Sunday. Is that also part of an exercise?" Tim replied.

Shaking his head, Nathan said, "Tim, I think you're just a little too paranoid."

"This coming from the man who says the Bilderberg group is real," Tim answered.

"Hey, they are real!" Nathan shouted, and Ares just plopped down on his stomach, making the bed bounce.

"Nathan, I have a bad gut feeling on this," Tim said.

Letting out a long puff of air, Nathan said, "Okay Tim, I'll be on the road today."

"Thank you, Nathan," Tim answered with relief.

Nathan smiled to himself. "If something happens, stay with the plans, alright? Why don't you and Sherry stay at the house until this is over," Nathan offered.

"Okay. We'll move over and stay in the guest room. We have all our stuff packed already," Tim told him. Nathan was shocked that Tim agreed so fast, and then the last sentence hit him.

"You're packed?" Nathan asked.

"Yeah, Sherry packed up after I talked to you yesterday," Tim said.

That alarmed Nathan some. Tim might be the husband in that marriage, but Sherry was the boss and she very rarely got shook up. You might say Tim wore the pants, but Sherry picked them out.

"Tim, it's Friday. I will see you early Sunday morning," Nathan replied.

"Thank you, Nathan, I'll tell Sherry. She's feeding the baby," Tim told him.

"How is little Nolan doing?" Nathan asked.

"Great, all he does is yell, eat, pee, and poop," Tim answered.

Laughing, Nathan answered, "That's what all babies do."

"Yes, so everyone keeps telling me," Tim answered.

"I'll call you when I get on the road," Nathan said, standing up.

"Cool, be careful," Tim said.

"Will do." Nathan hung up. Then he looked over at Ares. "Will you get up, lazy bones, we have to get ready," he said.

Ares sat up on the bed. "Awwe-shhff," he whined as he yawned, ending with a puff of air. Nathan gave him a hug and moved to the bathroom, knowing if he lay back down he wouldn't wake back up in thirty minutes.

Nathan had met Tim when Nathan was an instructor at the police academy five years before, and Tim was going through P.O.S.T. (Police Officer Standards and Training) certification. They were both reserve officers for the Kooteai and Shoshone Sheriff departments in Idaho. For his primary job, Tim worked construction and logging, while his wife was studying to be an accountant. They both lived on Nathan's farm outside of Coeur d'Alene in his guesthouse.

When Nathan met Tim, he'd instantly liked the kid, and to Nathan, Tim was a kid. Nathan was thirty-eight and Tim was twenty-five. Tim may have been young but was very mature for his age, besides being a good friend. What Nathan didn't know was that Tim's father and mother were drunks, and Tim was determined to make something of himself.

Three years ago, when Nathan had invited them out to his house to eat, he'd offered to let them stay in the two-bedroom guesthouse. They were living in some apartments in town, fighting to make ends meet. Tim at first refused, thinking it was a handout, but Nathan told him if they moved out there they had to help with the farm. The farm was only fifty acres but Nathan had chickens, rabbits, horses, cows, greenhouses, and gardens. It was a farm, albeit a small one, but with only Nathan running it, at the end of the day the farm felt like a plantation.

Tim finally agreed and to Nathan it was a match made in heaven. He no longer needed to pay someone to watch over the place as he traveled around the country taking classes or thirteen-week nursing contracts. Nurses made fair money but travel nurses made *good* money, and if you were single it was great money.

For the past year, Nathan had been a part-time ER nurse at the hospital in town. He didn't make as much money, but that was okay. The farm had been paid off after Nathan's parents died. Thinking about his parents, Nathan fought back the grief.

It had been over twenty years ago but it still hurt. He'd been two weeks from his eighteenth birthday and a senior in high school when a drunk driver hit them head on, killing both instantly. Thankfully a

judge ruled Nathan competent and an adult so the state didn't provide an administrator for the estate.

His dad had been a retired Special Forces sergeant major and Nathan received those benefits for ten more years. Nathan's mother had been a nurse and her benefits were more than his dad's. The insurance paid off the farm and all bills, leaving a lot left over.

Nathan's father had made him promise not to join the military and reluctantly Nathan had agreed. He was pretty sure if his father would've lived, he would have joined anyway, but since his death Nathan just couldn't break that promise. That was why he became a nurse, to follow in his mother's footsteps.

In all reality, he really liked being a nurse, but wanted to do more. When he was twenty-one he joined the Sheriff's Department as a reserve deputy. Two years later, Nathan joined the Special Response Team (SRT), most commonly referred to as SWAT.

Nathan walked into the bathroom and turned on the shower. Walking back into the room, he saw Ares had burrowed back under the covers. In a moment of weakness, he left Ares alone. Since the death of his parents, Nathan had always had a German Shepherd. When they were five years old he would breed them and take the male pick of the litter so he would always have one in his life. Ares' father, Apollo, was at the farm with Tim and Sherry.

Ares was two and a half and was massive for a German Shepherd, weighing one hundred and eighteen pounds of solid muscle. He was a certified police-trained attack dog like Apollo, but Ares had more personality and intelligence than any other dog Nathan had ever owned. Apollo would just do what he was told like his father before him, but Ares wanted to play, a lot. Not to say Ares was a bad dog, but he definitely had his own personality.

Nathan had been in Georgia for five days for a nursing conference to get his education points for the year. It was only March, but he wanted them out of the way now. After the conference, he had planned on visiting several large gun and surplus stores in the area, and since he had a Federal Firearms License (FFL), he wouldn't have to wait for any guns he bought. Now, because of Tim's tight tinfoil hat, he was just going to visit one and then head home.

After his shower, Nathan stood at the end of the bed and ripped off the blankets. "Get up, lazy bones," Nathan said, looking down at Ares who was feigning sleep. "I know you're awake, Ares, your eyes were just cracked," he said. Ares rolled over on his stomach in a bowing position.

"No, begging won't change that we have to get up," Nathan told him, and Ares put his paws over his face. "You're turning into a sissy," Nathan said, turning around to get dressed. "If you don't get up, you don't eat."

Hearing 'eat,' Ares jumped off the bed and headed to the door. "We have to get our stuff first, moron," Nathan said, pulling on his shirt. Ares narrowed his eyes and lunged toward Nathan. Nathan, thinking Ares was fixing to tackle him, turned his body in a side stance.

Before reaching Nathan, Ares lowered his head down and grabbed one of his penny loafers and bounced onto the bed. "Those shoes cost two hundred dollars, buddy boy," Nathan said, moving toward him. Reaching out to take the shoe out of Ares' mouth, Nathan glared at him. Just as his hand touched the shoe, Ares bounced off the bed.

"Damn it, Ares, give that back!" Nathan snapped, jumping up and running across the bed. Ares took off around the room, playing 'keep the shoe away from Daddy.' Nathan spent the next five minutes retrieving his shoe before they were finally ready to hit the road.

CHAPTER 2

Nathan had arrived at the gun store (which had also been a police supply store) thirty minutes early to find the owner opening up. When Nathan walked inside, he'd felt like a kid in a candy shop. He'd wanted to stay for a long time and probably would've if Tim and Sherry hadn't called him every thirty minutes.

Leaving Atlanta, Nathan looked in the rearview mirror to see Ares looking at him from the back of the Suburban, his head cocked. "No, you're not getting another hamburger," Nathan said, and Ares groaned, flopping down in the back seat. Nathan chuckled, then looked at the passenger seat where he'd placed the box for his new laser and flashlight for his M-4. The laser could fire green or IR (infrared) and the light was 500 lumens. Nathan reached over to open the box just as Ares barked at him, causing Nathan to jerk the steering wheel.

"Stop that, damn it, you scared the shit out of me!" Nathan snapped. Ares looked up at him with his head cocked to the side, as if he were saying, 'Keep your eyes on the road idiot.' Nathan smiled at Ares, then glanced at the bags of clothes he had bought. They were the new MultiCam pants and shirts with the knee and elbow pads built in. He had wanted some for a long time, but before he spent two hundred dollars on a pair of pants he wanted to try them on. Sure, the khakis he had on now were that much, but he'd tried them on first.

After trying on the new uniform, Nathan bought three sets of them. Then he picked up some more boots, another tactical flashlight, a switchblade, a case of MREs, a new custom 1911 high capacity, and a few other things. He just loved .45 caliber handguns. The owner of the store was a little sad to see Nathan leave after seeing him drop over six grand on his credit card, and he could tell Nathan wanted more. One secret Nathan held close was that he loved to shop, even for clothes. He didn't care. Whether it was online or in a store, he enjoyed it, but had to pace his spending. He wasn't rich but he was very well off. To Nathan, rich meant you could buy what you wanted all the time.

Looking over again at the passenger seat, he spied a tater tot hiding in the bottom of the drive-thru bag. Popping it in his mouth, he emptied his Route Forty-Four cherry-limeade. Hearing a whine behind him, Nathan said, "Hey, you don't like tater tots so pipe down. You ate a hamburger and a hot dog." Leaning forward, he adjusted the bullet-proof vest he was wearing so it wouldn't keep hitting everything he had on his belt.

"Woof," Ares barked. Nathan didn't know if that meant "more" or what, so he just ignored him. Hearing his phone ring, Nathan hit his Bluetooth ear piece.

"Hello Tim, I'm on the road," Nathan said.

"About time," Tim shot back.

"You'd think I'm married to both you and Sherry the way you guys bug me," Nathan told him.

Tim didn't answer for a second, then replied, "Sherry said we can go see the justice of the peace when you get here."

"No, thank you," Nathan replied, smiling.

"So you're really on the road?" Tim asked.

Nathan picked up his cellphone and hit video. "Look," he said, aiming the phone out the front window. Then he pointed it in the passenger seat. "I have ten energy drinks," he said, mounting the phone on the carrier on the dashboard.

"Don't drink them too fast or you'll get heart palpitations again," Tim warned.

"Hey, I'm the nurse here," Nathan snapped.

"I'm just saying," Tim said. "I see from you panning the camera around you bought a ton of shit," he added.

"I would've bought more, but two people kept bugging the shit out of me," Nathan replied.

"Hey brother, I'm sorry but we really think something's up. Rusty is already at the compound with his family. Billy and Aidan are taking their families up tomorrow," Tim told him.

Rusty, Billy, and Aidan, along with their families, were the closest thing Nathan had as family, not including Tim, Sherry, and Nolan. Hearing that made Nathan sit up straight. "What has you guys so worked up?" he asked.

"I'm sending you an e-mail with an attachment. I should've sent it to you this morning, but with everyone calling me to get you home, I forgot," Tim replied.

"So what of the others in the group?" Nathan asked. The group was twenty-two families strong that had formed an LLC and bought a thousand acres on the northern Idaho-Montana border. They used it for a hunting ranch, but it was really their bug-out area. Rusty was the first one asked to join eight years ago; then he asked if Billy, Aidan, and Nathan could join. Once they were voted in, they each were allowed to build structures on the land. Tim and Sherry were part of the group, but they were classified as Nathan's family and stayed with him at his house at the compound.

Nathan stared at Tim on the screen, then looked up at the road. Tim had close-cropped brown hair and a very boyish face, but was stocky as an ox. "The others that aren't at the compound now are all getting ready to roll," Tim told him.

"Everyone?" Nathan asked in surprise.

"Yeah," Tim replied with a serious expression.

"Okay, if something happens, make sure you follow the plan. Wait for a day if you can before bugging out," Nathan told him.

"We will, just get back here," Tim replied. "We're in your house now and I pulled my truck into your empty garage slot."

"That's cool, brother, and if you leave, remember to get all my shit," Nathan said.

"We already pulled your stuff out in the living room. I'm not emptying the gun safes till we have to leave," Tim said.

"When did you hear all this that got you all fired up?" Nathan asked.

"An hour before I called you yesterday afternoon," Tim told him. "Then everyone keeps sending me more stuff to reaffirm it. I just don't want to say more over a cellphone," he added.

"You really need to change your tinfoil hat," Nathan replied.

Tim shook his head on the screen. "When you stop for gas, read what I sent, then say that," he said.

Shaking his head, Nathan changed the subject. "Has Patrice called?"

Suddenly Tim was pushed out of the phone's screen. In his place was a very cute, short-haired brunette. "Your bimbo hasn't called here or us," she told him. Hearing Sherry, Ares started barking.

"I'm talking, Ares, knock it off!" Nathan shouted over his shoulder. "Sherry, she's not a bimbo. Patrice has a bachelor's degree," he added.

"In cosmetology. I can have a better conversation with the chair she sits in than her," Sherry told him.

Nathan laughed at her. "Sherry, she does make pretty good money."

"She models women's lingerie. To listen to her trying to explain what she does, it sounds like she's trying to find the cure for cancer," Sherry said disparagingly. "I'm actually surprised she has the intelligence to get mad over something," she added.

"Well, if she calls the house, tell her I'll be home Sunday," Nathan replied as Tim joined Sherry in front of the camera.

"I wish you would've left yesterday," Tim said.

"Shit, I want to go back to that gun store. He had an M-60 for sale," Nathan told him.

Tim and Sherry both shook their heads as Tim replied, "You have one already."

"Well I could've had another one," Nathan answered, bobbing his head from side to side.

"Please get home as quickly and safely as you can," Sherry urged him.

"I will," Nathan promised. "I'm stopping to let out the gallon of soda I drank and top off the tank, then I'll not stop until I have to get more gas."

Sherry glared at him over the little screen. "Oh, you can stop and pee, but when we go with you, I have to hold it," she snapped.

"I don't have an empty bottle and Ares wants something else to eat. I had to feed him all of his emergency food," Nathan told her.

"You better be nice to Ares," she threatened. Ares heard her say his name and stuck his head between the front seats, looking for Sherry. "Hey Ares, you take care of Nathan and hurry home," she said, kissing the screen. Ares barked and started licking the phone on the dashboard.

"Damn it Ares, get in the back. This is my area, that's yours!" Nathan yelled, pushing Ares back. Tim and Sherry laughed as they watched Nathan struggle with the big dog.

"We'll call you later today to check on you," Tim said when Ares finally moved to the back.

Nathan looked at the screen and could see worry on both of their faces. "Guys, I'll get home. If something happens, just do like we've practiced. You both know what to do. Just remember to stay safe," Nathan told them. "Don't worry. When I get home we can pick on Rusty for scaring everyone," he added, trying to break the tension.

Tim smiled but it didn't reach his eyes. "Okay Nathan, be careful, we miss you," he said.

"Miss you too, guys," Nathan said.

"We love you," Sherry said, then Tim hung up.

"Me too, guys," Nathan said as the screen went blank. His phone's screen lit up, saying he had new mail. Tapping the screen, he opened it and told it to download the attachment. As it downloaded, he replayed the conversation in his head. Both Tim and Sherry seemed worried, but Nathan couldn't dream of anything that could upset them like this. Finally he just blew it off as them being young.

Then he thought about the rest of the group. They were all near his age or older and they were getting ready or had already bugged out. The group was all composed of professionals or what Nathan called ordinary people that were relatively successful in life. They were not supremacists; they had two black families, three Hispanic and two Asian families in the group. The group could be called survivalists, but Nathan just preferred to think of them as prepared.

When Rusty asked him to join, Nathan thought he was crazy. Then he listened and realized he was already doing what the group was doing. He just did it at home. The group could provide a place to run to if something happened. Plus the area where the compound was at had some choice hunting and fishing areas, not that that was a factor in Nathan's choice to join. Well, it might have had a little to do with it.

Nathan's bladder reminded him it was past capacity and he noticed signs coming up on the Interstate. The first let him know Alabama was twelve miles ahead, and the next told him a truck stop was at the next exit.

Pulling off the next exit and heading down the ramp, Nathan didn't see the truck stop but a sign pointed south. Driving under the Interstate, his bladder informed him it was getting close to taking emergency measures. Finally, Nathan saw the station a mile down the road. It was a pretty large truck stop but there were only a few trucks parked at it, and several cars in the parking lot. He looked at the phone and noticed it was just after eleven a.m.

Pulling in, he eased up to a pump and jumped out. Ares started barking letting him know he had to go as well. Grumbling, Nathan opened the door and Ares bounded out, heading for the grass. Taking a card out of his wallet, Nathan swiped it on the pump. Grabbing the nozzle, he opened the tank and started filling it up. With both forty-gallon tanks full, he could go twelve hundred miles and figured he wouldn't have to stop again till he hit Kansas. He just had to get a bottle to take a whiz in.

Ares came running over as the pump stopped. Nathan put up the nozzle and opened the door for Ares. Seeing his phone on the dash, he grabbed it and threw it in his new tote bag in the passenger seat and closed the bag. Not that he was worried about someone stealing it with Ares in the truck, but he didn't want Ares to pull an arm off when they tried it. Lowering the driver's window halfway, Nathan closed the door and hit the alarm button, then speed walked toward the store.

The young girl at the counter looked up. She had seen that walk many times. When the man walked inside, she looked him over. The measuring tape on the door frame told her he was just over six-foot-two. He was clean shaven with broad shoulders and a muscular appearance, and thick, light brown hair that went just past his shoulders. Stopping just inside the door, he looked over at her, and even with his dark sunglasses on she could tell he was cute. As the man drew a breath, she pointed to the back of the store.

Nathan smiled upon seeing the restroom sign. The small clerk giggled as he walked by really fast. *Well at least she knew what I needed,* Nathan thought. Walking in the men's room, he saw the urinals and sighed. Making sure the 1911 he was wearing with an inside-the-waistband holster and the extra magazines and flashlight didn't pull his pants down, he sighed as relief hit him.

If I'm fixing to do a marathon driving run, I'm taking some of this shit off my belt, he thought as his bladder told him it was nowhere near done.

Nathan started running through drink bottles that he could use as a urinal when the lights in the bathroom went off.

Standing there in the dark as his bladder finished, Nathan thought of an old song: 'Shot in the Dark,' and laughed. Buttoning back up, he wondered why some kind of emergency light hadn't come on. Reaching for his flashlight, he turned it on, washed his hands and looked in the mirror. Then he noticed his Bluetooth earpiece wasn't blinking. Taking it off, he pressed the button to turn it on but nothing happened.

"I bought the good one so this wouldn't happen," he groused, putting it in his pocket. Grabbing his flashlight, he headed out the door to find the only light was that coming in through the windows at the front and side of the store. Putting his light back in its holster, he noticed the young clerk pushing buttons on her cellphone. On the other side of the store a security guard was taking his cellphone apart. "Weird," Nathan said, walking over to the windows.

Outside he saw one of the semis had stopped on the road; then he looked across the road to a little strip mall with four stores. In the middle of the parking lot, a man had the hood up on his car looking at the engine. With growing uneasiness, Nathan stepped outside and the first thing he noticed was how quiet it was. The Interstate was only a mile away but he couldn't hear any vehicles. He lifted his arm up and looked at his watch to find it dead. Closing his eyes, he said a silent prayer as he pulled out his keys.

He hit the automatic start and nothing happened. Then he hit the button to disarm the alarm and again nothing happened. Walking over, he could hear Ares barking in an alarmed tone. Unlocking the door, he sat down, took off his sunglasses and put the key in the ignition. No chime came on and nothing happened when he turned the key.

Fear gripping his stomach, Nathan climbed out and looked up. "Oh shit!" he yelled out.

CHAPTER 3

Day 1

Putting his hands over his face, Nathan fought the urge to start cussing and crying. Then he heard a humming noise, which rapidly grew louder. Nathan looked around for the source, then looked up. The power lines running along the side of the road were humming.

Nathan looked up in the sky and didn't see anything out of the ordinary. "Well I would've missed the explosion in space," he said out loud. Then a thunderous KA-BOOM shattered the quiet. Nathan crouched defensively as his right hand went for his pistol. Looking at the power pole at the front of the store on the road, he saw four transformers were in flames. Then he heard more explosions in the distance and the transformer for the small strip mall exploded.

"This is impossible," Nathan said, standing up. Just then the florescent lights on the awning started glowing.

Turning around, he walked over to his truck and grabbed his sunglasses. "Ares, come," he said and walked to the back of the parking lot. Looking across the field, he could see the Interstate and vehicles stopped everywhere. Then he started hearing a screeching sound in the air. Looking up, he didn't see anything, but when he turned around he could see a big jumbo jet falling out of the sky toward the east.

"Damn," he said in shock, watching the plane plummet.

The plane hit the ground about five miles away with a loud boom and Nathan felt the earth shake through the soles of his shoes. Panicked, he spun around, searching the sky for more planes. Particularly ones heading toward him. Off to the north he saw two more, but they were way off. He saw several more coming down in the east. Several booms rolled in over the next few minutes as Nathan just stood there in disbelief, watching as planes rained down.

Then he noticed another humming sound, but much fainter than the ones from the power lines. Looking around, he edged over to the field and stopped, noticing it was getting louder. Looking down, he traced the sound as coming from the three strands of barb wire on the fence. Looking out across the field, he figured it was miles of barb wire and stepped back. Ares edged closer to the fence and Nathan yelled, "Ares, back!"

Ares jumped and started looking around to see who was attacking them, and then looked up at Nathan. "Boy, if you piss on that fence your goober will get fried and so will you," Nathan said, pointing down at the ground beside him. Ares walked over and sat down next to him.

"I've never read anything about an EMP that could release this much energy," Nathan said to himself. "Then again, the assholes who said it wouldn't hurt your car were full of shit. Yeah, you listened to a government-run study, idiot," he answered himself.

He started pacing the parking lot, arguing with himself. Finally he looked up, then down at Ares. "Okay, guard the truck. I'm going to get us some stuff," he told his dog.

Ares barked and ran over to the Suburban. Nathan followed and pulled out his keys, hitting the unlock button, "Dumb ass," he muttered, sticking the key in the rear door and opening it. Moving bags over, he uncovered his backpack and opened a side pocket, pulling out a roll of cash. He tallied up his money and put it in his pocket.

Okay, I have close to three grand cash plus two ounces of gold and five ounces of silver in my belly band. Credit cards will be worthless soon, so let's try those first, he thought. Ares jumped in the back of the truck. Nathan left the hatch open since it was pointing directly at the store.

Walking inside, watched closely by Ares, he grabbed a shopping hand-basket and started walking the aisles. For the first time he studied the lay-out, realizing the store was actually quite large. There was a diner on the far side with a closed-off area that held poker machines, and at the back were the restrooms and showers for truckers. Throwing stuff in his basket, he studied the store aisles and saw they held a lot of food items, but also many other things mostly related to camping. In the front of the store was a gift area for souvenirs. With his first basket full, he headed to the counter and set it down. Taking out his wallet, he set a credit card on the counter and turned around, grabbing another basket.

The young girl looked at the full basket and started pulling stuff out and writing down the cost. Just then an older woman walked out from a door behind her. "I found one that works," she said, putting a calculator on the counter. "What is all this?" she asked and the young girl pointed at Nathan filling another basket. Turning around, she helped the young girl add up the stuff.

Nathan walked back over and set another basket down as the young girl looked up. "Sir, can you afford all this?" she asked.

"Young lady, I have more than enough money in the bank to cover this and could probably buy everything in this store," Nathan snapped back.

The girl looked down. "I'm sorry, sir, I was just asking," she replied.

Nathan let out a long sigh. "Miss, I'm sorry for my rude behavior. It was uncalled for. If you want I have cash to pay for that," he told her, and she looked up and smiled at him.

The woman looked up at Nathan. "Renee didn't mean anything, sir, and we can take cards for one hour if the power fails," she told him.

"I apologize, ma'am, this is just a lot to handle," Nathan said, turning around and grabbing another basket. Walking the aisles, he filled up basket number three and sat it on the counter. Then, looking at a display on the counter, he noticed Zippo lighters and watches. "I'll take two of those, fluid, flints, and the watch on the end," he said, then walked back down an aisle and grabbed two ten-pound bags of dog food.

When he put them on the counter, Renee looked at him and asked, "What's wrong with your watch? It looks expensive," she asked.

Nathan lifted up his arm so she could see it. "It is expensive but it's not working anymore," he told her. "Not after what just happened."

She looked down at her watch. "Mine works," she said.

"Mine too," the woman said, looking at her watch.

"This one has a transparent membrane on the front to gather light, and I think that's what fried it," Nathan told them as he turned around to fill another basket.

"What do you think happened?" the woman asked. He noticed she had a tag that read 'Manager' pinned to her shirt.

"Name's Nathan, Nathan Owens," Nathan told her, filling his fourth basket. "I'm not sure but I think we got hit with an EMP. I just haven't read about one that could do what this one is doing."

"Connie, Nathan," she told him. "Who do you think did it?" she asked.

Nathan shrugged his shoulders. "Have no idea," he said, setting the basket on the counter.

The young girl looked puzzled. "What's an EMP?"

Nathan looked at her and smiled grimly. "An EMP is an electromagnetic pulse, sometimes called a transient electromagnetic disturbance. They can be caused by a nuclear weapon." The girl gasped.

"Have you got a radio here?" he asked.

"Yeah, but it doesn't work," Connie told him.

Nathan looked behind the counter and saw several emergency crank radios of different brands. "Open the end of one of them, and if it's wrapped in a silver bag I'll buy it," Nathan told her. Connie opened two brands and found the third one wrapped in Mylar. "Of course it's the most expensive one," Nathan said as Renee totaled up his sale.

"Six hundred and twenty-one dollars and seventy-three cents," she told him.

"Damn," Nathan said, pointing to the credit card on the counter. Taking the radio, he pulled it out and cranked the handle. Then he turned it on only to find static. Hitting the scan button, he handed it back to Connie. "I'll be out in my truck. If you hear something let me know," he told her.

"Don't you want it?" she asked.

"I have one in my backpack but I'm not going to turn it on; I don't want people around my truck," he replied.

"Okay," she said as a man came from the diner area yelling.

"Damn it Connie, I want my money!" he bellowed. Nathan looked at the man closely as he walked over. He was clearly a bum. His body and clothes were beyond filthy and his odor preceded him by yards.

"Mel, I told you until the power comes on I can't give you anything," Connie replied in a very kind voice, Nathan thought.

"I was up to eight hundred dollars and you're going to give it to me. It might erase before the power comes back on!" he screamed.

"Mel, I'm sorry but I have to wait and you know it," she told him.

"Like hell, if you won't give me my money I'll just take stuff!" Mel hollered as the security guard walked over.

"Mel, like you have ever won on that damn machine," the security guard responded.

"Brian, don't you be startin' nothin'. I won me some money and somebody is going to give me some!" he shouted at the guard. Nathan looked at the guard, who was tall and physically big, but it was all fat. Mel may have been the smaller of the two but Nathan would put his money on him in a fight.

Shaking his head, his jowls jiggling with the movement, Brian asked, "Mel, do you want me to throw you out again?"

Mel grinned. "What you going to do, porky, call the cops?" he asked.

Brian took a step back as Connie moved to the end of the counter. "Mel, that's enough now. When the power comes on, *if* you won anything I'll give you the money," she told him.

"Listen bitch, I said give me my money!" he roared.

Getting a headache from Mel's shouting, and feeling guilty about snapping at Renee, Nathan stepped to the end of the counter. "Sir, Connie told you she'll pay you your money. Just leave her your contact information and when the power comes on she will get your receipt from the machine and pay you," Nathan told him.

"Pretty boy, I never talked at you so shut your trap!" Mel yelled at him.

"Sir, yell at me one more time and I will plant your face in this concrete floor and laugh as you bleed out," Nathan calmly told him. Brian took another step back and shock hit Mel's face.

"You can't talk to me like that," Mel said in a normal voice.

Lifting up the front of his shirt, Nathan exposed the Sheriff's badge on his belt. "Sir, you have threatened physical violence and theft from peaceful people. I can and will body slam your nasty ass on this floor, then scrub the funk off of me for touching you," Nathan told him, dropping his shirt and moving toward Mel.

"Hold on now," Mel said, stepping back.

Nathan stopped. "Sir, you are either leaving this establishment voluntarily or getting body slammed, your choice," he said calmly.

"Alright," Mel replied, shuffling toward the door and grabbing a filthy backpack. "I'll be back for my money," he said, heading for the door.

"Thank you, sir, but wait till I'm gone please. Have a nice day," Nathan said as Mel walked out. Mel looked at Nathan with a little fear on his face as he started into a fast trot across the parking lot.

"Thank you, Nathan," Connie said as the door closed behind Mel.

"You're welcome, Connie," Nathan said, walking over and grabbing bags. "Add two of those cases of bottled water by the door and a bag of ice please."

"No, it's on the house," Connie told him.

"I had it under control!" Brian barked at Nathan.

"Yes you did, Brian, but lower your tone please. Like I said, I'm trying to get a headache," Nathan told him as he headed to the side door. "I'll come back for the rest," he said as he walked out.

Ares saw him carrying bags and started panting with his tongue hanging out the side. "This is not all yours," Nathan said, putting the bags in the back beside him. Ares started sticking his nose in each bag. "Quit that!" Nathan snapped, and Ares looked up, trying to look innocent.

"You're not fooling anyone," Nathan said, scratching Ares' back. Ares started panting, then closed his mouth and looked past Nathan. Nathan turned around to find Connie and Renee walking over, both carrying as many bags as they could. "I was coming back," Nathan said, walking over to help.

"We can help you," Renee said.

"Ares, back, let them in," Nathan said and Ares backed up as the two set the bags down.

Renee looked at Ares. "Aww, he's beautiful," she said, reaching toward him.

Grabbing her arm, Nathan said, "Hold on. Ares, come here." Ares walked over. "Say hi to Renee," he said. Ares sat down and panted at her. "You can pet him now," Nathan told her.

Renee was unsure after that, although she was still holding her hand out. Ares moved over and put his head under her hand, startling her. "He's that well-trained?" she asked.

"He has to be, he goes on patrol with me," Nathan told her.

"So he's the department's dog?" she asked.

"No he's mine. I paid to train him," Nathan said.

Renee moved closer and Ares put his head on her shoulder. "He's a big teddy bear," she said.

"Yeah, after he knows you," Nathan replied. "Ares, this is Connie," he said, and Ares looked over at her and Connie scratched his head.

Now that the introductions were over, Nathan headed back to the store and grabbed more of his items and Connie and Renee helped.

Once everything was in the back of the truck, the women headed back inside. Nathan opened the back passenger door and pulled out what he called a sissy tool kit. It only weighed two pounds but the Suburban was only a year old, and with all the electronics there was actually very little Nathan could work on if something went wrong.

Moving to the driver's door, he threw the tool kit in and opened the center console. He took out another holster. This one was worn outside the belt for his pistol. Taking out his pistol, he removed the inside-the-belt holster and put on the new one. Reaching back in the console, he pulled out another magazine holder that clipped to his belt, giving him a total of four magazines with eight rounds each. Next, he pulled out his handcuff carrier with two sets of cuffs and clipped it to his back. With all the stuff hanging off his belt now, Nathan felt like Batman.

Feeling better, he popped the hood and moved to the fuse panel. Looking at the fuses, he saw all of them were blown. Then on a hunch, he pulled one of the relays off and looked at it. On the small circuit board he could see several burnt spots. Throwing it down, he went to the back of the truck and dug through the bags till he found the cheap watch he had just bought.

Throwing his diving watch down, he put the cheap one on. He had another good watch in his bag but didn't want to take it out yet. The power lines were still making the humming sound. The radio he had left with the girls was working, but he was not pulling out his electronics until he felt more sure of the situation.

Unpacking the bags of stuff he had bought, Nathan arranged everything in piles and started breaking them down. The bags of beef jerky he put in one zip-lock bag. He continued with breaking stuff down till he heard a metal groan from behind the store.

Looking up, he saw an old man in a white cook's apron raising the hood of an old truck.

"Ares, come," Nathan said, heading over to the old man. "You might be able to get that one going," Nathan said when he got closer, noticing the truck was a 1958 Chevy stepside.

The old man jerked around. "Scared the bejesus out of me," he said, patting his chest. "Yeah, I'm getting lights but nothing else," he said, turning back around.

"May I?" Nathan asked, stepping to the driver side.

"Help yourself."

Climbing in, Nathan turned the key and the lights came on but he only heard a clicking from the engine. Turning the key off, he climbed out and looked under the hood, then pulled off the distributer cap. A few minutes later he looked at the old man. "You need a new starter solenoid but I would just buy a whole starter," Nathan told him, and added several more items to the list.

"Damn, that's mighty expensive," the old man replied, looking at the truck with a long face.

"You work here?" Nathan asked.

"Yep, me and the missus run the diner in the mornings. I expect we will be here for a while since our relief hasn't shown up," he said. "I'm Jessie," he said holding out his hand.

"Nathan, Jessie," Nathan said, shaking his hand.

"Yeah, the girls told us your name. Thank you for handling Mel. Brian can't do much 'cept eat and hassle the girls," Jessie told him.

"Funny, that was my first impression," Nathan said with a grin. "Why don't you go over to the parts store and get the parts?" he asked.

"I ain't got that much cash and they put a sign up no sooner than the lights went out. Cash only," Jessie told him. "You think a 1972 Ford Bronco would be easier to fix?" he asked.

"No, it will need a few more parts," Nathan said. Then he noticed a semi tow truck behind the store. "You have a shop here?" he asked.

"Yeah, but they only work on semis and don't keep parts here. Atlanta is only a hop, skip, and a jump away," Jessie told him.

"The Bronco yours?" Nathan asked.

"Yeah, I use it to hunt in," Jessie replied.

"I'll be back in a minute," Nathan told him. "Ares, guard the truck," he said, pointing at his Suburban. Ares barked and took off running, then jumped in the back. Nathan looked up at the power lines that were still humming loudly. He was very nervous about going underneath them. In all reality, he probably wouldn't have but he'd seen Mel do it and live so he tried it.

Walking across the road, he noticed there were three stores in the strip mall: a parts store, a thrift shop, and a pharmacy. The last one was vacant. "These could come in handy," Nathan said, walking toward the parts store.

As soon as he walked in, an old man came out from behind the counter. "Cash only," he snapped.

"No problem," Nathan replied.

"I ain't got the computer board or injection relays here. I have to order them from Asia," he told Nathan.

Nathan walked over to the counter and wrote down what he wanted and handed it to the old man. "I need this," he told him.

"Be just a minute," the cranky old fart said. Nathan shook his head. He'd written down what he wanted because he didn't trust his mouth to stay silent. Twenty minutes later, the old fart walked back to the front carrying a box. He sat it on the counter and started adding up the total on a calculator. Then Nathan noticed he didn't see a cash register.

"Where's your cash register?" Nathan asked and the old fart took a step back, getting nervous. "Relax, I'm a cop," Nathan said, lifting his shirt up and showing his badge. "Is that the calculator you always use?" he asked.

"Yep, don't like registers," the old fart popped off.

Nathan smiled. If the little calculator still worked then the parts should be fine, but just in case, he said, "Sir if these parts don't work I want my money back."

"Nope," the old fart said, stepping back.

"Sir, first of all, this is an emergency. If you don't assist law enforcement you will be held accountable. Now let's keep this cordial please," Nathan said.

"Don't have to sell them to ya," the old fart said.

"You're right, you don't, but I can sign a piece of paper saying I took them and you will have to wait until the government pays you for them," Nathan told him. The old man grumbled and continued adding up the total.

"Four hundred and sixteen dollars," he said. Nathan handed the man the money and waited for change, which came out of the old fart's pocket. Nathan picked up the box and walked out, feeling a little sorry for the old fart.

Walking up to the front of the store, Nathan heard a motorcycle start up and watched as a man pulled out from the side of the store with another man riding on the bitch seat. Both were dressed like mechanics. "Well something works," Nathan said, walking inside and heading toward the diner. He saw Jessie talking to an elderly lady that Nathan took for his wife, and another man dressed in mechanic overalls.

The man looked at Nathan. "Mister, there is no way you are going to get your ride started. I'm afraid you wasted your money," he told Nathan. "My truck is a '99 and I pulled out the mother board and it's fried along with every injector," he added.

"This isn't for me," Nathan said as the man looked back at Jessie.

"Tell Mitch I closed the shop and sent the boys home. I'm riding Kevin's bicycle; he rode with Shawn," the man said, then walked out.

Jessie came over with the lady. "Is that for my truck, Nathan?" he asked.

"Yeah, and your Bronco. Help me push your truck over by my Suburban under the awning and I'll start to work on it," Nathan told him.

"Thank you," the woman said, wrapping her arms around him.

"Nathan, this is my wife Lenore," Jessie told him.

"Ma'am," Nathan said as she let him go.

"The young lady over there is the waitress. Her name's Monica," Jessie said as Nathan nodded to the young black female.

The two men left and pushed the truck over where they could work on it. Nathan looked at Jessie. "You have a real tool box?" he asked.

"Don't need one. There's a whole shop back there," Jessie replied.

Nathan nodded. "Go on back to work and I'll see about the truck," he said, reaching inside his truck and grabbing a pair of mechanic gloves.

"You sure you don't need help?" Jessie asked.

"Nah, you're getting busy in there," Nathan said.

"Yeah, people have been walking in from the freeway. Don't know why they come this way, since town is the other way," Jessie replied, then headed back to the store.

Nathan looked at Ares. "Well, at least I can do something," he said, opening the hood of Jessie's truck.

CHAPTER 4

It was a little after four when Nathan pushed the tool box back to the shop. He had replaced everything, and before he mounted the starter, he turned the key over just long enough to hear the starter whine. There had been a lot of people showing up lately. Several people had walked over and asked if he could fix their vehicles and Nathan told them he was doing this for a friend. That was why he didn't want to start the truck. He was sure he would have to kill someone to stop them from taking it.

Walking back over to his truck, he pulled out Ares' bowls and poured him some food and water. "Ares, guard," Nathan said, pointing at his truck and Jessie's. Ares just gave him what could only be called a grin. Throwing his gloves in the back, Nathan turned around and strolled to the store where he headed to the restroom and washed up. Inside they had put a small battery-operated light.

When he was done, he headed over to the diner and stopped. The place was packed wall to wall with standing room only. He saw Connie helping wait tables and Jessie and Lenore cranking out food. Then he noticed that people were paying for food before the order was even placed. Chuckling, he walked behind the counter and stopped by Jessie. "Hey, you have a second?" Nathan asked.

Jessie looked up. "Yeah," he said and pointed to the back of the kitchen. He led the way. When they were out of sight, Jessie asked, "You couldn't fix it, huh?"

"No, I'm sure it will work but I didn't want to start it with all these people here. I would have to shoot someone," Nathan said, handing him the keys.

"Shit, I didn't think about that," Jessie said. "Gives a whole new meaning to 'In the land of the blind the one-eyed man is king.'"

"Yeah, let's wait till tonight and don't go near your truck without me or Ares will attack you," Nathan said.

"Thank you. I won't ever be able to repay ya," Jessie said, laughing.

"Later you can fix me some food and we'll call it even," Nathan said, clapping Jessie on the shoulder and then walking out. Moving past the people in the diner, he saw the store wasn't much better. He walked behind the counter and stopped beside Renee. "Renee, you need to let Connie know she needs to put a sign up outside that says you guys are closing at dark and the diner closes an hour before that. If you stay open tonight it's going to get bad," he told her.

"It's already bad," she said, looking over her shoulder at him. For the first time, Nathan really looked at her. She had dirty blond hair to her shoulders with a few freckles across her cheeks and nose. She was no taller than five-foot-five and had that country girl cute look.

"No, if you don't close at dark it will be a lot worse," he told her. "I'll be over at my truck if you need me," he said, walking away. Nathan noticed she motioned Brian over as he walked outside. Getting closer to his truck, he saw Ares lying on his back with his legs in the air.

"You let an EMP take out our ride, then sleep on duty," Nathan said, getting closer. Ares slowly rolled his head over and looked at him, then closed his eyes. Laughing Nathan climbed in the front seat and closed the door. Looking down at his shirt and pants, he saw they were covered in dirt and oil. At least his loafers weren't that bad off. Reaching down to recline the seat back with the electric knobs, he cursed under his breath when it didn't move. Grumbling, he reached over to his tote bag.

He had bought it at the gun store and the man told him when it was closed it would act as a Faraday cage. Crossing his fingers, he reached inside and pulled out his cellphone. Holding it up, he was shocked to see the screen on but 'No Service' on it. Loading the e-mail attachment, Nathan started reading what Tim had sent him.

One was about the military doing an active alert for Homeland Security across the globe to test readiness status. Then another one about how all federal officers had to report for weekend training for the exercise. On another page he saw the notice for the nuclear reactors to begin shut-down procedures dated four days ago. Next was a notice to military families to stay on base through the weekend. Reading several more messages that corroborated what he had already read, he scrolled down. The last ones were military memos. At the top of each memo was 'Operation Dark Titan.'

The last one he read made a chill run down his spine. 'Government has ordered ammunition and fuel stock piles to be distributed to all military bases.' "Bases had stockpiles, why would they need more," he asked out loud. He read more and knew why Tim and Sherry were worried, but until the power stopped he still could've blown it off.

Suddenly, he heard a yell. "Nathan, come here quick!" Turning around, he saw Renee standing at the side door of the store, waving at him. Jumping out, Nathan ran to her and she held the door open for him. Stepping inside, he noticed a crowd at the counter and heard the NOAA (National Oceanic and Atmospheric Administration) alert going off. Walking closer, he saw the radio he had bought sitting behind the counter. "It just suddenly went off," Renee told him, leading him behind the counter.

"What's it mean?" someone shouted.

"Radios are coming back up," Nathan said, sitting down on a stool behind the counter.

"Does that mean the government is getting it fixed?" another person yelled.

"Hell, I don't know. I don't speak NOAA alert alarm!" Nathan shouted over the blaring alarm.

"Well, what do you know?" someone else yelled.

"I know the next fucker that asks me a stupid question I'll shoot 'em in the face!" he shouted. Suddenly the alert stopped and a voice came on.

"This is NOAA weather radio broadcasting from Savannah, Georgia. We are notifying the public that the Earth was hit with a massive CME at 11:18 a.m. local time. This CME is rated a Z-class and so far numbers are putting it a hundred times as massive as the Carrington event of 1859. When this CME hit the Earth it caused several satellites in orbit which were carrying plutonium or uranium to detonate. We don't know how many yet but the EMPs that resulted—," The man suddenly stopped and the Emergency Broadcast system alarm came on.

"Why did he stop?" Renee asked.

"He was kicked off the air," Nathan told her. "That warning is from the Emergency Broadcast system, not NOAA," he informed her.

"Why did they stop him?" she asked.

"Undoubtedly he was saying shit they didn't like," Nathan told her. He reached over and patted her arm reassuringly.

She looked at him with tears running down her face. "Is it going to be okay?" she asked.

Nathan looked at her and thought about lying to her, then shook his head. "No, but we can try to make it better for ourselves and our families," he told her.

"My husband is a deputy. Do you think he's going to be alright?" she asked.

"If he's smart and strong he will be fine, but's it's only going to get worse as time goes on, so be ready," he told her.

She gave him a weak smile. "Okay I will," she said, standing up. Outside he heard engines and saw a line of four school busses pass in front of the store.

"Where are they heading?" someone yelled.

"They're heading to the school. The county has set up a crisis center there," someone replied. As one, the mass of people dropped what they wanted to buy and took off out of the store after the buses. Those in the diner that had their food left, and when those that were waiting got theirs, they also ran out the door.

In ten minutes, the store was empty with only one customer, a man, standing at the magazine rack. "And people don't like to be referred to as sheep." He laughed out loud.

"Hey Jim," Connie said, walking over from the diner. "Did the school really set up a center?" she asked.

"Oh yeah, but they don't know anything. Your radio is the first I've heard since the event. What they said sure makes sense," Jim answered.

Nathan nodded his head in agreement. "That it does," he said, and Jim looked at him.

"I like how you handled the stupid questions. I wish I could do that in class," Jim told him, chuckling.

Connie turned to Nathan. "Jim is the senior science teacher," she told him.

Jim looked at Nathan. "I think you know something about CMEs and EMPs," he said, not asking.

"I know a little," Nathan told him.

"I think more than a little. How widespread do you think the EMP hit was?"

"Can't even begin to guess, but I hope it only affected the eastern seaboard," Nathan replied.

"Where you from?" Jim asked.

"Idaho," Nathan replied.

"Yeah, I can see why you would hope that. It's a long walk home," Jim told him.

"Can't they just turn the power back on?" Renee asked.

Before Nathan could answer, Jim spoke up. "No Renee, I'm sure by now the power plants are on fire and all the substations are burnt out. I only hope they are able to shut down the nuclear power plants before they have a meltdown. The Earth's magnetic field is overloading the system. Any long stretch of wire is gathering electricity. Hell, this afternoon one of the kids touched the fence around the school and it shocked the hell out of him. That humming you hear outside is power running through the lines from the Earth's magnetic field."

"We can make new power plants," Connie said.

"Oh, we will have to if we want power. None of the big transformers are even made in America anymore, and they take years to build not to mention the actual turbines at the plants. The EMP was probably the worst thing that could've happened. It broke the system so it couldn't be shut down, the important parts that is," Jim replied.

"What about the reactors?" Brian asked.

"Well Brian, the reactors have generators to pump water but they are not EMP proof. The Nuclear Commission didn't think that was relevant," Jim answered.

"How long if they aren't able to cool it down?" Jessie asked.

"Few days," Jim answered, grabbing a magazine and walking over to the checkout. "Y'all need to be careful, I've heard a lot of gunshots around town," he said, laying money on the counter.

"You too Jim," Connie told him.

Jim picked up his stuff and walked out. Connie turned to the others, "Let's get this cleaned up," she said, pointing at the mess the crowd had left.

Brian stomped his foot. "I've been here for almost twenty hours," he snapped.

"Like you're the only one," Renee told him.

Nathan left as the group started cleaning up. Walking to his Suburban, he climbed in the back and sprawled out, trying to relax. Off in the distance, he heard what sounded like a lawn mower approaching.

Lifting his head up, he saw a gigantic man driving a riding lawn mower. Only when he pulled in the parking lot did Nathan realize there was a woman sitting in his lap. The woman climbed off and went into the store. The man saw him and waved at Nathan and he waved back. Then, to Nathan's surprise, the man drove over and parked behind his truck and turned the mower off. Nathan scooted to the back, letting his legs hang out.

"Ain't this a river of shit," the man said grinning.

"Big, deep and wide," Nathan answered, making the huge man laugh. The man was wearing overalls, a hat, and boots. To top it off, he was huge, not fat, maybe a little porky, but an easy six-foot-seven, four hundred pounds. He was country through and through. "Name's Fred," he said, holding out his hand.

"Nathan," he replied shaking Fred's hand. Looking at the lawn mower, Nathan said, "You need to drop the deck off, put a better muffler on it, and I would start riding with a gun."

The man reached behind him, pulling out a .357 magnum with an eight-inch barrel. "Yeah, I've heard some gunshots around," he said. Nathan knew the gun was massive but in Fred's hand it looked like a pea shooter.

"You dropping your wife off at work?" Nathan asked.

"Yep, I got sent home from the plant after it happened. Luckily one of the old men had drove a 1934 truck and it started right up," Fred told him.

"He drove everyone from your plant home in one truck?" Nathan asked amazed.

Fred shrugged his shoulders. "It's a chicken farm," he admitted.

"Oh," Nathan replied. "You have a trailer for that thing?" he asked.

"Sure," Fred replied.

"Bring it tomorrow with some gas cans and I'll siphon the gas out of my truck for you," Nathan told him.

"Thanks," Fred grinned.

"No problem," Nathan told him.

"Well, I'm heading back home to work on my truck. I think I can have it running soon," Fred said as he started the mower up and took off.

Shaking his head, Nathan looked at Ares. "If that wasn't country I don't know what is," he said, and Ares barked, agreeing.

Nathan climbed back up in the cargo area, closing the rear hatch, and laid down, closing his eyes. He didn't know how long they'd been closed when he heard a deep-throated growl. Cracking an eye open, he saw Ares looking out the window toward the road. Nathan slowly rose up till he could just peek out the side window.

A white man with a shaved head was walking across the parking lot holding his hand inside a leather vest. The man kept looking around and stopped when he reached the front door. "Now he's not acting suspicious at all," Nathan observed. With a last look around, the man stepped inside. "Well just kiss my ass," Nathan complained, opening the door behind the passenger seat and climbing out.

"Ares, follow," Nathan said, walking toward the side door. He checked his gear and carefully moved his shirt off his pistol. Tightening his vest, he looked down at Ares. "If he shoots Daddy you better kill him," Nathan told him. Ares just gave a low growl as they eased toward the door.

As they reached the side door of the store, Nathan heard a man's voice yelling, "Get your old asses in here and you, sweet thing, give me the money now!" Nathan was going to guess it was Kojack as he pulled out his pistol. "I'm taking the sweet thing with me, and if anyone tries anything I'll cut her up, understand?" the man yelled as Nathan opened the door and eased inside in a crouch.

Coming around an end cap, Nathan saw the man had everyone on the floor and Renee by the wrist. Nathan stood up, aiming at the man's back. "I'll be your huckleberry," Nathan said in a plain voice, causing the man to spin around and bring up his pistol. Nathan squeezed the trigger, filling the store with a thunderous BOOM.

As the first bullet raced for its target, Nathan sent two more. The first shot hit the man in the neck, completing his spin and making him release Renee, slinging her to the floor. Then the next bullet hit him in the center of the chest and the third shot hit the man in the left chest wall right over his heart. Kojack dropped his pistol and reached for his neck as he dropped down to the floor.

Keeping his pistol aimed at the man, Nathan eased forward as the man coughed, holding his hands on his neck. Reaching the man, Nathan bent over and picked up the pistol he'd dropped. Ejecting the magazine, Nathan racked the slide back, ejecting the round in the chamber, then laid the gun on the counter. Never taking his aim off the man, he moved over and quickly frisked him, finding a knife and two magazines.

Nathan holstered his pistol and looked down at the man as he coughed up blood. "Help me," the man gasped, holding out a hand to Nathan.

"Help you? After all the trouble I went through to kill you? You've got to be kidding me," Nathan said. He turned around. "Is everyone alright?" he asked the others as he helped Renee up.

"That son of bitch was going to kill us all!" Jessie shouted, standing up.

"Yeah, I'm pretty sure he was," Nathan agreed, looking back at the man. "Dude, you just had to pick this store, huh?" Nathan asked as the man fought to breathe. "You know I'm an ER nurse and could probably buy you some time, but I'm choosing not to," Nathan said as the man started to gurgle.

"Oh God," Monica cried and took off running to the diner.

Nathan watched her run off, followed by another woman who he took to be Fred's wife. He turned to Jessie. "Jessie, lock the doors, I'll be right back. Nobody touch anything," Nathan said, running out to his truck and coming back with a digital camera.

"That works?" Connie asked.

"Yeah, it was in a shielded bag," Nathan said, taking pictures. "I want everyone to grab a piece of paper and write down what happened," he told them, taking more pictures. The group moved to the counter and started writing as Nathan finished taking pictures. Putting the camera in his pocket, he knelt down next to the now dead man. Opening his leather vest up, Nathan saw a holster shoved in the front of his pants. Taking it out, he tossed it to the side. Looking at the inside pocket of the vest, he saw a bulge and carefully opened it up and found two rolls. Reaching in, Nathan pulled them out to find they were rolled hundred dollar bills. Searching the other inside pocket, he found a bag with a shitload of blue pills.

Tossing them with the holster, he reached down and pulled the front pocket inside out and found a bag of crystal power. "Damn, that is a lot of meth," Nathan said to himself, figuring it was close to seven ounces. Rolling the man over, he pulled out a wallet and undid the chain holding it to the belt. Opening the wallet, Nathan gasped. "Shit, you have more money than I do and you want to rob the place?" Nathan asked the corpse.

Everyone looked over at him. "Someone bring me that pistol and a bag to put this shit in please," Nathan asked. Lenore brought one over as Nathan finished his search, not finding anything else. Taking some pictures of what he'd taken off the man, Nathan put the stuff in the plastic bag and stood up. Tying the bag to his belt, he walked down an aisle and grabbed a roll of duct tape and a tarp.

Walking back, he laid the tarp out beside the body. "You can't move him till our police get here," Brian snapped.

"I'll take that under advisement," Nathan told him as he reached over and grabbed two shirts off a rack and stuffed them around the man's neck. Walking over to another rack, he grabbed a pack of Playtex gloves. Pulling on a pair, he handed the other to Jessie and headed over to the body.

"I'm telling you, Nathan, you can't move that body till a real crime investigator gets here," Brian yelled.

Nathan stood up. "Brian, I'm glad you paid attention to CSI but in case you haven't noticed, nobody is going to show up anytime soon, and the air is off, that's why it's hot in here. I've been around dead bodies and they start to stink fast. Kojack is already shitting himself," Nathan told him.

"I can arrest you if you move that body," Brian challenged him.

"Dude! You couldn't stop a wet dream," Nathan snapped as he continued to work.

"I'm placing you under citizen's arrest. Hand over your weapon!" Brian shouted.

Slowly, Nathan stood up and said, "In your dreams, Brian."

Brian took a step back.

Nathan grinned. "Hey Brian, you pissed your pants," he said, pointing at his crotch. Brian looked down and saw the large wet spot on his pants and took off running to the back of the store. Nathan could almost swear he was crying.

Moving over to the body, he and Jessie rolled it onto the tarp. Then, rolling the tarp around the body, they folded the ends over and taped them down with duct tape. They were both breathing hard as they stood up. "I don't expect you guys have a dolly or something we can move his ass with?" Nathan asked.

"Yeah, hold on," Connie said, running to the back of the store. She came back with a flat-box dolly. The others moved over and helped move the body onto the dolly as a knock was heard at the door, making everyone jump.

They looked up and saw three men and a woman dressed in business attire pounding on the door. "We're closed!" Connie yelled at them.

"I'm a lawyer and I demand you open this door. This is an emergency!" one of the men shouted.

"We're closed. Go back the way you came and go under the Interstate and head to the school. They have a shelter set up there!" Connie yelled at him.

"I will break this damn door down if you don't open it!" he yelled at her.

"I'm not opening the door!" Connie yelled. Just then, the man looked down at the floor and saw all the blood. Then he noticed the bundle wrapped in a tarp.

"What the hell are you doing?" he yelled, his eyes bulging.

"This is the last bitch that banged on our door threatening to break it down, so I shot him!" Nathan yelled.

The four stepped back from the door. "I'm going to tell the police about this!" the man shouted.

"Good, tell them to come and get the bodies. We're starting to pile them pretty high here!" Nathan shouted, and the four took off running.

Connie turned around, shaking her head at Nathan. "Where have you been all my life?" she asked.

"Ah, up in the northwest," he told her.

"What do you want to do with this?" she asked.

"Roll him outside and throw him in the woods on the other side of the parking lot. The law can pick him up when they can."

"He will really be stinking by then," she said.

"Well we don't really have a lot of options. He damn sure isn't going in my truck. It may not run but I still like it," Nathan told her.

"Let's put him in the back freezer," she suggested.

"Connie, the power is out and that's a sealed room. You want to talk about stink?" Nathan replied.

"The freezer is run off propane and those two tanks out back are full. They will keep the freezer on for a year unless it breaks down," she said.

Thinking about it for a minute, he said, "Well it's better than he deserves, but okay."

"How about we put him in the freezer outside?" Jessie asked.

"That's better," Connie said as she started to push the cart. "We have a freezer out back that we store extra food in," she told Nathan. They rolled the cart out and dumped the body and headed back inside as the sun was setting.

"What are you guys going to do now?" Nathan asked.

"We were talking about that and most of us are staying here. It's not much of a job but it's the only one we have, and I'm sure they are fixing to get real hard to come by," Connie told him.

"Don't open until daylight," Nathan told her as they dropped off the dolly and headed back into the store. The others had mops out, cleaning up the blood, and were done in minutes. Nathan grabbed the statements and photographed each one as Connie brought over Allie, Fred's wife, for a formal introduction. Grabbing a memory card from behind the counter, Nathan put it in the camera and saw it was working, then moved everything to the memory card.

Lenore walked over and looked at him. "You're a mess. Those clothes must have cost a fortune and they're ruined. And you did it working on our truck," she said.

Nathan laughed as he walked to the side door and opened it up. "Ares, guard the trucks!" he yelled and Ares took off out the door. "Lenore, I helped some good people today so it's all good," he told her.

"What are you going to do?" Connie asked.

"First I'm going to get cleaned up, then I'm going to remind Lenore she owes me a meal. Then I'm going to eat and watch the sky. When I have my fill of that, I'm going to crawl in my truck and go to sleep," he told her.

"Watch the sky?" she asked.

"Yep, if they were right about the CME this will be a night that will not be soon forgotten," he told her.

"Well, go get you some clothes and come back and take a shower. Then how about you sleep in here?" she asked.

"Hell yeah, I want that," Monica said.

"Guys, I have a lot of stuff in my truck I can't leave. Some of my gear is dangerous and I can't let Ares stay out there alone," he told them.

"You can put it in my office and I'll give you the keys," Connie offered.

Nathan looked at the group and groaned.

"Please Nathan," Renee pleaded.

"Okay, I'll put my gear in your office but please don't mess with it. I have a lot of weapons that can hurt you," Nathan told them. "If you want to see some of it, that's fine, as long as I show you," he added.

"I don't care if you move Jimmy Hoffa in here as long as you stay," Lenore told him.

"Aren't you and Jessie going home?" he asked.

"Not tonight. One of the grandkids rode up here on a bike and told us everyone had made it to our house. Two of our kids live on our farm with their families and the other three brought in their families so everyone is safe," she said.

"Okay, let me go and get a load," Nathan said, heading to the side door.

"Hold on, I need to get something out of my truck," Jessie told him, following him out.

"Ares, come here!" Nathan called out. Ares ran over and started running around them. "Ares, this is Jessie. Say hi," Nathan said, and Ares moved over beside Jessie.

"That is one smart dog," Jessie said, scratching Ares' head.

"Sometimes," Nathan said.

"Think I can see if the truck will start up?" Jessie asked.

Nathan looked around and didn't see anyone. "Yeah, but pull it into the open bay in the garage and close the door. That way if someone comes for it we'll know and can talk them out of it," Nathan told him.

Jessie nodded and climbed in his truck. He looked at Nathan, held up crossed fingers, then turned the key. The engine chugged and died out. Jessie pumped the gas pedal and turned the key again and the truck fired up. Jessie closed his door and drove around the other side of the store into the shop.

Nathan grabbed his backpack and sat it on the ground. Then he looked at all the crap he had bought. Shaking his head, he heard Ares bark and take off running toward the store. Turning around, he saw Connie, Renee, and Monica walking toward him with empty boxes. Ares started jumping around them wanting to know what was in the boxes.

"You know I have a lot of crap," Nathan said.

"Well we carried a lot of it out," Renee told him, holding out a box. Grabbing the box, he started loading it up. "Why did you take the wrapping off of everything?" she asked.

"To save space and weight. I'm going to have to carry this out of here," he said.

"Nathan, that's over fifty pounds of stuff," she told him.

"Pretty close, and with the rest of my gear I'm figuring close to one hundred and ten pounds of gear," he said, handing her the full box back.

"And you're carrying it to Idaho?" she asked.

"Unless I can find a bus going that way," he said, taking Connie's box.

Connie shook her head. "You can stay here," she offered as he filled the box up.

"No, I have to get home," he said.

"You have to get back to your family?" she asked with a quizzical look.

"In a way, they are my family," he said, handing her the full box.

"You're not married?" she asked.

"I've never even been engaged," he said, smiling.

"I find that hard to believe," she told him as he took Monica's box and started filling it up.

Letting out a chuckle, he turned to Connie and said, "My last girlfriend told me I'm pretty difficult to live with."

Connie looked at him with a faint grin. "Hell, anyone is difficult to live with," she told him.

"You may be right there," he said, handing the full box back to Monica.

"We'll put these in my office stacked in the corner," Connie told him as they headed back to the store. Before they made it to the door, Jessie walked back out, heading toward Nathan. He was wearing a western gun belt around his waist.

"I like what you got out of your truck," Nathan told him.

"It's a modified .357. I used to shoot cowboy competition," Jessie said proudly.

"Cool. I shoot three-gun and open class," Nathan told him, setting the last of his bags on the ground. Walking around to the passenger door, he grabbed the stuff off the seat and floorboard, stuffing it in his tote bag. Then he went around to the back, took out his keys and stuck one in a lock on the floor of the cargo area. When he turned it, a drawer popped out.

"Damn, that's some James Bond stuff," Jessie said with raised eyebrows.

"Not really, it's just a cargo storage drawer. I had it installed then had the original carpet placed over it. Since the drawer's only four inches deep it doesn't look like much, especially with how big this damn thing is," Nathan said, pulling out the drawer.

Jessie just stood in amazement watching Nathan pull out equipment. "How many guns do you have in there?" he asked.

Nathan pulled out an AR-15 with a fourteen-inch barrel, a suppressor, and an ACOG scope on the flat-top upper. A single-point sling hung down and Nathan slipped it on. Reaching back into the truck, he pulled out his tactical vest with ballistic plates and drop platforms on each side. Sliding his arms in the vest, he let it hang down. Next, he pulled out a Springfield XD 45 with a tactical light and laser. Emptying the drawer, Nathan threw the rest of the stuff in his tote bag. "There's a Glock 21 in the glove box, it's a .45 caliber, and a Glock 19 under the backseat on the driver's side, it's a 9mm. Then I have a .38 strapped to my ankle." Nathan picked up a box and handed it to Jessie. "I just bought that pistol today. It is a beauty," Nathan told Jessie, who was speechless. "I want to make sure I have a weapon I can get to," he admitted.

"No shit!" Jessie agreed. "Is that your service rifle for the police department?" he asked.

"I wish," Nathan said, picking up his keys and unlocking a panel behind the passenger wheel well. "If it was, I wouldn't need this," he said, pulling out a plastic box.

"Why, what's it do?" Jessie asked.

"Evens the playing field," Nathan said, grabbing up stuff.

"What's this?" Jessie asked, holding up what looked like a weird suitcase.

"That's Ares' backpack," Nathan told him.

"You're kidding," Jessie said.

"Nope. Ares can carry twenty-five pounds on it. We go hiking a lot and he has to tote his own food and woobie," Nathan replied.

"Woobie?" Jessie asked.

Reaching down, Nathan picked up a camouflaged poncho liner. "His woobie. I won't let him use mine," Nathan said. Jessie let out a laugh and grabbed two armfuls. The girls returned and helped with the last of the stuff and Nathan's two suitcases.

They stacked everything around Connie's office and Nathan laid out the vest and weapons on her desk. Connie handed him the keys as he headed out into the store. He grabbed several packs of chemlites and opened them up. "Don't get any lights around the windows. I don't want people to know where we are in case they start shooting inside. Let's all sleep in the casino area since it's in the center of the store. Someone put a sign on the door saying armed guard and attack dog inside," Nathan said, heading back to Connie's office.

As he cracked a chemlite, the room was lit up with a soft red light. Grabbing a pair of tan tactical pants, an UnderArmor base shirt and a t-shirt with 'Sheriff' across the front and back, he laid them in a pile. Digging out a pair of suspenders he picked up his shaving kit and flip flops. Locking the door, he headed to the showers and scrubbed what felt like a year's worth of worry and grime off of him.

Throwing his old clothes and his penny loafers away, he walked back to Connie's office with his flip flops just a popping. Pulling his hair up into a tassel, he opened the box with his new boots, then opened a bag and pulled out some boot socks he'd bought as well. All he had packed in his suitcase were the half bitch socks. Making sure his gear was on tight, he left the office and headed to the diner.

He found Ares sitting by a plate that was laid in the floor with everyone telling him to eat. Ares just looked at them. "Ares, eat," Nathan told him. Ares lowered his head and dove down on the food.

Everyone looked back at Nathan and Renee asked, "You have him trained to only eat when you say?"

"Well yeah, what good is an attack dog if he eats when he wants?" Nathan asked.

Lenore set down a plate with a steak and baked potato. "I cooked it medium," she said, putting down some silverware.

"Perfect," Nathan said as he started wolfing down his food. He noticed everyone staring the front window. Gazing past them, he saw colors rippling across the sky. "Get some chairs and let's sit outside and watch the show. We won't see something like this again for a long time, hopefully," he added.

Brian turned around. "I want the gun you took off the man you shot," he told Nathan.

"Let me think about that," Nathan said, then put his hand on his chin. After a second, he looked at Brian. "Ah, no," he said.

"I saw you carry in a machine gun. I want a gun," he said.

"So you can shoot yourself or someone in here?" Nathan asked.

"I can have a gun if I want," Brian snapped.

"Sure you can, but not one of mine," Nathan responded.

Connie stepped over beside Nathan. "Ah, Brian, you aren't allowed to have a firearm," she reminded him.

"I can now," he said.

"You're a convicted felon," she said, and Brian looked around at his other co-workers.

"You can't let them know that!" he shouted.

Monica looked at him like he was totally stupid, which wasn't far from the truth. "Everyone in fifty miles knows that, Brian," she said.

"That was a long time ago," he whined.

"Yeah, two years is a long time ago," Allie smirked.

"If I don't get a gun, I leave," Brian challenged.

"Fine, the door is right there," Connie said, pointing at the door.

"I'm the security here!" Brian shouted.

"No, you were hired to lower the insurance premium," Connie told him.

Grabbing a bag, he walked over to the door. "I'm serious, I'll leave," he said, looking around at them. It was obvious he was hoping that they'd beg him to stay, but they just waited on him to leave. Nathan knew Brian couldn't believe nobody was arguing for him to stay; perhaps they didn't think he was really serious. Grabbing the handle, Brian looked at Renee like he expected her to run over and hug him, begging him to stop and not leave.

"You just have to pull it to open it, Brian," Lenore told him.

Brian looked at Monica. "Don't you want me to stay?" he asked.

"Not really," she told him honestly.

He turned to Renee. "Aren't you going to stop me?" he asked.

"Ah no, I'm sick of you staring at my tits and trying to look down my shirt," she answered. Brian let out a huff, threw the bolt and walked out. Monica ran over to the door and locked it.

"That man has always given me the creeps," she said, watching him walk across the parking lot.

Renee let out a shudder. "He's so weird," she said, turning to Nathan. "My husband Mark has had to talk to him several times."

Connie looked away from the window. "Don't you want to know what he did?" she asked.

"My guess is stalking and stolen property," Nathan said. Everyone gawked at him. "What? I'm a cop," he said matter-of-factly.

"But stolen property?" Jessie asked.

"Yeah, he was stealing every time I saw him today from the aisles," Nathan said.

"You didn't say anything?" Connie asked.

"Hell, I know you saw him once so I figured you guys let the retard take little things," he told her.

Everyone laughed as Monica came over. "He stole a car and went to stalk a girl that moved away just to get away from him," she told him.

"You think he'll come back?" Allie asked.

"Not here, but if he knows where you guys live, he'll show up there in a few days," Nathan told her.

"You think he's dangerous?" Connie asked.

"He will be in time, because the law of the land is going to be violence of action," Nathan advised. "Let's get some chairs and sit out back and watch the show." Nathan turned and headed toward the office.

"Why the back?" Renee asked.

"The light you see off to the east is Atlanta burning, and it will take away from some of the colors," Nathan said. Opening the door, he went inside and grabbed the pistol from the man he'd shot. Picking up the holster and two magazines, he stuffed them in his belt and relocked the door. Everyone was waiting on him at the side door. "Connie, can I have a key to the outside doors?" he asked.

"You have one, it's on the key chain with my office key," she said and showed it to him.

"I'm putting it under the driver's side floor mat of my Suburban in case any of us gets locked out by accident," he told them, and they all nodded. Each carried out a chair and sat watching the colors ripple across the sky. It was so bright there was enough light to read by. Nathan took out his camera and started taking pictures and several video shots, then he just leaned back and took in the beauty with the others. The group stared in awe at the shimmering colors.

"It may be pretty but this still sucks," Nathan commented.

"No shit," Connie said, tilting her head up and looking at the sky. They fell silent.

CHAPTER 5

Day 2

It was after midnight before the first one spoke. They were all mesmerized by the lights.

"How long will they last?" Allie asked.

"Don't know, we might see some tomorrow even up to a week out," Nathan told her.

"I've never seen anything like this," Renee said.

Nathan leaned forward and looked down the row. "Does anyone in any of your families have any health conditions?" he asked.

Jessie sat up suddenly, along with Lenore. "Oh my God, my granddaughter has diabetes! We keep about two months' supply, but with the power out it's going to go bad!" Jessie shouted.

"Don't be so loud, Jessie," Nathan told him. "Do you have a camper?"

Jessie gave him a bizarre look. "Yeah, a thirty-footer, but what good is that going to do me?" he asked.

"It has a refrigerator in it—" Nathan started to say.

"And it runs off propane," Jessie finished. "But I need to leave tomorrow to see if I can find her more insulin," he said.

"Let's talk about that tomorrow," Nathan said. "Anyone else?" he asked.

"My brother has asthma real bad. He gets put in the hospital at least twice a year," Monica told him.

"How much medicine does he have?" Nathan asked.

"We have to get it filled every month."

When no one else spoke up, Nathan started talking. "Okay guys, you all see this is going to be bad. If any of you live in the city or town, get out. Live with someone in the country. You need to get in groups of around twenty to forty. Any smaller and you are an easy target, and much bigger is hard to provide for unless you have a farm established. Your primary focus is food and water after protection and shelter. There's more, but those are what you focus on. Always have a bag packed with three days of supplies that you can grab and leave. That is called a 'go bag.' Only bring in people you can trust, and don't hesitate to throw people out that will hurt the group. You need to choose a leader that will listen to others but will make decisions and live with them. Each of you can survive this. I can see the strength in all of you."

Renee looked over at him. "How long do you think this will last?" she asked.

"Forever. It will never be the same," he answered.

"I saw a show on this one time and it said half the world would die if it happened," Allie told them.

"I put it at seventy-five to ninety percent," Nathan replied, and everyone sat up. "It's not that hard to see, guys. Two percent of the population grows the food for the rest. Tractors have to harvest it and trucks have to carry that food to the cities. It's planting time now. Even if the tractors are running, the refineries aren't producing the diesel to move the produce."

"We're going to die," Renee said, looking down.

"Think like that and you will," Nathan popped off.

Jessie looked over at Connie. "Connie, you come out to the house with us," he told her.

"Thank you Jessie. I was really worried about that," she admitted. "I live in an apartment," she told Nathan.

"Okay everyone, think about this and I'll write more stuff down if I can, but you need to read. Find books about edible plants, how to hunt, trap, fish, and preserve food. Don't throw anything away until you know you can't use it for something else. Water is what you secure first," Nathan told them.

"When will it get really bad?" Monica asked.

Nathan stood up. "Like it's not now, but I know what you mean. In about a month, and it will continue until next spring," he told her.

"Come on, let's get some rest. I'm going to walk around the area then come inside. Don't worry, I won't be out of sight. Tonight if you hear Ares growling, come and get me. That's what he does when danger is near," Nathan said, walking over to Renee. Holding out the pistol from the man he'd shot, he asked, "Do you know what this is and how to use it?"

"It's a Glock 17, nine millimeter, and yes I know how to use it. If I would've driven to work I would've had one in my car," she told him.

He gave her the pistol. "If you point it at someone, shoot them. Don't ever use it to scare someone or you'll die," he told her as she took the pistol.

"Mark told me the same thing," she said, clipping the holster on.

He led everyone back inside, then went to the office and grabbed several items. Locking the door as he went outside, he reached down and rubbed Ares' head. "Stay alert," he said, then headed across the street to the little strip mall. Going around the back of the building, he crouched down and listened. Not hearing or seeing anything, he moved to the back door of the pharmacy. Pulling out his lock picks, he prayed nobody was inside as he broke in.

Slowly turning the dead bolt, he moved to the doorknob. When the lock clicked, it sounded like a tree falling in the quietness of the night, and Nathan almost took off running. Standing to the side of the door in case someone was inside and started popping shots off, he cracked the door. Looking at Ares, he whispered, "Get 'em." Ares stuck his nose at the crack and looked back at Nathan.

Relief flooded over Nathan as he stood up and eased inside with Ares leading the way. Closing the door behind him, he moved over behind the counter where a skylight overhead lit up the store. A large locked shelf was over in the corner and Nathan passed it up, heading to the refrigerator under the counter. Opening it up, he searched, finding a lot of vials of regular insulin. Taking them out, he set them on the counter. Then he grabbed ten vials of Lantus insulin, placing them with the others. Looking around, he found the inhalers. Nathan grabbed twenty.

Moving out into the store area, he found cloth shopping bags and headed back to load up his haul so far. He poked around until he found the syringes. There were only fifteen bags and most diabetics used around a thousand a year. Nathan took them all. Next he found the glucose

THOMAS A. WATSON

meters and started opening each brand until he found one that was sealed in Mylar. Grabbing the six off the shelf, he took all the test strips for it.

Next he looked till he found the Prednisone and took a big supply bottle of five hundred, twenty milligram tablets. Dropping it in the bag with the inhalers, he grabbed an empty bag and moved toward the shelves. He started grabbing antibiotics like Cipro, Penicillin, Zithromax, and six others, all of them in the big supply bottles. Taking two of each, he laid the eighteen bottles in the bag, then found Tamiflu and Relenza and took half the supply of each of them.

Moving over to the locked cabinet, he took out his picks and unlocked it. He had been a nurse a long time and recognized what was in there. He grabbed four of the big bottles of pain medications and two of the muscle relaxers. Then he looked down at the Adderall. He had taken Adderall since he was twelve years old. Even now he had a bottle in his tote bag. It stopped his day dreaming but he really didn't like it much; it made him feel flat emotionally. Sighing, he grabbed several big bottles, figuring day dreaming wouldn't be healthy now.

Taking a last walk around, he grabbed some more supplies, then locked the cabinet back up and carried the seven bags to the back door. After he cracked the door, Ares let him know it was clear so he stepped outside and relocked the door. Easing up to the road, he didn't see anything so he trotted across and headed to the side door of the diner. He opened the door with the key, then slid inside and moved toward the office and put the stuff away. Locking the door back up, he headed out into the store and found a small ice cooler.

"Took you long enough," he heard behind him. Nathan dropped down, reaching for his pistol, only to see Jessie behind him holding up his hands.

"Dude, you scare me like that again and I'll shoot you in the leg on principle," Nathan told him as the adrenalin crash hit him and he just sat down on the floor. Ares came over and licked his face. "Some guard dog you are, didn't even tell me he was there," Nathan said, rubbing the massive head.

Jessie laughed and kneeled down beside him. "I could've gone with you," he said.

"No, if someone would've been in there I would've had to run. I wasn't going to kill for it," he told Jessie.

. 48 .

"I understand. You think I might have," Jessie told him.

"It's a moot point now," Nathan said, standing back up.

"How much were you able to get?" Jessie inquired.

"Enough for two years but only enough needles for a year."

"We have more than enough needles. You think that will be enough?" Jessie asked.

"Don't know, but I figure the higher ups will have drug manufacturing back up in that time. You just have to make sure you're important enough around here for them to give her the medication," Nathan told him.

"How do I do that?" Jessie asked.

"Have your son and other members of your family become part of the police force and have your farm pumping out food," Nathan said.

"I can do that."

"Who else is awake?" Nathan asked.

"Everyone," Jessie replied. Nathan slumped his shoulders and Jessie chuckled. "It wasn't that hard to figure out, Nathan. You're trying to help us," Jessie told him.

"But now you guys are accessories," Nathan said.

"I don't know what you're talking about and neither does anyone else," Jessie said, patting Nathan on the arm.

Nathan handed the cooler to Jessie. "Find a box we can put the insulin in so it doesn't touch the ice," he said, then headed to the office. He unlocked the door and grabbed the two bags for Jessie. "Put the vials in there and get rid of the bags," Nathan told him.

"Okay," Jessie said, taking the supplies.

Nathan grabbed a box and set the supplies for Monica in it and carried it to her. "I found these and you can have them," he told her.

Monica looked at him with tears running down her face. "Thank you Nathan," she said.

"No thanks required. I found them, just don't tell anyone," he told her.

"What, that I traded a bottle of Jack Daniels for them?" she said, looking up and smiling. Nathan grinned at her approvingly.

"Okay everyone let's get some sleep," Nathan said. He headed back to the office where he pulled the stuff out of the other bags and shoved them in his pack. Then he gave the bags to Jessie, who burnt them. Sitting down behind the desk, Nathan saw the bag with the rest of the dead man's possessions. Pulling out the wallet and wads of cash, he started counting. He counted it twice and each time came up with seven thousand six hundred dollars. Throwing the wallet back in the bag, he shoved the money in his pocket.

"This will do more good with me," he said to himself. Picking up his AR, he took it apart and pulled out the small plastic box. The chemlite was now very dim so he pulled out his flashlight and turned it on. He almost hit the floor as he jumped back from the light. "Damn, that's bright," he mumbled.

Taking the parts out of the lower receiver of the AR, he laid them to the side and put the parts from the box in the lower. When he was finished, his selector switch rotated all the way around with four clicks: safe, single shot, auto, and burst. He had a tax stamp for the suppressor, but what he had just done was beyond illegal, cop or not. If he was caught, he was toast. Somehow he didn't think that would matter too much in the end.

Picking up his backpack, he started packing it with supplies and food. When he was done, only the top bag that could be pulled off for a fanny pack was empty. He figured he was carrying close to forty pounds of food now along with thirty pounds of ammo just in his pack. Then when he threw in the other supplies it would be another thirty pounds.

Reaching down, he lifted up a small nylon case and unzipped it, pulling out a Ruger 10/22 take-down. Putting it together, he put it in the gun scabbard on the side. This is what would feed him on the road home. Not in the mood to go through his pack to see what could be left behind, he headed out into the store. Looking out the window, he saw the Northern Lights still lighting up the sky.

Turning around, he saw the magazine and book section. Looking at the magazines, he picked up a bodybuilding one, another on assault weapons, and froze upon seeing the topographical books of states. He picked up the ones for Alabama, Mississippi, and Arkansas; then, thinking about it for a second, he grabbed six other states on his route. Walking over to the maps, he picked up a map wheel pen and a map of the United States. He left the electronic ones and grabbed the one with the dial. Sitting down at a table in the diner, he started going over routes, finally falling asleep an hour before dawn.

Nathan woke up to a long, wet tongue licking his face. "Ares, you better have a good reason to wake me up," he mumbled, opening his eyes. Ares was looking at Nathan with his tongue hanging out. "You need to go outside?" he asked and Ares ran for the door.

Standing up and stretching, Nathan looked around and saw Jessie and Lenore in the kitchen cooking. Ares barked one time real loud, "RAAF!" to let Nathan know he was waiting. Nathan moved out from behind the table. "Chill out, I'm coming," he told Ares, who was dancing in a circle. Throwing the bolt, Nathan opened the door and Ares took off like a rocket across the parking lot.

Chuckling, Nathan stepped outside and looked around. The sun had not yet risen over the horizon and the only sounds he heard were birds and insects. "This is just weird," he said out loud as Ares ran back over to him. "That's all you had to do and you woke me up for that?" he asked Ares.

Ares lay down on the ground and rolled on his back and groaned. "Ahhw."

"I'm not rubbing your belly, fool, you woke me up," Nathan said, looking down at him. Undeterred, Ares raised his paws over his head, exposing his chest. "Oh alright," Nathan said, kneeling down beside him and scratching his belly. Ares started grunting as Nathan rubbed his belly. "You are pathetic," Nathan said, standing back up. Ares, still resting on his back, cocked his head and looked at Nathan as if to say, 'Yeah, but you're the one that rubbed my belly.'

"Come on, we have work to do," Nathan said, heading back inside. Ares jumped up and followed. Inside, Nathan found everyone up and cleaning the area. Walking into the diner, he stopped in front of Connie. "I'm going to put together a survival box for everyone here. Start a tab for me, okay," he told her.

"You want me to charge you for putting together a box for us?" she asked, speaking volumes with her raised eyebrows.

"Yeah, I'm buying it and giving it to you," he said.

Connie shook her head. "You are a very weird man. I think you were born in the wrong time period," she told him.

"I think you don't know me that well," he told her before walking to the back.

Renee walked past him and called out, "I think you don't give yourself enough credit."

Ignoring her, he walked to the back storeroom and grabbed ten packing boxes and carried them to the store. "Does everyone have a backpack at home?" he called out, and everyone said they did. Grabbing a box, he headed over to the camping aisle first and saw a rack of JanSport backpacks. There were ten in all, so he grabbed four just in case they needed one extra. Looking at the price tag, Nathan almost collapsed. He could pick these things up for fifty bucks and here they were eighty.

He dropped his box and looked at the packs, noticing they were all hydration-compatible. Moving down the aisle, he grabbed four, two-liter bladders and strode over, showed Connie the packs and then threw them in the office. Heading back to the first box, he started grabbing basic supplies, then moved to the food aisle. Placing dried food like rice and beans in first, he then moved down to the canned goods where he selected items carefully. Finally, he moved to the hygiene area and put in the important toilet paper. Grabbing other supplies, he filled the box up and stopped at a display where he threw in a pack of lighters.

Putting the box on the counter, he looked at Connie. "Add this up and put nine more on it," he told her.

"There are only six of us," she reminded him.

"In case we want to help out someone or one of you need more," he told her.

"You're going to need some of this money to get home on," she told him.

Nathan started laughing. "Connie, in a few weeks this money is going to be worthless. I'm trying to get some use out of it. Currency is fixing to be barter and ammunition is going to be at the top of the list," he told her.

She looked in the box. "You didn't put any ammunition in here though," she pointed out.

Nathan shrugged his shoulders apologetically. "I'm sorry, I don't have that much," he told her.

She turned around and pointed at a closet behind the counter. "We sell ammunition," she told him.

He walked around the counter as she unlocked the doors and opened them up. There were rows and stacks of ammunition. Granted, he knew he had way more at home but he wasn't at home. "You have to love a country store," he said, looking at the ammunition.

"This is Georgia, Nathan, and hunting is big business here," she said.

"You don't sell guns by any chance?" he asked hopefully.

"Ahh, no," she admitted.

"This will be enough then," he said, picking up a brick of five hundred .22 caliber. "Ask everyone what type of guns they have at home. I would like to buy each of you all in that caliber, but your prices should be illegal," he told her.

"That's the owner. He buys cheap and sells dear. One of his grandkids came by yesterday to check on us and told us he was in the next county emptying out his liquor stores," she told Nathan.

"He has working vehicles?" he asked.

"Yeah, for some reason he has a big box truck, a station wagon, and a motorcycle," she said.

The first thought through that crossed his mind was that the owner was a complete ass; then Nathan thought about that a minute. The liquor stores would get hit first and that would always sell. No, he concluded, the man was just thinking ahead.

Connie grabbed his arm. "I'm giving you the employee discount of twenty percent since you're working here," she told him.

Nathan twisted his head around to look at her. "I have to see what kind of retirement plan you have before I commit to employment," he said with a wink.

She hugged him. "It sucks but the people here are good co-workers," she said.

"Yep, I can see that," he said as she let him go. Looking back at the ammo, he grabbed a box of .45 and .38 for his other guns, then grabbed another brick of .22. He had fifteen hundred rounds of .22 now and that should keep him fed as he crossed the continent. "Connie, go sit with Renee and let her show you how the Glock works," he suggested.

With a dumbfounded look, Connie just stared at him and said, "You don't think I know how to use a gun?"

Nathan took a step back. "Well, I just figured that—" he stumbled to a halt.

"What, because I'm a woman and dress up I don't know how to use one?" she asked indignantly .

"No, I know plenty of women who hunt and dress up. You just didn't strike me as the type," he admitted.

"I hunt every year and fish all the time. I even bait my own hooks," she said, crossing her arms.

Nathan laughed. "Well, you'll do fine then," he said. "Wait here." He headed to the office, where he dropped the boxes of ammo and pulled out his Glock 19 and the extra magazine. He truly wanted to keep it for trade, but looking at his stuff he knew he had to start paring down the weight.

Walking back to Connie, he held out the pistol and magazine. "Here's a present for my callous remark. Please be careful with it, but use it if you have to," he told her.

Slowly, Connie took it and pulled the pistol out of the holster and ejected the magazine, then racked the slide, popping out the shell. "You always keep one under the hammer?" she asked.

"A gun is useless if it's not ready to fire," he told her.

Connie smirked. "Point taken," she said, putting the round in the magazine. Then, putting the magazine back in, she racked the slide, chambering a round, and holstered the pistol. "I have a shotgun, a rifle, and a revolver at home. You should take this with you and trade it," she said, holding it out to him.

"I think it will do more good here with you, and it's a gift. I just want one promise in exchange for it," he told her.

"What?" she asked.

"Never trade it for anything and keep it close, always. This is going to go on for a while and you are a beautiful lady, which means 'target,'" he said gravely.

Connie smiled at him. "Thank you, and it's a deal," she said and bent down and opened a drawer at the bottom of the ammunition closet. Inside were packages of magazines of many different calibers and models.

"Holy shit," Nathan said, stepping back. "What else is back here?"

"The next cabinet is electronics and the next one is tobacco," she told him, pulling out three more magazines for her present. Then she grabbed two for Renee's pistol. Tearing the drawer apart, she found three dual magazine belt clips and took them out.

Leaving her digging through the drawer, Nathan continued filling boxes and stacked them along the wall of the office. Then he headed to the storeroom just to see what was in there. Walking the aisles, he found it was mostly canned and dry food goods and a lot of it. The storeroom was about fifteen hundred square feet and full. Noticing a case of hiking food bars, he pulled it down. He didn't remember seeing these in the store. Opening one of the boxes and taking out a bar he grinned. *These will come in handy.* Continuing his exploration, he found two cases of emergency meal replacement bars. Nathan was not fond of them as they tasted like the protein bars he ate after lifting weights, but it was food in small containers. Grabbing the three cases, he moved them out and divided up the stuff among the boxes he'd put together and his stuff. When he was finished, he looked at his pile and knew there was no way he was carrying that much shit. Doing a rough calculation, he had now over a hundred and sixty pounds. The most he'd ever carried was a hundred and ten, and he'd barely managed fifteen miles the first few days.

"Nathan, come and eat!" Lenore shouted.

I'll decide what I'll take when it's time to leave, he thought as he walked to the diner. He pulled out a chair and sat down at the table, joining everyone else. Lenore set out plates full of food.

"Oh yeah, now you're talking," Nathan said, looking at the fried eggs, biscuits, and bacon with pancakes on the side. Pouring himself a cup of coffee, he looked around as everyone ate.

"How long are you guys going to stay here?" he asked

Connie looked down the table at him. "The grandkid that stopped by yesterday said Mitch, the owner, would be here as soon as he could to empty the store. We were to just keep going on till he gets here," she told him.

"Seems like an asshole to me," Nathan said.

"Nah, Mitch is okay, it's his son Steven that's the asshole. He runs the stores but his dad owns them," Connie said.

"Okay, I'll stay till he shows up," Nathan said, and everyone thanked him. Then they heard lawn mowers outside coming down the road.

"That's Fred. What is he doing here this early?" Allie asked.

"That is more than one mower," Nathan said, standing up and heading to the front window, followed by the rest of the group. Coming down the road was a sight Nathan would remember for a long time. Fred was on his lawn mower, pulling a small trailer. He was still in his overalls, with a straw cowboy hat and a rifle slung across his back. A second man, the same size as Fred and dressed the same, was riding another mower. Between them was another man. He was dressed identically and was just as massive as the other two, but he had a beard that was down to his chest and was riding a tiny moped. When Allie saw them she took off running.

Nathan pulled out his camera and started taking pictures because nobody would ever believe him without proof. Here were three human giants riding down the road. He had about a dozen pictures as the group pulled up in the lot. Putting his camera up, Nathan followed with everyone else.

When they reached the three men, Fred had Allie wrapped up in a bear hug and was holding her off the ground. Way off the ground. Allie wasn't a small woman, but next to Fred, she seemed damned near diminutive. The man on the moped got off and Nathan could swear he heard the moped sigh with relief as the giant laid it on the ground. Then the moped giant joined the other giant with Fred as they both walked over and hugged Allie.

When Fred released her, the other two picked her up. When they were done greeting her, Allie turned around to the group.

"Everyone, y'all know Fred, but these here are his brothers. This is Billy," she said, gesturing to the one with the beard, "and the other one is Andy."

"You're going home Allie? You not goin' to stay?" Monica asked.

Allie shook her head. "No they's just checkin' on me. Billy's wife works at the school cafeteria and was helping at the center last night. Seems some people came runnin' in tellin' the folks someone here was shot. They described all of us so the sheriff didn't send nobody. They just couldn't figure out who Nathan was, but since he had a badge on the sheriff figured we was fine," she told them, then turned around and hugged Fred. "He thought I was havin' troubles and him and his brothers was goin' to do some fixin'," she said proudly.

"What happened, Allie?" Fred asked, and she told him the story. Fred took off his hat and handed his rifle to Billy, then walked around her, heading to Nathan.

Nathan could swear he felt the earth shake with each step Fred took. Seeing Fred walk toward him like that, Nathan wasn't sure if he should pull his gun, and if he did, who he should use it on, Fred or himself. Looking at Fred's face as he came closer, Nathan had to keep tilting his head back to look up at him. When Fred reached Nathan, he wrapped his arms around Nathan and picked him up, hugging him.

"Nathan, you saved my Allie. I'm indebted to ya," he said, putting Nathan down.

Feeling kind of small and weak, which he didn't like, Nathan smiled up at Fred. "Fred, it was my pleasure," he told him.

"Me and the brothers are goin' to be stayin' today in case trouble starts," Fred told Nathan.

"Shit, sounds good to me," Nathan said. Be damned if he was telling 'em no.

Lenore came out and hugged the three. "Boys, go put those up and come get some food," she said, pointing at the mowers and moped.

Billy put his hands in his pockets. "Ms. Lenore, we don't be havin' money fo' food stuffs," he told her.

Lenore spun around. "Billy, if I tell you to get in there and eat a bite, you better be doin' it. You want me to tell your Ma?" she threatened.

"No ma-am," Billy said meekly, moving to the moped.

"That's good, boys. Now we'll have a busy day, so eat up," she said, heading inside.

Nathan watched as the two pushed—not drove, pushed—the lawnmowers with one arm. Billy just picked up the moped under one arm and followed the others to the back, with Allie leading them. Mesmerized, Nathan just watched, since the two mowers had trailers and neither man showed much effort. Jessie came over to stand beside him.

"Those are some good boys there," he said as the three disappeared around the corner.

"Damn, they're big," was all Nathan could say.

Jessie started laughing. "You think they're big, wait till you see Renee's husband, Mark," he said, still laughing.

"You know them well?" Nathan asked, still looking at the corner they'd gone around.

"Oh yeah, they live right down the road from us. They have a rather large family and are dirt poor. The brothers work at the chicken farm that's called The Fowler Plant. They work hard and the family has a large plot of land. They don't consider themselves poor, though. They have all they need," Jessie told him.

"Shouldn't they be guarding their farm then?" Nathan asked.

"There's two more brothers and two sisters and their husbands not counting Ma and Paw. Then you have the kids, some as old as sixteen. But even the young'uns can shoot in that family. Trust me, anyone who goes out there for trouble will get more than they can handle," Jessie assured him.

"I can imagine," Nathan said, finally turning to look at him. "He really loves his Allie," he said.

"You have no idea," Jessie told him. "Allie was the high school prom queen and is from a pretty well-off family here. Fred always wanted to date her but was intimidated by her standing at school and her family. He never really talked to her or asked her out. Allie took care of that in their senior year. They've been married fourteen years and have three boys and a girl. We visit them a lot," Jessie said.

"Then you'll be fine," Nathan said.

"Of course we'll be fine. My boys aren't much smaller than them, and my daughters can almost beat down their brothers," Jessie told him proudly.

Nathan laughed at that as he headed back inside with Jessie. "Thank you for taking in Connie," he told him, and Jessie grabbed his arm.

"That is a good woman and for nothing else I wish you would stay for her," Jessie told him.

Nathan looked at him and sighed. "I wish I could, but I have a home and friends that are counting on me. I hope you understand," he told him.

"Of course I understand. I'm just sayin'. You're a good man, Nathan, it's been nothin' but an honor to know ya," Jessie said.

"Damn, thank you." Nathan smiled at him.

"Come on, let's eat before it gets much colder," Jessie said, opening the door, and Nathan headed back to the table.

CHAPTER 6

Nathan sat down and started shoveling food down as Lenore set a plate on the floor for Ares. Nodding his head at Ares, Nathan watched as Ares started wolfing down the food. He looked up as the brothers sat down and Lenore and Jessie set plates down for them. Nathan thought he ate fast till he saw the three brothers pile in. They were human vacuum cleaners.

He cleared his throat. "Fred, I haven't had a chance yet to siphon some gas out of my truck for you."

"That's okay, we can do it. We brought cans, and Paw gave us some money to give ya," Fred said, shoving a whole biscuit in his mouth.

Nathan slapped the table. "No sir, I will not take money for it. It's a gift."

"Paw said we needed to give ya somethin' for it since it's goin' to be scarce," Fred told him.

"Fred, there are eighty gallons in my truck that are goin' to ruin. I want it to go to some use," Nathan said. "I'm not taking money for it, understand? Besides, you're helping me guard everyone here," he added.

"Paw will get right mad," Fred said, and the brothers nodded in agreement.

Jessie leaned over the table, putting down another plate of bacon down. "Boys, I'll tell 'im, he can't say nothing to me," he said, and that seemed to satisfy them.

"Thank you Nathan," Fred said.

"No, thank you, Fred, for not letting it go to waste," Nathan told him.

The three brothers grinned at him and he had to admit he really liked them. "Connie, since we have more help in the guarding department, and you, Jessie, and Renee are now armed, I want to limit how many people are inside. How many you figure for the diner and the store?" Nathan asked.

She thought for a minute. "The diner can seat a hundred, but let's keep it at fifty, and the same for the store," she decided.

Nodding his head in agreement with her, Nathan cleared his throat. "Sounds good to me. Fred, you and your brothers rotate around the store. One of you on the inside of the diner door, one at the front door of the store, and the other walking around making sure everyone plays nice. I'll be walking around and giving you guys breaks," he said.

"You want us to count out fifty people to let in, then count out fifty more?" Billy asked in horror.

Nathan just looked at the brothers, not knowing what to say. Connie spoke up. "We will have fifty tickets in a box. When people come in, they have to take one, and when they leave, have them put it back. That way if you see tickets in the box you can let one person take it and come in. When they leave they put it back in the box and another person can come in," she said.

The three brothers thought about that and Fred grinned in relief. "That sounds better," he said.

Wiping his plate down with a biscuit, Nathan popped it in his mouth and stood up. "Come on guys, let's get the gas before the crowd gets here."

The brothers got up and followed Nathan into the store, but not before each one grabbed a biscuit and more bacon. Nathan walked over to the automotive aisle and grabbed three, five-gallon gasoline cans. "Connie, put three gas cans on my tab!" he yelled.

"Bite me!" she yelled back.

Nathan looked at Fred. "You're going to let her talk to me like that?" he asked.

Fred nodded his head. "Allie likes Connie and is her friend, so I'm not going to make her mad," he told him.

"Smart man," Nathan said, patting his shoulder. "We just need to find a water hose now."

"We brought one," Fred said. "It's in my trailer," he added.

"I'll get it and the cans," Billy offered, walking through the store and heading to the shop.

Nathan led the other two outside to his truck, with Ares bouncing around and wanting to play.

"That is a nice ride," Fred said, walking up to the truck.

"It was. It's only a year old with all the bells and whistles," Nathan agreed. "Now if you're around here in the next few months, I want you to get what's left," Nathan told him.

Fred looked at the three cans at Nathan's feet and closed his eyes. Nathan was fixing to ask if he was alright when Fred spoke. "We can get it all now if that's okay with you," he said.

"You said you only brought two fuel cans," Nathan said.

"We did, but we also brought a drum with us," Fred told him. Before Nathan could question him further, he saw Billy walking around the back of the building. In his right hand were two, five-gallon cans and a green water hose. Under his left arm was a fifty-five gallon drum, carried as casually as a stack of schoolbooks. Left speechless, Nathan watched as Billy walked over and set down the stuff.

Then, as if on command, the three brothers reached into their pockets. They each pulled out a pack of chewing tobacco and pulled out a cud, shoving it in their cheeks. Then together they put it up and turned to Nathan.

"Oh I'm sorry, Nathan," Fred said, and pulled his tobacco back out. "Want a chew?" he asked.

Nathan shook his head in spellbound wonder. "No, I dip. Chewing gives me indigestion," he said. In reality, he'd quit dipping four years before and had only tried chewing once. He'd thrown up for an hour and had a headache for a day after that one chew.

"I tried the dippin' but went through the cans too fast," Billy said, grabbing the hose.

Nathan opened the tank and grabbed the water hose from Billy. Then he started taking deep breaths, psyching himself up. "I hate this shit," he said.

"Why?" Fred asked.

Nathan looked up at him. "Because I hate drinking a mouthful of gasoline," he explained.

"Gas tastes nasty. Why would you want to drink it?" Fred asked.

"You have to siphon it out," Nathan answered, running the hose down the tank.

Fred grabbed the hose and pushed Nathan back. "I know it's your truck but let us do this. I don't want to see you drinkin' gas helpin' us out," he told him.

"You'll have to drink it too," Nathan warned him.

"You must siphon gas different out west," Fred told him as he blew in the hose and sucked on the end. Then he quickly pulled it out of his mouth and held the end over a can just as the fuel came out. "You don't have to be drinkin' it," he told Nathan.

"That was cool," Nathan said admiringly. "I've been siphoning gas since I was a kid and every time got a mouth full," he admitted.

Billy moved over with another can, taking the full one and pouring its contents into the drum. "You need to keep your hand where it goes in the fuel tank, and when you feel the gas hit it, take it out of your mouth," he said.

"Damn, that's smart," Nathan admitted, feeling very stupid.

They emptied the tanks and tightened the lid on the drum. Nathan bent down to pick up the cans but Fred stopped him.

"We can get this. You have on good clothes and new boots," he said.

Nathan looked down at his tan tactical pants tucked into his new boots and his black t-shirt with 'Sheriff' across the front in big white letters. "Guys, these aren't good clothes and I'm breaking the boots in," he told them.

"That's nice stuff you're wearin' and you have all that stuff around your waist," Billy said, agreeing with his brother as he tilted the full barrel on its side and laid it down. What shocked Nathan was that he did it without any effort.

"Nathan, you givin' us this. Please let us do the work," Fred begged him. Nathan just nodded as Andy walked over to join his brother Billy. Each one bent down and picked up a five-gallon can, and with the other hand they grabbed the half-inch lip on the barrel, Billy at the front and Andy at the back. They lifted it up and carried the drum of fuel off between them.

Gawking at them in disbelief, Nathan followed them with his stare as they calmly carried a drum weighing over four hundred pounds with their fingertips. Fred put the cap on his tank and closed the fuel door, wrapped up his hose, and grabbed the other three cans.

"We'll meet you inside," Fred said as he followed his brothers.

Nathan was still standing there after they left his sight. "What the hell do they feed these boys down here?" he asked out loud as Ares came over and sat down beside him. "Did you see that?" he asked Ares. Ares just looked up at him, wondering what he wanted.

Nathan shook his head and walked back to the store. "Anyone insane enough to screw with them deserves what they get," he told Ares, holding the door open for him. Walking inside, he headed to the cooler and pulled out a pop and took a swig.

"Yeah, I'm going to miss these," Nathan said, taking another long drink and walking to the counter. He looked at his cheap watch, seeing it was almost eight. "Shouldn't be much longer," he said, looking at Connie and Renee. They each had their pistols on their right hips and magazine holders on their left hips. "You guys look intimidating," he said, motioning to the guns.

"It keeps pulling my shorts down," Renee told him, pulling up her cut-off blue jean shorts.

"Get some suspenders," he suggested.

"I'll look funny," she said.

Nathan shook his head. "I wear them. I think I would look more funny with my pants falling down. You two are pretty enough that no one would say anything."

"You're not wearing suspenders," Renee said.

Setting his Coke down, Nathan pulled his shirt out of his pants and lifted it up. Moving his bulletproof vest, he showed them the suspenders he was wearing to hold up his pants.

Renee spun around. "I'm doing that," she said, heading to the camping aisle.

"Get me some too," Connie called after her.

Nathan smiled, tucking in his shirt. "You two could've let your pants fall down once," he said, grabbing his drink and waggling his eyebrows.

"Shame on you," Connie said, giggling.

Nathan drank in her smile, noticing she was a very sexy woman. She had dark brown hair and was just a little taller than Renee, and not much younger than he was. "I'm a bad boy," Nathan said as Ares came over, butting his leg with his head. "You're not getting any pop," Nathan told him sternly.

Ares whined at him and Nathan sighed. He walked over to the counter and grabbed a cup and poured some pop in it, then held it in front of Ares. "Here, tiddy baby," he said, and Ares started lapping up the soda. When he finished the cup, Ares raised his head, his tongue lapping in the air. Connie started laughing. "He does that with fizzy drinks," Nathan explained.

Renee came back over carrying the suspenders and started laughing at Ares. "Your dog is so cool," she said.

"He takes after me," Nathan said proudly. "Come on, let's gather up one last time," he said, heading to the diner.

They followed him and Nathan called everyone over. "Now the people that come in today will have the shock wearing off, and many will be angry. Their world is turned upside down and they will want to take it out on someone," Nathan said.

"That's just mean," Billy said, and his brothers agreed with him.

"The power's off and it's freaking them out," Nathan explained.

"We didn't have power till I was in high school," Fred told him.

Nathan fought the urge to laugh and continued. "Like I said, some will be mean. Don't get into an argument with them. Remain calm and ask them to calm down. If they refuse, ask them to leave, and if they don't, help them leave. Once they're outside they can't come back in. Now a lot of people will be armed, so keep your weapons visible. An armed society is a polite society.

"If a person that comes in goes for a weapon, shoot them and don't think about it first. Just do it," he said, looking at everyone to make sure they understood. "If you think something is getting out of hand, motion to me or the brothers and we will take care of it," he continued. "Fred, Billy, and Andy, don't be scared to throw someone out, okay," he said, looking at them.

The three looked at each other, furrowing their brows. Allie stepped over to them. "He means it's okay. Use muscle to throw them out and don't worry about hurting them as long as we are okay," she told them.

Nathan was fixing to clarify what he meant but decided not to. If someone was stupid enough to fight the Oakridge boys from hell then that was on them. "Our first concern is to keep everyone safe, and I want you to take some breaks, okay," he said, and they all nodded in agreement. "Now some people will be coming in and will only have a little cash. Some of those people I want to help," he told them. "And I want you to help me do it," he added.

"How can we do that? We don't make good money here," Monica said.

"If I see any of you giving your money or supplies to anyone but family, I will bend you over my knee. Then I'll take my belt to your ass. If your house and your neighbor's house is on fire, you don't give your neighbor your water hose. You use it, *then* help them. Take care of you and yours first," Nathan said, pulling out a wad of cash. "I'm giving each of you two hundred dollars to help people today. Don't give any money to them, just help them on purchases. Nobody getting beer gets anything," he told them.

"You really need to be savin' yo money," Monica said as he handed her the money.

"I already told him that, Monica," Connie said.

"We had this talk, Connie," Nathan said, handing Jessie and Lenore money. "If you guys help me do this, I will give each of you two hundred tonight when we close, and you can spend it on extra supplies." He moved over to Connie. "What's my total now?" he asked.

"Right at two grand," she told him, and the brothers whistled in unison.

Reaching into his pocket, Nathan pulled out another wad and counted out two thousand dollars. "Here's for my tab," he said, holding it out.

"This will clean you out after you give us money tonight," she said, taking the money.

He winked at her and pulled out another wad of cash. "I found some more," he told her.

"You could get in trouble," she said.

"I saw that man pick it up from the parking lot when he walked in. I knew I had lost some money and couldn't find it. I won it at a casino. Read my report," he said, grinning.

"I saw him with that money before hand," Jessie said, looking at Connie. Connie's eyes became wide when she heard that. "He showed it to me to prove you could win at a casino," he told her.

Connie laughed. "Yeah, I think I remember him saying something about that," she agreed.

"Okay, let's take our places and stay safe. I'm going to lock the side door and every other door into this place," Nathan said, then looked at the brothers. "I want you guys to help me make sure they stay that way unless we unlock them. I don't want someone sneaking in to get the drop on us," he told them, and they nodded.

The three brothers looked at the money in their hands, then each other. As one, they stepped over to Allie and handed it to her. "Allie, you, Connie and Renee give ours out," Fred told her and stepped back, joined by his brothers.

Allie passed the money to the others, then walked over and hugged the three brother. "Y'all be careful and don't get hurt," she told them. Nathan wanted to tell her if someone could hurt those three they were all screwed and dead, in that order.

Fred picked her up, hugging her gently. "Don't be worryin' bout us. We're big boys," he said. "Andy, you take the door to the diner and Billy, take the door to the store first. We can switch when y'all get tired," he told them.

"Get tired doin' what?" Andy asked.

Fred exhaled a long breath. "Makin' people be good and only lettin' people in when we have tickets in the box," he told him.

Connie took off running. "I'm getting the tickets and boxes now!" she hollered out.

"We're goin' to get tired doin' this?" Andy asked.

"No, but we can switch up anyway," Fred said.

Nathan stepped over to Andy. "Andy, he means if you need to go to the bathroom you can switch up," he told him.

Andy looked at Fred. "Why didn't you just say that?" he asked.

"You should've figured it out," Fred barked at him.

Nathan was fixing to say something when a knock at the door stopped him. Turning around, he saw two people standing at the door and several more coming across the parking lot. "It's game time, people," he said as everyone moved to their area.

Billy moved to the front door as Connie set a box down beside him, handed him a bundle of tickets, and carried another to Andy. Billy turned the bolt and opened the door as two men in their twenties walked in. He held out a massive arm, stopping them. "Take a ticket and put it back in the box before you leave. Only fifty people at a time in the store," he told them. The two men looked at the giant with a rifle across his back, grabbed a ticket and moved inside.

Nathan left the front and walked around the building, making sure the doors were locked. When he walked inside the shop, he saw the two lawn mowers with trailers full of gas cans and a drum. Leaned against the wall was the moped. He walked over and patted the little scooter. "You are one tough machine," he said, looking around to make sure the doors were locked and admiring the equipment.

When he was done, he headed back to the store to find about twenty people in it and about that many in the diner. He looked at his watch and saw he had only been gone fifteen minutes. Shaking his head, he went behind the counter to stand beside Renee, who had Ares on the other side of her. "Ares is protecting you," he told her as she was ringing up a customer.

"Yeah, Fred was going to walk back here and Ares growled at him," she said with a laugh.

"I'll bring him back," he told her. "Ares, follow," he said, and Ares fell in behind him. Nathan walked around and introduced him to everyone. Fred just about refused till Allie came over and started hugging Ares. "Fred, I have to tell him your name and you have to pet him before he knows that you're a friend," Nathan explained.

"Shoot fire, that dog is smart," Fred said, petting Ares. Ares licked his hand and looked up at him, panting.

"Yes he is," Nathan said, walking back over to Renee with Ares following. Ares sat down beside her as Nathan started pulling boxes of ammunition out and carried them to the office. Grabbing a pen off the desk, he wrote names on the boxes and put the ammo in order by what caliber everyone had.

By ten, Nathan was glad Connie and the others had restocked the store the night before. They were averaging ten people in the store and twenty in the diner at all times. Everyone was paying cash. He continued his walk around and let the brothers trade out, even though Andy yelled at Fred he wasn't tired and didn't have to pee.

It was just before noon and Nathan was sitting behind the counter with Renee. Connie and Allie were helping in the diner when Nathan saw a family walk in. They were dressed identically, all wearing polo shirts, khaki shorts, and loafers, but that was not what caught his attention.

They were all textbook attractive. The man was tall with an athletic build; the wife was knock out gorgeous. As for the kids, one was an older girl around ten and the spitting image of her mother; the boy was around six and just like his dad. They all had golden blonde hair and perfect skin.

He looked at Renee and was glad she was gawking at them as well. "Glad I'm not the only one staring at them," he whispered to her.

"Shit, you can't help but stare at them. I look at the woman and want to crawl under the counter. Even the brothers are staring at them," she whispered back.

Nathan laughed and looked at Fred at the door and Billy walking around. Both were looking at the family. Two men walked in after the family, both wearing backpacks, and Fred told them to set them against the wall before shopping. The men complied, each taking a ticket and putting their packs on the wall, then walked into the store.

Turning back to look around, Nathan saw most everyone was staring at the perfect family shopping. He stood up and stretched, then walked around the counter, telling Ares to stay beside Renee. He watched the two men that followed the perfect family in his peripheral vision. He could tell both were armed and studied them closer. One was black, about five foot ten and one hundred and seventy pounds, and the other was white, close to six foot and two hundred pounds. Both were filthy.

Moving back to the front of the store, he continued to watch the family and the two until he heard yelling at the counter. "You have to take a credit card!" a short man yelled at Renee.

"No I don't, sir," Renee said as Ares stood up, putting his front paws on the counter and growling at the man. Nathan fought not to laugh seeing as Ares was almost as tall as Renee. The man backed away from the counter.

"That's a health violation!" he shouted.

"Ares goes where he wants to. If you try to stop him he bites your arm off. Since I have both of mine, you see I haven't tried to stop him," Renee said with a gentle smile.

"I don't have that much money," the short man told her.

"I'm sorry sir, cash only," she said as Nathan moved over to the counter.

The man saw Nathan and turned to him. "Make her take my credit card!" he shouted.

"Sir, don't yell, please," Nathan said calmly. "It's cash only, and if you need something else there is an aid station at the high school. They are serving food and water there," he told the man in a calm voice.

"Well I want to buy something here," he popped off.

"Of course sir, but it's cash only," Nathan told him.

"You can't do that!" the short man yelled. Billy came up behind him and grabbed the man by the back of the neck. Then Billy just lifted him up off the floor, holding the man in the air like a doll, with one arm.

"You heard Nathan say don't be hollerin', why you have to be rude? Then you yellin' at Renee. She just a little bitty thang and you being mean," Billy grumbled, holding the man out at arm's length two feet off the floor. The man couldn't see Billy since he was behind him, but he could sure feel the grip of steel on his neck.

Billy looked at Nathan who was just staring in awe at the sight. "Yeah, what he said," Nathan mumbled.

Billy started moving toward the door when Renee hollered for him to stop and came around the counter followed by Ares. She held out a bottle of water to the man. "Here," she said.

"You're giving me some water?" he asked.

She pointed at Nathan. "The officer bought several cases and asked us to give one to each person till they're gone," she said, walking back behind the counter. "Have a nice day," she said, and Billy carried him to the door and Fred took his ticket.

Billy walked back Nathan. "That was just being rude, Nathan," he said.

"I'm not going to be rude, Billy, I promise. If I am, let me get a running start first," he said, still in awe and praying the massive giant wouldn't get mad at him.

"I know you ain't goin' to be rude, Nathan," Billy said, walking down an aisle.

Nathan turned and saw the perfect family at the counter. They were all holding an armful of stuff and were putting it on the counter. The dad stepped up to the counter, holding a gold wristwatch out. "Can you take this in trade?" he asked Renee.

Renee looked at the perfect looking man with a pleading look. She had used up all her helping money already. "Sir, I'm sorry," she finally got out.

"It's a Rolex, a real one I swear," he told her.

"I can't, sir," she told the perfect looking man.

The man smiled at her and she wanted to melt. "That's okay, I have a little money," he told her. "Will you add up till I get to thirty-nine dollars?" he asked.

She nodded, wanting to cry as Nathan walked over. "Renee, will you get me a roll of Skoal long cut please?" he asked her and she turned around and grabbed one, handing it to him. "Ring up their stuff and add it to this," he said. Renee smiled at Nathan and mouthed 'Thank you' at him.

Nathan turned to the family, smiling as the dad held out the watch. "Here, sir," he said, trying to hand it over.

"Nah, you keep it. You might need it later," Nathan told him.

"Sir, please," he persisted, holding out the watch and shaking it.

"I got one so I don't need another one," Nathan said, smiling at him. He turned to the little girl. "I think you're as pretty as the morning sunrise, little one," Nathan told her, making her giggle and smile. "Hold on baby, you have something behind your ear," he said, reaching out and popping his wrist. "Told you something was there!" He held up a folded hundred dollar bill.

The girl gasped.

"You just heard your dad say he needed some money and you could've given it to him," Nathan told her.

"I didn't know it was there," she said, holding her ear. Her brother pulled her hand away, grabbed a handful of his sister's hair and pulled her head down to him so he could look to see if there was more.

The little girl screamed and his mom popped his hand. "Raymond, stop that," she told him.

Nathan looked at Raymond and grinned. "You too," he said, holding out his hands, then reached over behind Raymond's ear and popped his wrist and held another hundred dollar bill up.

The man turned to his wife. "Honey, check their ears. I was watching his hands that time," he told her and turned back to Nathan.

"Your kids were holding out on you," Nathan said, holding out the two bills.

"Sir, I can't," he said, looking at the two hundred dollar bills with longing.

"Sir, please take 'em before Billy comes over here thinking we are being rude to each other," Nathan whispered.

The man cut his eyes toward Billy without moving his head, then looked at Nathan. "Okay," he said, taking the money. "At least let me buy this stuff then," he said.

Nathan smiled. "Renee will do what I ask before what you ask," he said in a teasing voice.

"I already rung it up and bagged it, Nathan," she chimed in, smiling.

"See, told ya," Nathan said, then kneeled down, looking at the two kids. "Do you guys like hamburgers?" he asked, and their eyes got wide as smiles filled their faces. They both nodded together and stepped up to Nathan wanting more information.

"I have a friend in the diner over there that makes the best hamburgers in the world. You go over there with your mom and dad and ask for Lenore and tell her you're my friends. Then tell her what you want, okay?"

They both looked up at their mom and dad with pleading smiles. "Kids, Nathan has done too much to help us already. We can't take more from him or he won't have enough for himself and his family," the dad told them.

The kids looked at Nathan with sad faces and Nathan smiled. "Kids, tell Daddy to be quiet before Billy thinks someone is being rude," he said.

"Rude, who's being rude?" Billy asked, walking up to them.

The kids moved behind a kneeling Nathan as he looked up at Billy, still smiling. "Nobody is being rude, Billy, I swear. I was just telling the kids I wanted them and their parents to eat and it was my treat," Nathan said, looking up at Billy. "Please don't pick me up by my neck?" Nathan begged.

Billy shook his head at Nathan. "Nathan, I can't hurt you for nuthin'. You helped my family. Besides, you saved Fred's Allie. If I was to try and hurt ya he'd be liable to get real mad at me and hurt me," Billy told him.

"You can get hurt?" Nathan asked, not believing that.

Billy shrugged his shoulders. "Well yeah, the last time we tussled we were at it for six hours. Paw shot us with rock salt to break us up," he said.

"When was that?" Nathan asked. He had to know.

"Thanksgiving," Billy said.

"I just want them to eat and let me pay for it. If you're going to hurt me, let me know so I can hide behind Fred," Nathan pleaded with a smile.

Billy turned to the mom and dad, taking his straw cowboy hat off and holding it over his heart. "Ma-am and sir, please let Nathan get sum vittles in y'all. He's right nice and all," Billy told them. "It would just hurt my heart if I had to say anything unkind to y'all," he added.

The mom stepped over to Billy and smiled at him. "We will, sir, and thank you," she told him.

"Thank you, ma-am," he said, bowing down. As he bowed down, she reached out and grabbed his face and kissed his forehead.

"Thank you, sir," she said, smiling.

Billy stood up grinning with his face turning red. "Aw, shucks, ma'am," he said, putting his hat on.

"Can I stand up without someone grabbing me by the back of the neck?" Nathan asked.

Heavy footsteps sounded across the store. "Who's gonna grab you by the neck?" Fred challenged, walking over.

Nathan lowered his head toward his shoulders and the kids got closer to Nathan, thinking their parents were too far away for protection. "Nobody, Fred, I promise," Nathan said.

"Well don't be sayin' stuff like that. I don't want to have to be unfriendly to someone," Fred said as Nathan stood up.

"I'm taking them to the diner," Nathan told him.

Fred held out his hands. "Y'all go get some food in ya. Y'all look starved," he said as Nathan whispered to hand the tickets to Fred. When they gave the tickets back, Fred took his hat off. "Thank ya," he said, throwing the tickets in the box.

When they turned around, Andy walked over, holding out tickets. "Take the tickets," Nathan told them, leading them to a table in the diner. Nathan pulled out chairs for them to sit down as the dad was looking at his ticket. "Don't ask," Nathan said as the dad sat down.

Dad held out his hand to Nathan. "Bradwin, Bradwin Bedford, but everyone calls me Brad," he said.

"Brad," Nathan said, shaking his hand.

"My wife Abigail, my daughter Ashlee, and my son Raymond," he said as Nathan moved his hand around the table, shaking hands.

Allie walked up to the table carrying the menus. "Alright folks, what will it be?" she asked and looked up. "Oh my," she said, looking at the family.

Nathan smiled. "Allie, these are my friends. The kids want hamburgers," he said, then introduced the family. When Allie finished taking their order, Nathan looked at Brad. "I don't want you to leave before talking to me, okay?" he said.

Brad pinched his brows together, trying to figure out what Nathan was getting at. "Huh?" he asked.

"I just want your word that you won't leave this building till you talk to me," Nathan said.

"I have no reason not to, but with the kindness you've shown me, yes, I'll talk to you before I leave," Brad told him.

"That goes for your whole family. Please don't leave till you talk to me," Nathan said. Brad looked at him, bewildered. "You'll understand later," Nathan told him.

"Okay," Brad said, shrugging.

"Thank you," Nathan said. "Enjoy," he said with a smile, then stood up and walked back to the store. "Fred, watch that family," he said as he passed by him, then headed to the office. Grabbing two backpacks, he took two of the boxes and filled the packs with their contents, then put in the hydration bladders. Throwing them on the desk, he dug into his suitcase.

He pulled out a pair of jeans, his tennis shoes, and a t-shirt and threw them on the desk. He walked out to Renee who was at the counter with Connie. "Renee, do you have any clothes here Abigail can wear?" he asked.

"Who's that?" she asked.

"The pretty momma," he told her.

She thought for a minute. "I might have some sweatpants in my locker," she said. "But she won't wear them," she said, then added, "I don't know if I want someone that pretty to wear them."

"I'll take 'em," Nathan said, then walked to the front of the store and grabbed t-shirts for the kids and one for Abigail. Then he went to the counter and waited on Renee. She came back carrying a pair of gray jogging pants.

"They're clean," she said, handing them over.

"Thank you." He went back to the office where he dug out his Glock 21 and the two clips still in their holster and shoved them in one of the

backpacks. Throwing the backpacks over his left shoulder, he walked out and set them behind the counter with the armload of clothes.

He walked over to Connie and Renee, pulled them shoulder to shoulder and whispered in their ear. They both looked up in alarm and nodded. He went around to the brothers and did the same, then walked back behind the counter and grabbed the stuff and headed to the side door.

Billy was waiting and held it open as Nathan jogged out to his truck. He unlocked the driver side door and opened the back passenger door on the driver's side, then put the packs inside. Opening the one with the gun, he pulled it out and put it in the center console with the magazines. Then he threw his clothes in the passenger seat and laid the rest out in the back.

Closing the doors, he ran back to the side door and Billy held it open for him. Billy locked it as Nathan stopped and looked out the window. He saw some people walking along the road out front, but not much out of the ordinary. He glanced at Billy.

"You ready?" he asked.

"I'm ready," Billy said, taking his rifle off his back.

"Let's see if I'm right," Nathan said as he walked toward the diner. As he passed the counter, Connie and Renee both nodded at him and Nathan nodded back. Fred and Andy did the same as he headed into the diner. Nathan smiled as he walked over to the family's table to see empty plates and happy faces.

"Was it good?" he asked, pulling up a chair and sitting down.

"Yes, it was the best," Ashlee told him with her little face split with a smile.

"Nathan, it was great," Brad told him.

"Where are you guys from?" Nathan asked.

"California," Brad said.

"I'm glad you enjoyed. Now I have a favor to ask?" Nathan said, leaning over. "Do you know how to protect yourself?" he asked.

"Yes, I have a black belt in Aikido," Brad answered, not understanding.

Reaching down, Nathan palmed his knife and passed it to Brad. "It's a switchblade, so be careful," he told him and before Brad could speak, he continued in a low voice. "My Suburban is parked out on that side of the building," he said with a nod of his head. "Walk out of here and head to the driver's side. Open both doors and wait for me before you get in, and no, it doesn't run but just wait on me, okay?" he asked.

Brad took a breath to ask a question and Nathan stopped him with a low voice. "Don't talk loud about what I just told you; just act happy and walk toward my truck okay? I'm begging you," Nathan said calmly.

Brad nodded. "Kids, tell Nathan thank you," he said in a loud voice.

Nathan shook their hands and walked them to the diner door as Fred held it open for them. Seeing the filthy men get up from where they'd been sitting, Nathan walked through the store and nodded at the girls at the counter. Billy was waiting by the back door and held it open as Nathan walked out to see Brad leading his family to the Suburban. Brad opened the doors as Nathan walked up.

"What's going on?" Brad asked.

"Don't have long, I think, but there are two backpacks inside with enough food for you guys to last a week or more," Nathan told him.

"Nathan—" Brad started.

Nathan held up his hand for Brad to stop. "Wait Brad," Nathan said. "In the passenger seat are some clothes and shoes. I want you to get in and change into them," he said. Then he turned to Abigail. "There are some clothes in the back for you. All I could find was shirts for the kids," he told her.

"You want to change our appearance?" Abigail asked and he nodded. "We stand out that much?" she asked.

"Well Abigail, you already have some admirers that don't look too nice," he told her. "Don't turn around but bend down and look toward the front of the building and you will see two men standing at the corner wearing backpacks," he said.

"They could just be travelers," Brad said hopefully.

"They're not," Nathan said.

Brad's eyes became wide as it all fell into place. "Oh shit, what do we do?" he asked.

"Do you know how to shoot a Glock?" Nathan asked.

"Yeah, I have two. One for me and one for Abigail," he replied.

"And you're from California?" Nathan asked, actually shocked.

"Not everyone from Cali is a moron," Brad informed him.

Nathan smiled. "In the console is a pistol. Take it when you get out, but be careful, it's loaded. Get in and change as I walk back inside. They are going to either walk over here or wait on you to leave, but either way don't get out until I have them on the ground. Then get the backpacks on and walk to the side door over there. Billy will be waiting on you." Nathan turned to Abigail. "In the console are some of my ponytail holders. I want you and Ashlee to put your hair up," he told her.

"Okay," she said in a nervous voice.

"Hey, the hard part is over for you guys. I wanted to make sure they let you out," Nathan said.

Brad gasped. "You wanted to see if they had friends," he said.

"Oh, I'm sure they do, but I don't know where or who," Nathan said. "Now change, and if you hear shots, wait till they stop before you run back to the store." They both nodded as he turned around and walked casually toward the store. Billy held the door open as he walked inside.

"Connie told me nobody went out with those two," Billy said as Nathan walked in. He closed the door behind him.

Nathan nodded. "Ares, come!" he shouted. Ares bounded over with a playful face. "Time to work. Guard me," Nathan told him. The hair on Ares' back stood up and his body tensed up as Nathan checked his gear and looked out the window to see the two bums walk toward his truck.

"Wait till they're in before you come out. You have to hold the door open for the family," Nathan said, moving to the door.

"Don't worry, I will," Billy said as Nathan pushed the door open, pulling out his pistol. Stepping outside, he aimed his pistol at the two.

"Freeze assholes!" he yelled at the two. The two men turned to see Nathan aiming a pistol at them and a big ass dog with his hackles raised, growling at them.

"I can kill you before you twitch, and if you run, Ares will tear you apart," Nathan told them as Ares started baking. "Raise your hands high in the air!" he yelled over Ares' barking and the two men did what he told them. Out of the corner of his eye, Nathan saw Fred at the corner of the building aiming his rifle at the two.

Nathan smiled as he yelled, "Okay white man, on your knees and lay on your belly holding your hands out over your head." The man did as he was told as Ares crept closer to them.

"Black man, do the same thing!" Nathan yelled, and he did. Keeping his pistol aimed at them, he moved closer. "Either of you move, and you both die," Nathan said. "Ares, watch 'em," he commanded. "If you so much as twitch, he will attack," Nathan told them as Fred walked over, aiming his rifle at the two.

"Three men who were sitting on the side of the road took off running toward the Interstate," Fred told him.

Nathan kicked the white man's leg. "How many more?" he asked sternly.

"It was only them," he whimpered.

Nathan looked at Fred. "Will you know them if you see them?" he asked.

"Yep, they easy to pick out," Fred replied.

"If you see them again, kill 'em," Nathan said, holstering his pistol. Then he pulled off the white man's pack and took two pistols off of him and a large sheath knife. Then Nathan pulled out one pair of cuffs and cuffed him. Then he moved to the black man and did the same, taking the same off of him as Billy came walking up.

"Whatcha' need?" Billy asked.

"Grab their packs and take them inside," Nathan answered as Ares came closer, barking at the black man.

"Officer, control your dog," the black man begged.

Fred stomped on his back. "Nobody said talk," he said and looked at Nathan.

Nathan was just staring at the man. He could swear the guy bounced up six inches after Fred stomped him. "What he said," Nathan blurted out.

Connie and Jessie came running out with pistols drawn. "What do you need?" Connie asked.

"Get those weapons and put them in the office," he told her and looked at Fred. "Let's get them inside," he said, grabbing the black man's arms and pulling him up.

Fred just walked over to the white man and grabbed a handful of hair and picked him straight up. "Stand or I'll carry you like that," he told the man. The man screamed but stood up.

"You would make one hell of a cop," Nathan told him as they led the men to the store and Andy held the door open for the group. Billy dropped the packs by the door as Jessie and Connie carried the weapons to the office. The customers inside just watched the spectacle as they laid the men on the floor.

Fred grinned as he just threw his down. "I always wanted to be a policeman," he admitted. "Just couldn't pass the test.,"

"You can't do this to us!" the white man yelled.

"Billy, he's being rude to me," Nathan said. Billy walked over and stomped on the guy's back.

"You be nice," Billy said as the man gasped for air.

"Renee, bring me some rope please!" Nathan yelled out.

"You can't hang us, you're the police!" the black man screamed.

Nathan just looked at Fred and Fred walked over and stomped on him again. "You would think that once was enough," Nathan said as Renee handed him the rope. He tied up their feet then bent them at the knees and hog-tied them. "We need to get that dolly and move them," Nathan said, standing up as he finished.

"Where you want 'em?" Fred asked.

Nathan shrugged his shoulders. "I don't know, I guess the showers," he said.

Fred nodded and walked over and grabbed the rope connecting the handcuff and the feet together, using it like a suitcase handle to pick up the white man. Then Billy walked over and picked up the black man the same way. "Finish searching them for me, will ya?" Nathan called after them. They both raised their rifles over their head acknowledging him.

He turned to Jessie. "I'm almost tempted to stay just to have those three as my deputies," he admitted.

Jessie laughed. "Those three are having the time of their life."

"I'll probably be sued, but hell, it'd be worth it," Nathan said, grabbing the packs and taking them to the office, then heading to the diner. He stopped at the front door. "Andy, can you handle both doors till they get back?" he asked.

"Sure, but I want to arrest the next one," Andy said with somewhat of a pouty face.

"It's a deal," Nathan said, patting him on the shoulder. Then he walked over to the Bedfords. They were still handsome but didn't stand out so much. He sat down at the table with them and smiled. "I'm glad that went well," he said.

Brad looked at him with a solemn face. "You saved my family's life," he said.

"They might have just robbed you," Nathan lied.

Brad shook his head. "You know that's a lie," he told Nathan.

Nathan nodded his head. "Nothing happened and you're safe, so it doesn't matter," he said. "Now we can talk about my payment for lunch," he informed them. They all looked at him in shock and Nathan smiled. "I think a kiss right here from a little angel should cover it," he said, pointing at his cheek.

Ashlee stood up in her chair and wrapped her arms around his neck and kissed his cheek. "Wow, a kiss *and* a hug from a little angel," Nathan said as Ashlee sat back down. Abigail stood up and hugged him and kissed his other cheek. "Holy cow, and from a big angel," Nathan said, grinning.

Brad laughed. "Nathan, I would kiss you too but I don't think you would take it the same way."

"Dude, you're almost handsome enough so I don't really know," Nathan said with a wink, making Brad laugh harder. "You guys stay here and eat some more," he said, standing up. Brad was going to say something till he saw Nathan's face and just nodded. "Kids, tell Lenore you want some ice cream," Nathan suggested, getting cheers as Allie walked up and handed him a sheet of paper.

He read the paper and turned to her. "Are you kidding me?" Nathan asked.

"That's what they said and I wrote it down," she told him.

"Not that. They're questioning them without Andy?" he whispered loudly at her. Nathan turned to Andy. "Andy, go back there and find out the names of their friends, and tell Billy and Fred to come on back up here. Andy, just don't break anything or kill them, okay?" Nathan said as Andy started jogging to the back of the store, grinning devilishly.

"I'll be easy. I saw a picture show on how to do this," he called over his shoulder.

When he was gone, Nathan looked at Allie, "I hope it wasn't 'Saw.'"

Allie shook her head. "No, the Lethal Weapons."

Nathan shook his head as the two brothers came in. "Are you two insane questioning them without Andy?" he almost shouted.

"We figured you would want to know," Fred said, slinging his rifle over his back.

"I do, but he's pissed he didn't get to help arrest them!" Nathan shouted that time.

Billy waved his hand at Nathan. "He's the baby brother so he comes last," he said.

"Baby to you, maybe" Nathan pointed out.

"You don't have to be worryin' about Andy. I can fight him down in a few hours and Fred can usually do it in one," Billy told him.

Nathan stumbled back in shock. "Dude, I've never been in a fight that went over twenty minutes," he informed him.

Billy and Fred looked at each other, then at Nathan. "You need to come to the farm and wrestle the cows down," Fred suggested.

"You mean calves, right?" Nathan asked.

Fred looked at him with displeasure. "What good would wrestling babies do? You wrestle the cows till you're good enough to wrestle down a bull."

Nathan pulled Allie in front of him. "Allie really likes me and if you guys break me she will get mad at you," he told them.

Allie threw her hands on her hips. "Boys, don't y'all go and get Nathan hurt," she snapped.

"We ain't goin to let him get hurt, honey pie," Fred told her.

"Okay baby, and you did so good today. I'm so proud of you," she said, walking over and hugging him.

Fred blushed as she hugged him, then she hugged Billy and went to help with the orders.

"Guys, watch the doors. I'm going to check on Andy," Nathan said.

"Renee is with him," Fred told him.

"You let Renee watch?" Nathan asked incredulously.

"Yeah, she was watchin' us to make sure we didn't hurt 'em," Billy said.

Nathan started rubbing his temples. "I'm getting a headache," he said, walking back to the showers. He passed Andy on the way. "You got the names that fast?" he shouted.

Andy looked at him with a pouting face. "Yeah, I didn't even get to rub salt in a bleeding hole," he said.

Nathan walked into the showers to see the two men laying on their stomachs, hog-tied and crying. Renee walked over to him and handed him a piece of paper.

"Here's the rest," she said.

Nathan just took it, smiling as she walked out. He made sure they couldn't get loose then went to the office and started going through their packs.

The packs were dirty but were actually very nice large expedition packs. He pulled out six pistols, a lot of magazines, boxes of ammunition, and two complete police duty belts. Then he found two Georgia State Police badges. Laying them on the desk, he continued the examination to find six wallets and a bag of jewelry, some with blood on it.

He left the weapons, magazines, duty belts, and ammunition on the desk and threw the rest back in the packs and closed them up. He held the badges in each hand, rubbing his thumbs over them. The men had admitted to catching a group of people camping last night beside the Interstate. The two troopers had been part of the group, along with two men, three women, and two kids. None of the captured group saw the sunrise this morning.

CHAPTER 7

Connie walked in as he was holding the badges. She coughed to let him know she was there. "Mark is here; Renee's husband," she told him when he looked up.

Letting out a long, mournful sigh, Nathan laid the badges down and followed her out. When he came around the corner, Nathan froze as he beheld the biggest man he had ever seen in his life. The brothers were all between six foot seven to six foot ten. The man Nathan was looking at could lick salt of the top of their heads, and stood an easy seven and a half foot tall. His shoulder span was twice Nathan's, and Nathan put his weight well over four-fifty with very little of it fat.

The gigantic man was holding up Renee, hugging her; Renee's feet were over a yard off the floor. She looked like a little bird next to a skyscraper. "What the hell do you people feed the boys around here?" Nathan shouted. Everyone turned to look at him. Mark moved Renee over and just held Renee in the crook of his arm like a child so she could look at Nathan. "I swear to God if someone tells me Mark isn't the biggest person in this county, I'm leaving now," Nathan said, making everyone laugh, but he was serious.

Mark laughed and walked over to him carrying Renee. Nathan had to keep tilting his head back and felt like he was looking at the sky by the time Mark stopped in front of him. Mark shifted Renee to his left arm and held out his right hand. "Sir, I'm indebted to you," he said in a deep voice.

Nathan held out his hand, praying he would get it back in one piece. "I don't taste good," Nathan said as Mark's massive hand engulfed his. Mark laughed again, releasing his hand and pulling Nathan to his chest.

Mark's badge was just above Nathan's eye level, and Nathan felt like a small animal, wanting to run for cover. "I've heard nothing but good things about you and you saved my wife and friends. I couldn't hurt you," Mark told Nathan, hugging him tight.

"Ah, not to seem too ungrateful but you're really making me want to wet my pants," Nathan said, his face buried in Mark's chest.

Renee popped Mark's chest. "He can't breathe, baby," she told him and Mark let Nathan go. Nathan took a step back and bumped into Ares. He looked down and noticed Ares was hiding behind him with his tail between his legs.

"Damn, I've never see you scared even when you fought a bear," Nathan said. Ares looked up at Nathan, then at Mark as if telling him, 'I'm not attacking that!'

"Put me down," Renee told Mark, which he did. Renee got down on her knees. "Come here, Ares," she said, clapping her hands.

Keeping his eyes on Mark, Ares slinked over to her, keeping her between him and the giant. "Ares, it's okay," she said, hugging him. "Nathan, will you introduce them?" she asked.

"Ares, this is Mark," he told Ares. Ares looked at Nathan with a startled look, then turned to Mark and lowered his head.

Mark squatted down. He was still almost as tall as Nathan standing up. Renee was still much shorter. Mark rubbed Ares' head, then started talking to him. Ares started panting and moved over to the giant, letting Mark scratch him. Then Mark picked Ares up like a puppy and continued to play with him. Ares didn't mind a bit. Finally finished playing with Ares, Mark put him back down gently and Ares looked up at him, tongue lolling. He liked him now.

Nathan looked outside and saw an old Jeep Cherokee out front. "You got some wheels now?" he asked.

Mark looked over at him, grinning. "Yeah, we're slowly getting enough cars to patrol again," he answered.

"What's it like out there so far?" Nathan asked.

The smile fell of Mark's face and out of his eyes. "It's bad. We've lost two officers and three are unaccounted for. The state police have called and said they have five missing in this area. We've had over two dozen murders and that's just the ones we know of so far. I'm not even going to talk about rapes and assaults," he told him grimly.

"Let me guess, most right around the Interstate?" Nathan asked.

"Yep," Mark said.

"Any word from further out?" Nathan asked.

"Oh yes, and it's all worse. Half of Atlanta is a war zone and the other half is on fire. Birmingham and Savannah are the same except without the fire. The military is sending in troops to all the major cities and the government has imposed martial law for all cities with a population over a hundred thousand."

"When's the last time you ate?" Nathan asked.

"A candy bar an hour ago," Mark replied.

Nathan turned to Lenore and Jessie. "Will you fix Mark—" he hesitated. Then finished, "A cow." They laughed and then headed to the kitchen.

"I really can't stay long," Mark said.

Nathan coughed. "Ah yes you can. I have to tell you some things and this little lady has been worried sick about you. I can't physically stop you and I'm not sure if the brothers could either, but if you leave I'll tell Renee you were very mean to me."

Mark let out a deep, rich laugh. "Okay, I'll eat, but I think the three brothers could stop me," he said, but Nathan had his doubts.

"Follow me," Nathan said, walking back to the office with Mark and Renee following. Nathan picked up the badges and held them out to Mark. "I think you can safely say two of the troopers are dead," he said, handing them to Mark.

"Shit!" Mark yelled. "Is this from the two you have tied up?" he asked.

"How long have you been here?" Nathan asked, shocked.

"Not long, but we got word from people at the center at the school who've come from here. Last night, four lawyers came running in telling the sheriff that someone had been shot here for banging on the door. From their descriptions, we knew everyone but you, and they said you had a sheriff shirt and a badge on. We figured you were an officer who got stuck here," Mark explained.

"It's that bad out there already?" Nathan asked, thinking it should've taken longer.

Mark nodded. "I wanted to come and check but the sheriff and captain said if an officer was here then y'all were safe," he said and looked down. "I've been in two shootouts since this has started and shot one man."

"Don't feel bad about it. You couldn't have done anything different unless you preferred you were the one who died," Nathan told him, and Mark looked up. "It was their choice. Someone tries to kill you, you kill them right back," he said.

Mark chuckled. "That's keeping it simple."

For the first time, Nathan noticed the sergeant stripes on Mark's sleeve. "You're kinda young to be a sergeant," he said.

"The youngest the county's ever had." Mark beamed with pride.

Nathan handed over the transcript of the confessions. "It won't mean much, but this is what they told us," he said, and Mark took the pages. Then Nathan handed over the written statement for his shooting. "There is a memory card in there with pictures of the scene," he said.

Mark laughed. "The sheriff and the DA have already ruled it a justifiable homicide, but thanks," he said.

"Renee, please make sure they are getting his food ready while I show him around," Nathan asked her.

Mark bent way down so she could kiss him, and she took off for the kitchen. Mark followed Nathan to the outside cooler. When Nathan opened the door, he pointed at the body. "His personal effects are wrapped up with him. I don't know what will happen to them before you guys can collect them," he told Mark.

"Renee told me where her gun came from," Mark said.

Nathan shook his head. "His gun is wrapped up with him," he said.

Mark nodded. "Yeah, I see the bulge and thank you."

"I want to lose the weapons inside before you take those two. These people need them," Nathan said, closing the cooler.

"I'm not taking them in. I'm calling someone to get them. If they don't pick up the guns then that's on them," Mark said.

"You do have your officers riding double, don't you?" Nathan asked.

Mark sighed heavily. "We don't have enough," he said as they walked back.

"Tell the sheriff to start deputizing people and double them up with regular officers. You need to deputize those three brothers in there," Nathan said.

Mark nodded as they walked inside. "That's a good idea," he said.

"You'll have to put them with an officer who knows the rules; someone they would listen to," Nathan added.

"I can do that," Mark said.

"Jessie and his sons want to help also but I want your word that you will not take all the men from those farms at the same time. Someone has to guard the home front," Nathan said.

"Yeah I can see that," Mark replied. "We could really use that help."

"You need to get out of your house with Renee," Nathan told him. Mark looked at him in shock. "You're going to be a target that won't be home but she will be," Nathan warned.

"I'll take her to her parents' house. They live not far from Jessie," he said.

"Another thing. If Brian comes out there, kill 'im," Nathan said.

Mark just looked at him incredulously. "He's not really that bad," he said.

"Now he's not, but I think you'll only get one chance before he realizes that he can get away with a lot of stuff now," Nathan said. "He'll hurt Renee," he added.

Mark nodded. "I know a deep water hole," he said as they walked into the diner.

Renee pulled out a chair and Mark collapsed in it. Nathan was surprised the damn chair didn't break. "Fred, Andy, and Billy can I see you for a minute!" Nathan shouted and the three came over. "I asked Mark to present each of you to be deputies, and I'll write a letter of recommendation for you," he told them, and their jaws hit the floor. "You will be riding with other deputies to teach you the ropes for a couple of years, and you will have to listen to them," Nathan said, and they still just stood with their mouths open.

"Other cops aren't like me, so don't be questioning people till they tell you to, okay?" Nathan told them. "I know those guys fell down in the shower several times but other officers might not like them falling down that much," he added.

Fred closed his mouth and looked at Nathan. "Those two really did what they said, didn't they?" he asked.

"Yes they did, Fred," Nathan said.

Fred looked at his brothers, then back at Nathan. "Can we take them outside before we become deputies?" he asked.

Mark spoke up. "Guys, those two are cop killers and that is what I'm telling the sheriff. That you three helped to arrest them and got them to talk as you were treating their wounds after they fell down."

Damn, that's good, thought Nathan.

"Mark, they did other stuff, stuff you don't even see on the TV," Billy told him.

Lenore set down a plate for Mark as he looked up at the three. "Tell you what, when the truck comes to pick them up y'all can carry them out. Just make sure they don't try to escape," he told them.

The brothers started smiling and talking to each other as Nathan looked around. "Where are the customers?" he asked.

"The owner's grandkid came by and said to close the store. They'll be here tomorrow. They'll pay us and give us bonuses for staying," Connie answered. Nathan nodded and then turned to look at the Bedfords, who were sitting in a booth chatting amongst themselves.

Lenore came over to Nathan, already knowing what he was thinking. "Jessie and I asked the Bedfords to come and stay with us and they agreed," she told him.

"Thank you," Nathan relaxed back in his seat. He noticed Mark's sidearm, a Colt Python with an eight-inch barrel. He laughed and leaned across the table. "Damn, didn't think anyone carried those anymore. You a fan of 'Walking Dead'?" he asked.

Mark grinned. "Yeah, but the department required all sidearms to be a .40 caliber or larger last year and I haven't had the money to upgrade. I gave Renee my Glock," he said.

"You really need something better than a six shooter out there," Nathan told him.

"I know, and the sheriff is working on it, but I just bought a new trailer for me and Renee."

"Eat up. I'll be back," Nathan said, standing up and looking at his watch. It was just past three. He felt like this had been going on for two years. He walked into the office, where he looked at the pistols on the desk and smiled. There was a Beretta 92F, a Glock 19, a SIG 226, a 1911 and two Smith and Wesson .38s with six-inch barrels. Then the two pistols in the duty holsters. He pulled one out and saw it was a Sig P226 tactical .40 caliber with all the bells and whistles. Grabbing the other one, he saw it was just a plain P226 .40 caliber.

Sighing, he laid both on the desk and went to his luggage and pulled out his new toy, the custom 1911 high capacity. He opened the case and ran his hand over the gun with longing. It had an extended barrel, adjustable sights, the works. Nathan knew he couldn't carry it. "Almost three Gs with all the holsters and magazines, and I didn't even get to shoot you," he said sadly, closing the lid.

Grabbing the bag with the duty holster, drop holster, waistband holster, magazine holsters, and magazines, he walked back to the diner. Stopping in front of Mark, he said, "Stand up please, and take your rig off." Nathan opened the bag.

"Why?" Mark asked. Then Renee popped his arm and Mark stood up.

"I have something you need," Nathan said, taking out the duty holster with the retention lock.

"That won't fit my gun," Mark said, handing over his rig.

"You're talking," Nathan said, putting the holster on its mount.

Mark shrugged and laid his rig on the table as everyone gathered around. Nathan took off Mark's holster and speed loaders and laid them on the table and started mounting the holster and two double magazine holsters. Then Nathan opened the 1911 case and Mark sucked in a deep breath.

"Shit, man, I can't take that," Mark said, admiring the pistol.

Ignoring Mark, Nathan said, "Renee, go and get all the black boxes of the .45 caliber behind the counter." She scampered off. "That's the best load they have here," he said, taking out the pistol. "I take it you know what this is?" he said, looking at Mark.

Mark cleared his throat. "Yes, a customized Springfield G.I. 1911 high capacity, and it looks like you got everything for it," he said.

"Yep, it will do everything except fix you breakfast," Nathan said, running his hands over the gun, then passed it to Mark. "Here, my gift to you," he said.

"Dude, I can't take that. Renee said you're heading to Idaho. You'll need that for the trip," Mark said, not taking the pistol.

"I have the 1911 on my hip, a Springfield XD .45, and a snub .38 for pistols. I can't carry all of them. Renee seems rather fond of you so I want you to be prepared for some shit," Nathan told Mark, still holding out the pistol.

Mark just stared at the pistol. "Nathan," was all he said.

"You're being rude and we won't even talk about what the brothers do when someone is rude," Nathan said, and everyone started smirking.

"I can't pay you for this," Mark said, still looking at the pistol with longing.

Nathan laughed. "If you tried I'd kick you in the nuts. Then run like a bitch begging for mercy," he added, making everyone start laughing. Renee pushed her way back through the crowd, setting down an armload of boxes. "This will be one of four parts of the payment I demand for saving Renee, for you to have this. I may not be there next time. I want you to be able to shoot at them fourteen times and not six," Nathan said, still holding out the pistol.

Mark looked up at him, then back to the pistol before slowly reaching out and taking it. "I never even dreamed of having this," he said, rubbing the pistol. "Thank you seems kinda poor. You save my wife then give me this," Mark said, working the slide.

"It's my pleasure," Nathan said. "Take some of these boxes of ammo and run fifty rounds through it to see how she handles."

"What kind of groups have you shot through it?" Mark asked.

"None, but the owner told me he shot a two-inch group at fifty yards," Nathan said. "You have seven magazines total, hip holster for concealed carry, and a drop holster for a tactical set up." He took out the other stuff, laying it out.

"You haven't shot it!" Mark yelled.

"Mark, I just bought the damn thing yesterday," Nathan said.

"Come shoot it with me then," Mark said.

"I have one at home. It's not customized but it's great. But I really don't want to. I have to leave it but I really don't want to flirt with it," Nathan said, grinning.

Mark laughed. "What are the other three parts to this payment?" he asked, taking out the magazine.

Nathan thought a minute. "A kiss from Renee," he said, grinning.

Mark looked at Nathan, then looked at Renee. "Renee, kiss him with tongue," he said, looking back down to the pistol.

"Mark!" Renee exclaimed.

"What? He saved you and gave me this. Kiss him good," Mark told her.

Renee turned to Nathan who was stunned; his face was turning red. Renee started giggling. "Nathan, are you blushing?" she asked.

"I don't blush," Nathan said, fighting the blush but it wasn't working.

Renee started laughing. "You're blushing, it's so cute," she said, moving toward him.

"I don't blush," he said, fixing to back away.

"Okay, you don't blush but your face is getting so red," she told him. "Don't back away from a woman because that is rude," she told him.

"On the cheek," Nathan said, bending down.

She turned his face and kissed him on the mouth and let him go. "If you get much redder I think you'll explode," she said as the others laughed.

"That wasn't my cheek," Nathan said, trying to be cool. He looked at Mark. "That was not really necessary," he told him.

"Hey, I could kiss ya but I think you would fight me," Mark said, busily loading magazines.

"It wouldn't be much of a fight," Nathan admitted and put his hand on Mark's arm. "Use it well and stay safe. Part of my payment is also for trying to get the brothers on the force. I really like them, and with officers like you guys, there won't be much crime," Nathan said.

"I have to agree with that," Brad said, watching Mark load magazines. "Nathan, here is your pistol back," he said, taking off the Glock.

"Brad, you just heard me tell Mark that I can't take all that shit. I gave that to you," Nathan snapped. "Use it to protect your family," he added and looked out the front window at the strip mall. The parts store and the thrift shop were open. "Everyone stay here for a second please," he said, turning around and heading to the office.

He grabbed the Berretta, the two P226s and one of the revolvers. Then, grabbing all the holsters and magazines for the automatics, he walked back to the diner. "Fred, Andy, and Billy, come here," he said, laying the guns down. He gave Fred the souped-up P226, Billy the regular one, and the Berretta to Andy.

Andy looked down at the pistol and his hands started to tremble as he moaned, "Ahhhhh."

"Like it, Andy?" Nathan asked, grinning.

Andy looked up with kidlike excitement. "It's just like Riggs'!" he shouted. Allie put her head in her hands as the brothers patted Andy on the back.

Fred looked over at Nathan, grinning, "He can recite all four of them," he said.

Nathan smiled, then leaned over the table. "I have a mission for you, Andy and Billy," he said, and they both looked up at him. "I want you to escort Brad and Abigail over to the thrift store so they can get clothes, shoes, and other supplies. I don't want anyone to bother them. They've been through enough for one day. Fred, I need you in the parking lot. Look intimidating. When Mark is out back shooting, people may want to come and see. Make them go away. Just don't shoot them," he quickly added.

Allie leaned over the table, pointing her finger at Fred. "Nathan said look intimidating. Don't be bouncing any more people," she warned him.

"It wasn't so bad," Fred said, looking at her guiltily.

"Fred, you lifted that man over your head, betting Billy he would bounce up to your waist when you dropped him," she snapped.

The room was silent for a second and Nathan just had to know. "How high did he bounce?" he asked.

"Only to my knee. I lost a pack of tobacco," Fred told him with a sad look.

"No more bouncing," Allie said firmly.

"Allie baby, when they told us what they did you wanted us to bounce both of them," Fred told her.

"Yes I did, but not for Billy to stand on one's chest to see how many colors his face would change to," she said, crossing her arms.

"Billy got three colors on his face at one time," Fred said proudly.

"Fred!" Allie snapped.

"Okay baby," he said, looking down.

"Baby, if someone is bad then you do whatever you need to till they stop or someone asks you to stop," she compromised.

Fred's face filled with joy. "Okay baby," he said.

Nathan moved over to Brad, pulled out several hundred dollars and pushed them into his hand. "Since you have a place to stay, you need to get supplies. I want you and Abigail to buy each of you blue jeans, good shirts, and boots if they have them. Look for sleeping bags and better backpacks," he told Brad.

Brad smiled. "We were preppers, Nathan. Although a lot of good our stuff is doing us here," he said.

"Then you know what to look for. You have one hour," Nathan said and turned around. "Connie and Lenore, I need you to watch the kids.

Jessie, I want you to teach Monica how to shoot this revolver. Everyone back here in one hour," he said.

"What about me?" Renee asked.

"You're going with your husband as he shoots his new pistol. I want him to run at least fifty rounds through it. Make sure he gets used to changing magazines. Only put five rounds in each magazine so he get used to it," he told her.

"Come on baby," she said, picking up the other magazines and leading Mark outside.

Jessie walked over, picking up the revolver. "What are you gonna do?" he asked.

Nathan just looked out the window. "Repack my shit and go over my route," he said, turning around and heading back to the office.

CHAPTER 8

Whittling down his supplies to manageable portions, Nathan went out to the store and grabbed several boxes of the space saver bags. Then, grabbed his new tactical clothes he'd bought, he took out the knee and elbow pad inserts. Throwing them over his shoulder, he headed to the utility room and filled the sink up with water and threw the three uniforms in. Then he walked to the store and grabbed some soap.

As he was pouring soap in the sink, Lenore came around the corner and saw what he was doing. "Let me do that, you're just making a mess and not doing it right," she scolded, pushing him out of the way. "Go get some fabric softener," she commanded. Nathan took off and came back quickly, handing her the bottle. "Go help with the kids. They're in the diner," she said. Not wanting to get her mad because she was cooking for him, Nathan left, but not before grabbing his camera.

Nathan walked around taking pictures of everyone, then headed to the diner. He saw the kids were playing some game with Ares that involved running and a lot of laughing.

Connie was sitting at a table watching them. He walked over and joined her. "Tired of packing?" she asked.

"No, Lenore told me I was washing my clothes wrong and kicked me out," he told her.

"It's good you didn't argue then," Connie said.

Nathan smiled at her, then turned to the kids. "Have you ever told Andy you like him?" he asked.

Connie spun around in her chair so fast she almost fell out. "What?" she cried out.

"If you want everyone to know, keep yelling," he told her.

Connie looked over at Jessie and Monica to see he was still teaching her about the pistol. Then, turning back to Nathan, she leaned over the table. "What are you talking about?" she whispered.

Still smiling, Nathan just stared at her. "You heard the question. If you don't want to answer then that's fine," he said.

"What makes you think that?" she whispered harshly.

"I have eyes, Connie," Nathan said.

"I've made a dozen passes at you and you didn't take any of them. I'm not pretty enough?" she croaked at him.

"You are very pretty. In fact you're a hottie," he said. "But I'm not what you need," he told her.

"How—" she started, but stopped as he held up his hand.

"Trust me, I'm leaving and there is no way I would ever expose you to what I'm about to face. I'm not saying it will be easy here, but you're better off. Plus I've seen you look at Andy," he told her.

Connie sighed. "Okay, I've had a crush on him since high school. I'm thirty-three and he's thirty. I'm an old maid now and he's a stud," she popped off.

"Flirt with him," Nathan said.

"I have," she told him.

"Connie, you will have to be a little more forceful. Andy is smart just like his brothers, but they only know what they want and need to know. If they put their minds to it, anyone of them could become whatever they wanted," he told her.

"Fred failed the police test and he studied for it," she told him.

"No he didn't. I asked Mark. He scored third highest in the state," Nathan told her.

"Why—" she started.

"He didn't want to make his brothers jealous and feel bad. They have everything they wanted and that job was just a dream," Nathan told her. "That is another reason I wanted the brothers to do this together. They all need to know just what they can do."

Connie thought for a moment. "You think he likes me that way?" she asked.

"Oh I know he does. He watches you all the time," Nathan told her. "Just get a little more forceful," he said as Allie walked over.

"Y'all want something to drink?" she asked, looking at the kids try to wrestle Ares down.

"A Coke with ice would be great," Nathan told her, and Connie agreed.

"Listen to him, Connie," Allie said as she walked away. Connie started laughing as the front door opened up.

Brad and Abigail had arms loaded down with stuff as Billy held the door open for them. He had a load under his arm as well. They walked over to a table and dropped the stuff down. Billy joined them as Andy took off running to the back of the store with something under his arm. Nathan looked at Brad and Abigail. "What's that about?" he asked.

"Don't ask," they said in unison.

Nathan chucked as Fred came in and sat down. A few minutes later, Mark and Renee came in and joined the group. Mark looked over at Nathan. "That man lied," he said. "I shot three one-inch groups at fifty yards and hit a five-gallon bucket at a hundred," he said, grinning.

"Dude," Nathan said, holding a thumb up. "Any word from the government today?" he asked.

"Just over the Federal Law bands. Do this and this is what we're sending here," Mark said. "No official statement," he added.

Renee stood up and kissed him, then turned around. "That radio you had out has had people talking on it all day," she said.

"What?" Nathan said.

"Yeah, most of the people say a whole bunch of numbers and letters before they talk, but it's been going all day," she told him.

"I didn't hear it," Nathan said.

She smiled. "I had an ear piece plugged in it. I got tired of people asking questions about it," she said as Lenore walked in.

"Your clothes are hanging up. Don't touch them. I'll finish them later," Lenore said, sitting down.

Nathan just smiled at her. "Renee, anything important on the radio?" he asked.

"Basically what Mark said. The big cities are war zones and you have to turn in weapons at the crisis camps," she said.

"What of the rest of the country?" he asked, not liking that bit of news.

"Only one guy said it was like this everywhere. He talked to a whole bunch of numbers," she said.

"Those numbers and letters are their call signs, their handles," he told her.

"That's stupid," she said.

"Okay, does anyone have any flash drives?" Nathan asked. Connie and Renee raised their hands. "If they are here, get them for me," he said, and they headed to the back. "Mark, what are your plans?" Nathan asked.

"I'm going to call for a pickup of your bad boys then get back to work," he said. "I got to get some gas soon. I haven't siphoned gas since I was a kid and forgot how nasty that shit is."

Before Fred could speak, Nathan did. "Fred, not now. How about you ride over to the parking lot with Mark and help fill him up," he said. Fred nodded in agreement.

As Mark and Fred walked out, Nathan looked around. "Tonight I'm going to give you a fast lesson on survival and also give everyone the money that was promised. Then we are going to eat," he said.

Renee and Connie walked in, handing him a handful of flash drives. "What's on them?" Nathan asked.

"Music," they said together.

"Care if I erase it?" he asked, and they shook their head no as Andy walked in. He was wearing blue jeans with a red plaid shirt and a blue windbreaker. His pistol was stuck in the front of his pants and he had a huge grin on his face. "You look cool," Nathan told him.

Abigail walked over to him and pulled him down and kissed his cheek. "I told you it would look good," she said, walking back to Brad.

Nathan looked at Brad. "They had clothes that fit him?" he asked in wonder.

"Two complete racks," Brad said, separating his stack.

"I'm in the land of giants," Nathan said, looking back at the supersized 'Riggs'.

Mark and Fred pulled back up in Mark's vehicle and got out. When they walked in, they stopped and stared at Andy.

"You didn't get me some?" Fred asked, looking at him.

Andy smiled. "Yours and Billy's are in the bathroom," he said.

Mark laughed as he lifted up a huge handheld radio left over from the sixties and called in, asking for transport. When he was finished, he sat down and saw everyone looking at the radio. "It's left over from the cold war. We had boxes of them in the bunker under the courthouse," he told them.

"Mark, stop by tomorrow afternoon and I might have a pump rigged up for you," Nathan told him. "Okay everyone, three hundred dollars. Connie, pass it out please," he said, throwing her some more of the robber's money.

Nathan moved over to check the Bedfords' haul and was impressed. They had gotten one large hiking pack, another smaller military pack, and three sleeping bags. He counted six set of boots with four pair of smaller ones. He watched them sort out gloves, coats, pants, and shirts, and new packs of underwear and socks. They continued to make piles of other stuff and he grinned. "You guys did well," he told them.

Abigail turned to him with tears on her face. "We can never repay you for what you've done," she said.

Nathan hugged her. Brad turned around and he had tears as well. "You're wrong, you can repay me," Nathan said, and Abigail leaned back, looking up at him as Brad stepped closer. "Make sure those kids grow up in a place they can be proud of and know the true meaning of America," Nathan told them.

"We can do that," she said, hugging him again, and Brad leaned over and hugged both of them.

Nathan coughed. "Guys, I don't want people to start talking," he said, making both of them laugh. They let him go and he looked at Brad. "What area of medicine are you in?" he asked.

Brad smirked. "How did you guess?" he asked.

"I've been a nurse for a long time," Nathan answered. Brad's smirk fell off as he looked down at the badge clipped to Nathan's belt. "Oh, I'm a cop, but I was a nurse first and still am," he told him.

Brad smiled again. "I'm a family practice doctor," he told him. "Abigail is a dental hygienist," he said, nodding to his wife.

"Guys, you will be able to build here. I'm not going to tell you how to live your lives, but I wouldn't try to head to Cali unless the government can fly you," Nathan said.

They both nodded in agreement as Brad spoke. "We figured what we have will be gone before we get there and the violence will be ten times worse."

"You have any other family near here?" Nathan asked.

"Just an uncle in Tennessee," Brad told him. "We were coming back from his place heading back to Atlanta to catch our flight home when this hit. We slept beside the road last night and I used up most of our money the first day. Then we walked in here to be saved by a cop with longer hair than my wife's," he said.

"Yeah, but her hair is prettier," Nathan said. "Brad, you can help here but stay near Jessie and his family. They are close to the brothers and several other farms. People surviving in numbers are the only ones that are going to make it. Numbers to grow food and numbers to fight to protect it," he told them, putting his hand on each one's shoulder. "It's going to be bad but you have something to offer them with your services. You can do stuff to barter for things, and they can protect you. It's going to be a lot of hard work but each of you can do it," he confided.

"I'm going to need a few things," Brad told him.

"I'm working on that and should be finished tonight," Nathan told him. "Brad, no matter what happens, don't let anyone take your weapon away. If they want it, say it's lost or stolen, and don't go anywhere they will search you to take it. You will be dead in days without it. Not saying it will save you, but it gives you the option of staying alive," he stated.

"Don't worry, I'll never be unarmed again," Brad promised. "Again, thanks to you," he said.

"Glad I could help," Nathan said. "Finish up here, then I need you two to do something for me."

"Okay," Brad said, and he and Abigail went back to separating supplies.

"Don't forget to spend your three hundred dollars," Nathan said, walking away.

"No, and here's your change," Brad said, reaching in his pocket and pulling out a wad of cash.

"Keep it," Nathan said, not even turning around. He saw a truck pull in the parking lot and told Andy and Billy to get the bad boys as he went to grab their packs. When he came back out, they were toting them like suitcases again and both of the bad guys were crying. They carried them outside as a deputy lowered the tailgate, but the brothers just lifted them above their heads and threw them in the back. Nathan carried the packs out and the deputy put them in the front.

"I need my cuffs back," Nathan said. The deputy reached inside and pulled out zip cuffs and handed them to Nathan.

"I'd have to be nice about it," the deputy said.

"Not really. Watch," Nathan said. "Fred, can you and your brothers get my cuffs and put these on instead? And don't let them escape. They've been talking about it," Nathan said, handing him the keys.

Fred laughed. "They can't outrun us," he said as all three jumped in the back of the truck. Nathan noticed the truck got real low to the ground. With a lot of fists, knees and stomps they put the zip cuffs on. They jumped out and Fred handed Nathan his cuffs back. "Told ya they wouldn't be a problem," he said.

"My bad," Nathan said as the three grinned at him. "They're cop killers," Nathan told the deputy.

"Yes, it's confirmed. We sent out a team an hour ago after the sergeant called it in," the deputy told him. "I'm going to run over several curbs," he said, climbing into the truck. Nathan laughed as the deputy fired the truck up and pulled out. True to his word, the deputy drove through the ditch, almost bouncing the two out of the back of the truck. Turning around, Nathan saw Mark come out with Renee at his side, carrying his old pistol.

"Nathan, it's time for me to get back at it," he said.

"When's the last time you slept?" Nathan asked.

Mark closed his eyes, thinking. "I don't know," he answered.

"We will have someone awake here at all times, so stop and catch a few winks," Nathan told him.

"Nah, I'm telling the sheriff I'm taking a few hours off tomorrow to move our stuff out to Renee's parents' house. I have to run out there and make sure that it's okay first," he said.

Fred moved over to him. "You can stay at our place, Mark. Paw thinks he can have the logging truck running this week and we can hook up to your new trailer and pull it out there," he told him.

"Now that is a thought," Mark said.

"Mark, does your department have some gear for the brothers?" Nathan asked.

"Everything but guns, the legislature wouldn't approve the expense," he told him.

"Even vests that big?" Nathan asked.

Mark laughed. "Hell, they had to order five for me until they got one that could fit," he said. "They can have those."

"You be careful out there, and if you need us, send someone for us. We'll come," Nathan assured him.

"You've done more than enough," Mark said, kissing Renee and climbing in his Cherokee. Nathan fought the urge to laugh. Seeing Mark in it reminded him of a clown driving a tiny car.

As Mark pulled out, Nathan headed inside. "Men, you will wear those vests at all times while on duty. Unless you agree to that, I'm not going along with this. Am I clear?" he said.

"Don't worry, we will," Fred assured him and the others agreed.

Nathan took off his cuff holder and put both cuffs in it, then pulled the cuffs off the duty belt. He gave each brother a holster and two cuffs and keys. They smiled at him and went to spend their money. They each spent it all on ammunition and extra magazines.

Nathan walked over to the kids and pulled twenty dollars out of their ears and told them to go spend it. Then he went into the office and grabbed his tote bag and pulled out his laptop. Saying a prayer, he turned it on and wanted to jump as he saw it start up. "This one bag was worth its weight in gold," he said as Renee came in.

"You have a computer?" she yelled.

"Yeah, I bought this bag at the store I bought the gun from," he said, holding up his tote bag. "The guy told me it would shield from an EMP and he was right."

"It looks like a super-sized diaper bag," she said, looking at it.

"It's a tote bag or large messenger bag," Nathan hissed at her.

She raised her hands. "Sorry," she said. "What are you doing?"

"Going to give you information to help you solve this," he said, reaching down to his backpack and pulling out what looked like a book with a zipper. He opened it up and showed her twenty zip drives on each page for a total of five pages.

"I don't think we have enough zip drives," she said.

"You don't need all of it, but it would be nice," Nathan admitted. "You only need the first page. It contains information on how to build stuff. Like how to generate electricity, make fuel, a radio, suppressors, and a million other things."

"Cool," she said. "What's the other pages?" she asked.

"How to fight a battle, train snipers, survive in any climate, preserve food, and a lot more," he said, then flipped to the next one. "This page is survival stories and the last is my page. I have my information scanned in like my insurance, nursing license, social security card, music, and pictures of friends and stuff like that," told her.

"Are we on that page?" she asked, smiling.

He laughed and pulled out his camera. "You will be in a minute," he told her as he picked up his computer, carrying it to the diner. Renee took off running into the store. Nathan sat the computer on a table and called Brad over. He explained that he wanted Brad to transfer the zip drives on the first page to the ones the girls had given him. Brad sat down and got started.

Nathan went back to the office and grabbed the topographic map books, some scissors and tape. In the store he found a box of laminating plastic and carried it to the diner where he laid it on a table. He called Abigail over and showed her the pages he wanted and how he wanted them laid out. Abigail smiled and sat down to work. Nathan went back to the store and headed for the electronic aisle where he found several brands of power inverters. As always, only the expensive ones had the Mylar wrapping. He grabbed two and headed to the shop.

On one of his snoopings he'd found a fluid transfer pump. The ones he had at home were all hand pumps, but this one plugged into a wall. He had hopes for it since it was stored in a metal cabinet. He grabbed a car battery and put it on a roll-around cart, then moved it over to the work bench. He wired the inverter to the battery terminals and crossed his fingers before turning the switch on. The light came on along with the fan, and he fought the urge to jump up and down as he turned the switch off.

Next he rolled the pump across the floor to the bench and plugged it up. Turning on the inverter, he crossed his fingers as he pushed the button. This time he did dance when the pump came on. He unhooked the pump and put it back in the cabinet, then rolled the battery with the inverter to the diner and plugged in his laptop.

Looking down beside Brad, he saw a stack of flash drives still in packages. "Where did those come from?" he asked.

"Connie grabbed them from the electronic closet behind the counter," Brad told him.

"Damn, I have to see what's in in there," Nathan said, looking up to see Connie and Renee taking pictures of him. "Guys, I hope that is not what you spent your money on," he said.

"No, I'm telling Mitch we want these for our bonus," Connie told him. "You know you got almost all the camera batteries," she told him.

"All that I saw," he told her.

"That's alright. We found some more and some rechargeable ones," she said, looking at the battery with the inverter. "Oh my," Connie said, running back to the store. She came back with an inverter and a dash solar charger.

Nathan laughed and looked outside to see it was getting dark. Then he noticed several people standing in front of the pharmacy. "Shit," he said and ran to the office where he grabbed his M-4, chambered a round, and took off running. "Lock this place down," he shouted, opening the front door and running out. He was halfway to the road when one of the people threw a chunk of concrete at the window on the pharmacy door, shattering it.

As the first one moved to the door, Nathan yelled, "Dyin' time is here, let me give you some tickets!" The group turned and saw a man with 'Sheriff' across his chest running at them, aiming a machine gun at them, and three giants loping along behind him.

"Run!" one screamed and they all took off running toward the Interstate.

Nathan kept his rifle aimed at them until they were over two hundred yards away. "Damn, scared away a dozen," Nathan said, feeling proud.

"Yep, and they can run, can't they," Fred said behind him.

Nathan turned to see the brothers aiming rifles at the group. All three were now dressed like 'Riggs'. "No wonder they ran so hard, probably thought you guys were going to cook and eat them," Nathan said, feeling disappointed now.

"We had to back you up," Billy told him.

"I know, and thank you, Billy," Nathan said, aiming at the pharmacy. "Help me clear the building," he said.

"Nathan, nobody went in," Andy said.

"We don't know that. Rule one, always expect the unexpected," Nathan said, moving to the door with the busted-out window. Reaching in, he opened the lock and eased inside and then went over how to clear a building. The brothers took to it like ducks to water, performing beautifully. When it was clear, he looked at them.

"You don't see what I'm fixing to do," he said, grabbing some bags. He started moving through the aisles, grabbing medical equipment and supplies, and filling over a dozen bags. Then he moved over and filled bags with medical and pharmacy books. Laying the bags by the front door, he went back to the counter and started filling bags with medications. When he ran out of the cloth shopping bags he used the plastic ones.

Looking back at the front door, he saw the mountain of shit and figured he had enough for Brad to start a practice. Fred walked over to him, smiling. "That's a lot of stuff," he said.

"That's right, and you guys are going to need it," Nathan said, feeling bad but hoping they understood.

"There's a trailer out back," Fred told Nathan.

"I was just back there and didn't see a trailer," he said.

"It's back in the corner of the lot," Billy called from the back door.

Nathan walked to the back door to see Billy standing there. He was fixing to ask where Andy was till he saw him walking toward them from the field. "What's he doing out there?" Nathan asked.

"Checking it out. I was covering him," Billy said.

"Now that's what I'm talking about. Thinking about the unexpected," Nathan said, grabbing his shoulder and shaking it, proud of him. Andy walked up, grinning. "What's in it?" Nathan asked, gesturing toward the trailer.

"Camping gear for a Boy Scout troop," Andy said.

"You're kidding," Nathan said with a flat face.

"Naw, I opened it up to make sure," he said.

"Someone go get Jessie. We need that trailer," Nathan said, turning around to take the bags in his hands to the pile.

Twenty minutes later they were pulling the trailer into the shop along with the medical supplies. Shutting the door, Nathan led everyone to the diner to have a talk over supper.

"Everyone. I want to set something straight. I stopped those thugs taking the stuff because you guys needed it. Is what I did stealing? Yes it is. But I know you will use it for the greater good. I didn't know that about them. You will have to walk a fine line. If you come upon something that will help you and no one is around to claim it, take it. Now if you walk into an active camp or a house you know is occupied, that doesn't apply, of course. If you come across a dead body and it has something you need, take it. They no longer need it," he told them.

Everyone was staring at him in the low light. "With the best estimates, seventy percent of the human species is fixing to die. That's over two hundred million just here in America, and remember that's best case scenario. I'm putting it higher. Each of you are going to have to learn to survive and count on each other, and more than likely each of you will have to kill just to live. Accept it and move on unless you just want to die," he told them. "Now let me talk to you in the little time we have left together," Nathan said, and started telling them how to survive.

CHAPTER 9

Day 3

Nathan stretched out his arms, yawning, and noticed light coming in. He looked down at his watch and saw it was after six. He sat up suddenly and started putting his boots on. They had taken some cots out of the trailer and put them in the casino for everyone to sleep on. Looking around, he could see the kids but no one else.

He walked out to the diner to see everyone writing and Brad still at the laptop downloading flash drives. Walking over to the brothers, he stopped and looked down at them.

"I was supposed to have guard duty after you, Andy," Nathan said looking at him.

Andy started to blush. "Connie sat with me on guard duty and I took your shift too," he said.

Nathan smiled. "Well thank you," he said, turning away as Fred and Billy elbowed Andy. Nathan walked over to Brad. "How many have you done?" he asked.

"I'm downloading your books now," Brad said, looking up with a tired face.

"You better get another battery ready then," Nathan told him.

"Already changed it out," Brad said, stretching his arms over his head as Lenore brought him a cup of coffee.

Nathan took a sip of coffee. "What's everyone writing?" he asked.

"Monica took notes last night and they're copying them," Brad said, taking out a flash drive and putting in another.

Nathan saw Abigail writing and looked at Brad. "Did she finish my maps?" he asked.

"Of course, there in the office," he said.

Nathan sipped his coffee while heading to the office, where he found his maps on the desk. He had Abigail cut out the pages of the route he was taking. Instead of him taking ten books with hundreds of pages, he was only taking sixty or so, all laminated and joined together. He had the topo/satellite program on his laptop and tablet but he didn't want to use it. There would be too many people around here for him to be using electronics when he left.

He studied the maps as Lenore came in and handed him the uniforms she'd washed. "Here you go," she said, smiling.

"Thank you," he replied. He set one to the side and put the knee and elbow pads back in, then put the others in a compression bag and rolled the air out. Then he laid it on his pack. He saw everyone's boxes were now stuffed full, and he knew everyone had more boxes in Jessie's truck and trailer. He had talked to them till midnight, then they had all grabbed cans of spray paint and painted the trailer. Nathan never even remembered laying his head down.

Ares came in and looked up at him, whining. "Hey, I've been here, you could've found me," Nathan told him, walking out of the office to the front door and opening it for his dog. Ares shot out, heading to the ditch. Nathan chuckled and watched him, then heard a lot of gunfire to the north, close to the Interstate and town. "I need to hit the road before I get tied up in a freaking war," Nathan said, looking to the north.

Taking a sip of coffee, he heard something he wasn't expecting to hear again for a long time: helicopters. He stepped out from under the awning and looked up, searching for them. Then he saw them to the southeast; there were twenty-four of them flying in a line. He saw they were the big ones with two blades. Everyone saw Nathan look up in the sky and came running out and saw the choppers. Several of them started cheering.

Renee looked at Nathan. "Where do you think they're going?" she asked him.

"My guess is they're taking troops to Atlanta to fight a war the police are losing," he told her.

The smile fell off her face. "They might be taking supplies," Renee said hopefully.

"Land would be the best route for supplies, or fixed wing. They might be but I'm thinking troops," Nathan said, draining his cup.

Andy walked over to him. "With the military in the city, that means the bad guys will leave it and move out here," he said, and the others just stared at him.

"That's what I think," Nathan confirmed, glad they were thinking about their surroundings.

"How long till we start seeing them here?" Abigail asked.

"Two, probably three days," Nathan said. "Ares, come on!" he yelled, walking inside. The others followed, with Ares pushing his way through; he knew food was coming soon.

"Damn, I was hoping it was over," Connie said.

"Don't ever expect it to be over, Connie, and if it comes, be happy," Nathan told her. "Don't give yourself false hope, only a real hope. Like surviving the day, learning something new, or being thankful all your friends are still alive," he said. "I'm going to take a shower now," Nathan said, and headed to the office.

As he was in the shower, Nathan heard the door open and close several times. He dried off and stepped out, wrapping a towel around his waist, and walked over to the sink. He adjusted the light on the counter so he could shave and brush his teeth. As he was shaving his face, in the mirror he saw Renee walk by toward the door wrapped in a towel. Nathan spun around and walked to the line of showers. There were seven side by side and each one had a door on it. He looked down the row and saw Abigail drying off, looking back at him without a shy bone in her body.

Feeling uncomfortable, Nathan darted back to the sink and finished shaving and brushing his teeth in record time. Grabbing his stuff, he ran out of the showers to the office. He dropped his towel and dressed, hoping Abigail hadn't noticed him ogling at her. Those hopes were dashed as she walked in the office wrapped in a towel and carrying some flip flops. "You left these," she said, grinning as she handed the flip flops over. Nathan just nodded and smiled, taking the flip flops. Abigail moved toward him.

"Well?" she asked.

Over an hour later, grinning and wearing his new clothes and his M-4 across his back, Nathan headed to the diner to find Lenore and Jessie setting out plates of food. Looking around the table, he noticed everyone had taken a shower and seemed to be feeling much better.

"Jessie, I want you and the brothers to pull the vehicles out of the shop. I really don't want the owner knowing what's in them," Nathan said.

"That's a good idea. Steven would damn sure go snooping," Connie said.

"Steven?" Nathan asked.

"He's Mitch's son that's over this store," she told him.

"He have a key to the office?" Nathan asked with some concern.

Connie shook her head. "No, I had that lock put in after talking to Mitch. Steven kept coming in, digging through everything and scattering my paperwork. I've been the manager here for three years and the books are always balanced, so Mitch let me put a lock on it," she told him and started laughing. "Let me tell you, that pissed Steven off to no end."

Nathan looked at her grimly and she stopped laughing. "If he messes with my stuff, I'll kill him and anyone else that gets in the way," he said with a flat expression.

Jessie stood up. "Hey Nathan, Steven is just a stupid administrator with a short man's complex," he said.

Looking at Jessie and shaking his head, Nathan said, "You may have been listening last night but you were not letting it sink in. What I have and what you have are needed to survive. You will not be able to go to the store for more. It's all there is for some time to come. If he sees some stuff I have collected for you and the others and demands some or tells others, your life will become an instant hell. Others will come and try to take it."

Jessie's eyes got wide with horror. "I'll kill the fucker myself," he said.

"Now you understand what I've said," Nathan told him. He looked around the room. "This stuff here that we have not paid for is his and they have a right to it. I don't care what they do with it, but what I've bought for you and got for you is yours. If you band together, like we talked about, this group will make it. *If* you keep control of your stuff. You will see families starving to death in the days, weeks, and months to come. It's going to suck, but if you give them your stuff it will be you joining them starving. It's called self-preservation. Don't let people into your group that you don't need. Weigh their benefit against what it's going to cost the group to feed and protect them. If you hand out anything it will bite you in the ass. Handouts are not earned and become expected. Worse, it lets others know what you have," he told them.

"If we kill Steven, we'll have to kill them all," Jessie said.

"Then that's what we'll have to do," Nathan told them. "I'm not staying, so if it comes to that, tell everyone I did it," he said.

"That's a lot of heat," Andy said.

"Once I'm outside this county it won't matter," Nathan said. "Now I'll handle Steven. Fred, I want you by the vehicles at all times. Billy and Andy, I want you in here helping to load up and staying close to the group," he said, giving out assignments. "Now, let's eat," he said, sitting down.

After breakfast, they moved the vehicles out and Nathan put on his tactical vest. It was actually an IOTV or Improved Outer Tactical vest. He didn't have the shoulder guards, groin guard, neck guard, or side plates. He had the new ceramic plates which were a lot lighter in the front and back. Still, with all his equipment on the thing weighed thirty pounds.

He had four of the vests and used two for his SRT duties. The other two were extras and the one he had on was MultiCam like his new uniform. He looked down at the uniform and he had to admit he liked it so far. Granted, he hadn't done anything yet but the knee pads he used to wear were always falling down. It only took one time to fall to your knees and land on a rock to let you know: protect your knees.

Reaching up, he pulled off the Velcro flap that was covering his embroidered badge and headed toward the diner. He ran into Andy on the way there. "I want one of those," Andy said, walking around Nathan and looking at the vest.

"Andy, sorry but you can't have this one," Nathan said, chuckling.

"I know but I want one," Andy said.

"If I see one I'll hold on to it for ya," Nathan promised.

"Thank you," Andy said, admiring it one last time, then walked back to the diner. Nathan followed him and started taking pictures of the group as they sat around talking or copying Monica's notes. Brad was still downloading books but was getting close to finishing.

It was almost nine when a 1956 Chevy station wagon pulling a trailer and an ancient ten-foot box cargo truck pulled into the lot. The workers went through the diner to the south door to meet the vehicles. Nathan went and locked the office and put the keys in his pocket, then headed back out to the store. He was surprised not to see anyone, so he went to the back hallway. They had formed a chain from the storeroom and were loading the box truck.

Nathan shrugged his shoulders. He would've emptied the store first then the diner. The storeroom had a one-inch steel door on it. The other stuff was only protected by the windows and the group inside. He walked over and was amazed to see that they were taking everything. The line of people passed huge cases of paper plates, paper towels, cups, napkins, and other useless stuff. A gentleman who Nathan assumed was the owner, Mitch, was pointing at those boxes and leaving cases of food stuff.

In thirty minutes the box truck was filled and Nathan couldn't remember seeing one case of food put on it. The station wagon was pulled over and it wasn't until the trailer was halfway full that the first case of food was loaded.

"Connie, open this damn door!" Nathan heard behind him. It had only taken him two minutes to figure out who Steven was. The small redheaded prick irritated Nathan just by looking at him. He could tell that he loved trying to demean others even though he could rarely pull it off. Steven had yelled at everyone there including the two kids, only stopping when one of the brothers glared at him. Nathan had to agree with Connie. Steven had little dick syndrome.

Spinning around, Nathan walked to the office to see Steven kicking the door. "My stuff is in there," Nathan told him.

"I don't care, I want to make sure none of you are hiding stuff!" he yelled.

"I am hiding stuff. *My* stuff," Nathan growled.

"You aren't even a cop here so shut your mouth. I can have your job at will!" Steven yelled.

"Yell again and I'm shoving your face into the wall," Nathan warned.

"Open the door now or I'll get a gun and shoot the damn thing!" Steven screamed.

Nathan's right hand shot out, hitting Steven in the gut and doubling him over. Lifting his knee up, he caught Steven in the face, sending his head back up. Because he'd promised, Nathan grabbed Steven by the back of the head and shoved it into the wall. Steven slid down the wall, leaving a streak of blood as he sank to the floor. "I warned you," Nathan said.

"What the hell do you think you're doing?" Nathan heard behind him.

"Letting him know to not yell at me," Nathan said, turning around and seeing Mitch coming over.

"You didn't have to hit him," Mitch said, kneeling down by his son. Steven was moaning and looking around with a wobbling head.

"Actually I did. I wasn't in the mood to shoot him. But I'm getting there," Nathan informed him.

"You aren't a cop here!" Mitch yelled.

"Old man, this is a National Emergency. Any sworn peace officer has jurisdiction anywhere in the U.S. That means yes I am," Nathan said, trying to get his temper under control.

"This is my son," Mitch said, trying to help Steven stand.

"Then shame on you. You should've taught him some basic manners. I've known him less than an hour and I've seen him disrespect every person here, including two little kids. You just suck his tiny dick even though he's disrespecting you as well," Nathan growled.

"You are going a little far there," Mitch said, squaring off.

"Old man, I've killed one man who came in here to rob the store and kill and rape some of the employees. Your store and your employees. I've caught two more cop killers here and who knows what else I've stopped just by being here. Your employees stayed on the job helping your dumb ass. They could've left and had the right to. Where would that have left you?" Nathan asked. "This is how you repay them, letting your son run around and demean them?"

Mitch stumbled back. "I— I'm—"

"If that is the type of man you are, then you disgust me," Nathan said.

Mitch blinked his eyes as what Nathan said sunk in. He looked down at Steven. "Steven, get up," he said, and Steven looked up at him. Mitch kicked his leg, "Get up," he commanded.

Putting his hand on the wall, Steven struggled to his feet. Mitch grabbed his shoulder and spun him so Steven could see his face. "I want you to go and apologize to every employee here. Is that understood?" Mitch told him.

"I will not," Steven said.

Mitch swung his right hand and slapped the side of Steven's face with a loud 'crack' that resounded through the building. Steven's body spun around as he hit the wall. He caught himself with his hands on the wall and pushed off, spinning back around and balling up his fist.

"You hit me, boy, and you'll wish this officer had continued," Mitch told him and Steven unclenched his fist.

"They could be hiding stuff in there," Steven said, pointing to the office door.

"I don't care," Mitch said.

Nathan reached in his pocket, pulling out the keys. "Mitch, you just had to ask," Nathan said, unlocking the door and stepping inside.

"See, I told you," Steven said, pointing at the boxes on the floor.

"I paid for that and gave them as gifts to the employees," Nathan said, looking at Mitch.

Mitch nodded. "I know, Connie gave me the receipt book showing you spent several grand buying stuff for them," he said with a smile.

"I'm taking one of these," Steven said, reaching toward the pistols on the desk.

Nathan dove forward, grabbing Steven by the throat and driving him to the wall. Holding Steven a foot off the floor by his throat, Nathan pulled his pistol and put it to Steven's temple. "That is evidence," he told him. "You are going to leave this store now and go sit in that big box truck. If I see your face again, I'll kill you," Nathan grumbled. Steven's hands were holding the arm that had him pinned and he couldn't do anything as he started seeing stars in his vision.

"Do you understand me?" Nathan asked. With what little reserve of oxygen he had left, Steven nodded his head and Nathan let him go, shoving him out the door.

"Steven, you apologize before you get in that truck, you hear me?" Mitch told him as Steven sucked down air. "If you don't, I'll throw you off the property when we get home," Mitch threatened. Steven nodded his head yes. "Start with this officer first," Mitch told him.

Steve's jaw muscles clenched as he narrowed his eyes. "I'm sorry," he spit out. Nathan nodded his head as he holstered his pistol. With a stumbling gait, Steven walked down the hall, his shoulders slumped.

Mitch turned to Nathan. "I'm sorry, you're right. I'm indebted to you. If anything would've happened to these people it would've hurt me dearly," Mitch told him sincerely.

"Your son is going to get you killed," Nathan said as he stepped out of the office.

Mitch followed him as Nathan relocked the door. "You're probably right, but he's my child," Mitch said.

"How long till you make another run?" Nathan asked. "I want this group out of here tonight."

Mitch shook his head. "We're beat. We emptied two of our liquor stores and our other store. We haven't stopped since this happened. I'm taking everyone home and giving them the rest of today and tomorrow off. So we probably won't be back till day after tomorrow," he said.

"I'm telling these people to leave this evening. It's getting too dangerous here and they need to check on family," Nathan told him.

"They don't have to leave if they don't want to," Mitch said.

"They've only stayed because I was here, teaching them how to survive," Nathan said.

"I'll have to get them to come over and show me," Mitch said as Nathan chuckled. "How long you staying?" Mitch asked.

"I'm leaving tomorrow," Nathan said.

Mitch nodded. "The store will be alright then till we get back," he said.

"Mitch, if you see any broken windows or a forced entry, don't come in. Go find a bunch of people with guns before you do," Nathan warned.

"Sounds good," Mitch said, and pulled out an envelope and handed it to Nathan. "It's what you spent in here for them. I'm paying you for your service," Mitch told him.

Genuinely surprised, Nathan accepted the envelope. "Thank you," he said softly.

"I'm going to give the others theirs," Mitch said. "I'm sorry about my son."

"I'm serious about what I said. He's going to get you killed and probably worse," Nathan told him. Mitch just smiled and left.

After Mitch and his family left, everyone gathered in the diner. "What did they do wrong?" Nathan asked.

"Pissed you off," Renee answered, causing everyone to laugh.

"No, what did they do wrong?" he asked again.

"They didn't get hardly any food," Jessie said.

"That's right," Nathan said. "Jessie, you and the brothers pull the truck and mowers back in the shop and let's load up everything we can fit in and on them," Nathan said.

Connie looked at the store. "Nathan, even if we pool our money together it won't be anywhere near enough. There has to be over two hundred thousand dollars of merchandise left just in the store not including the diner," she said.

"Connie, when we leave this store it will get raided. I wanted everyone that came in to see everyone carrying weapons. That would let them know 'we will kill you.' Once we're gone, it's open season," he told her.

"You're that sure?" she asked.

Nathan just turned to the brothers, and Andy looked at Connie. "He's right. There are about twenty people by the Interstate watching us," Andy told her.

Connie looked at Nathan. "That means you need to leave when we do," she said.

"No, I'll be outside and visible. I'm going to stay the night here in case you guys need to come back," he said.

"How long will it take you to get home?" Renee asked.

Puffing his cheeks out and exhaling, Nathan looked at her then said, "I'm figuring six months."

"People walk across America all the time faster than that," she said.

"Not carrying over a hundred pounds and having to live off the land. I expect to make fifteen, maybe twenty miles a day in the south. In the mountains I think half that," he said.

"That should only be four months then; it's only two thousand miles," Connie said.

"Right, *if* I walked the Interstate, main roads and traveled through the big cities, taking the straight route. I'm taking back roads and logging trails. I mapped it out at twenty-six hundred miles and I have to stop and collect food," he told her.

"Steal a damn car," Connie said firmly.

Nathan nodded. "I've thought about it but I think it might prove a hindrance. Everyone wants one and I might spend all my time fighting to keep it. I only have six hundred rounds for the M-4."

Brad spoke up. "If they start putting up road blocks then you would surely get stopped," he said.

"Thinking outside the box," Nathan said, smiling approvingly.

"How will we know if you make it home?" Renee asked.

Nathan smiled. "Tell you what. I want you guys to unload what you have tonight when you get home. Then tomorrow head to the co-op and buy all the seeds and fertilizer you can. Find someplace you can get ammo and, if possible, long guns with large magazines. Tell Mark to keep an eye out for some. I want you to get a short wave radio," he said, leaning down and writing in a notebook. "Starting October fifteenth at eight p.m. mountain time, listen for this message on this frequency. If you don't hear it, listen for me on the fifteenth of every month till February. If I haven't made it by then, I'm not going to. Now if you hear it, don't try to call back because transmissions can be tracked fast," he told them.

"I don't want you to go," Renee said, her eyes filling with tears.

"Renee, don't think I haven't thought about it, but I need to," Nathan said.

"I feel like I've known you forever," she said, pouting and stomping her foot.

"That's no lie," Jessie agreed.

Nathan laughed. "Now I want pictures of everyone, then one big group picture," he said, taking out his camera. For an hour they took pictures and laughed, and then Jessie and Lenore fixed lunch.

Nathan was sitting at a table with Brad waiting on lunch. "You could stay," Brad told him.

"I have friends that are counting on me," Nathan replied.

"You have new friends here that could use you," Brad told him.

"I've tried to help you as much as I can," Nathan said.

Brad leaned toward him. "I'm not meaning that to be ungrateful. We don't want you to get hurt. I'm not a fool, I know you've saved me and my family from a fate worse than death. That goes for the others as well. The thought of you getting hurt out there with no one to help really hurts," Brad said with tears in his eyes.

"I'm glad I mean that much, but I've known these guys and their families for a long time. We agreed if anything like this happened, we would do it together. Granted, we never expected something like this, more of an economic collapse," Nathan told him as the kids jumped up in his lap and began hugging Nathan.

"I can never repay you for what you've done for me and my family," Brad told him.

Looking over at Abigail, Nathan said, trying not to blush, "We're even, trust me."

"I know about it and no, we're not," Brad said, smiling. Nathan coughed and laughed as Connie and Abigail came over. Connie held out several laminated papers to Nathan.

"Here," she said.

Nathan grabbed them and saw they were three by five laminated pictures. Looking through them, he saw they were of him with members of the group. The last one was of the entire group. "How?" he asked.

"Last year I ordered a picture printer. I told Mitch it was so we could print employee of the month pictures but I wanted it to print some pictures. I had it stored in the file cabinet and plugged it up to see if it worked and it did. I then used your computer, I hope you don't mind," Connie told him, smiling.

"Seeing how they are all on the computer anyway I don't mind," he said, looking through the pictures again.

"We printed some for us too," Abigail said, sitting down.

Nathan looked at Abigail. "Abigail, will you do me a favor?" he asked.

"Name it," she said with a teasing smirk.

"Take off your big diamond rings and earrings. They make a tempting target," he said.

"Shit, I should've thought of that," she said, taking them off. Nathan smiled and found it was still hard to take his eyes off her as he turned to Brad.

"Did you guys ever model?" he asked Brad. Nathan was not gay but even he had to admit that Brad looked good. Then when you looked at Ashlee and Raymond you couldn't help but think some kind of genetic manipulation had taken place. He had looked hard trying to find something wrong with all of them and was still drawing a blank. They were all smart, well mannered, fun to be around and physically perfect.

Abigail and Brad started laughing as she leaned over to another table and grabbed her purse. Brad reached over the table, grabbing Nathan's hand. "Yes, we modeled as a family. Our last shoot was for an RV line. I make more money as a model than a doctor, and with the family a lot more," he told Nathan. Abigail handed him a booklet advertising a class A motor home.

On the front cover he saw Brad at a grill with Abigail beside him and the kids playing in front of the motor home in front of a beach. Flipping through the book, he saw them with the motor home in the desert, mountains, and grassland. "I knew it," Nathan said, handing the book back.

"That shoot took two weeks traveling California," Brad told him. "We've done about fifteen as a family, then each doing a single shoot," Brad added.

"It's a busy lifestyle. I dated a model before," Nathan told him.

"Who?" Abigail asked.

Picking up the kids, Nathan walked over to his laptop and brought it over, pulling up a picture of him and Patrice. He sat the computer down and turned it around. "Her," he said.

Abigail looked at the picture and up at him. "You dated Patrice?" she asked incredulously.

"Yeah," Nathan replied, shocked she knew Patrice.

"She's a grade A bitch," Abigail said without any remorse.

"Ya think," Nathan said, sitting down. Connie turned the computer to see the pretty woman and caught her breath.

"This is the skank that had you upset?" Connie almost shouted.

"I wasn't upset, Connie," Nathan replied, looking at Abigail.

Abigail shook her head. "I've worked with her twice and can't stand her. I don't think she has anything but air between her ears. She acts like a queen and demands too much special attention," she told him.

Nathan started laughing and banging the table. When he caught his breath he looked at Abigail. "I had someone tell me just about the exact same thing fifteen minutes before the world crashed," he said, wiping tears from his eyes. Grabbing the computer, he started showing them pictures of him with his four buddies and their families. Nathan explained the photos and each friend and their kids. When it got to Tim and Sherry with baby Nolen, they could tell Nathan felt extra close to them.

Connie reached over and put her hand on his. "You do have family," she said. He had told her about his parents dying when he was young.

Thinking about that, Nathan smiled. "Well, I guess I do," he said.

Abigail and Brad reached over and grabbed his other hand. "You have another family here," Brad told him. "I want to see you again," he said as the kids jumped out of Nathan's lap to chase Ares.

"If it is possible, Brad, I swear you will," Nathan promised him.

"Yep, I got to teach you how to wrestle a cow," Andy said from behind him. Nathan turned around to see everyone standing behind him having watched the photo explanation.

"Andy, the only way I wrestle a cow is to eat it, and I prefer not to fight my food in hand to hand combat," Nathan said, standing up. Everyone laughed as Lenore left and started bringing out plates. Nathan walked to the office to grab the three pistols that were left and headed back to eat.

He gave Lenore the Glock and had Connie show her how to work it. Then he walked over and gave Abigail the revolver and Sig 226 9mm. "You know how to work those?" he asked.

"Yes, Brad showed me. I have a Sig but it's heavy. It doesn't kick though," she said, taking out the magazine.

"Everyone, make sure you always have your go bag packed and ready. After we eat, let's fill up the trailer, truck, and lawn mowers. I'm sorry, Billy, I don't think you can carry much on the moped. I'm amazed it can carry you," Nathan said. Billy just smiled and shrugged.

After they ate, they rearranged the trailer. They started out by shoving all of the camping gear forward then started loading food and all the ammo. Nathan made them take it all; what they couldn't shoot, they could trade. With every square inch holding something, they returned to the diner. Nathan carried one of the backpacks he'd bought out of the office.

"I'm giving you this," he told Brad. "It is only to be used for your group here and their families. The other stuff I got is for your practice; make sure you ration it out."

Brad looked in the bag to see several large bottles of antibiotics, pain killers, and muscle relaxers. "It's half of what I have," Nathan said as Renee brought over a Coke for him and he told her thanks.

"You should keep these, you can trade with them," Brad said, zipping the bag up.

"Can't carry them," Nathan replied and Brad nodded.

"On the flash drive you have with your personal information I typed in a code we can use to talk over the radio. Just make sure you have a tape recorder," Brad said.

"They can track you," Nathan told him.

"Yeah, but I'm a ham operator and there are ways around it. When you call back," Brad said, stressing 'when,' "listen the next night at the same time and I can update you."

"If it starts getting real bad that could be dangerous for you," Nathan pointed out.

"I know," Brad said, grinning. "But I want you to know how this part of your family is doing and you can talk back to us," he said.

"Fair enough," Nathan said. Ashlee and Raymond came over and climbed up in his lap again.

"We're going to miss you," Ashlee said, lying her head on his chest followed by Raymond.

"I'm going to miss you as well, and I want both of you to promise to always be where your mom and dad can see you or know where you are. Don't even go off with other kids without telling them. You could get hurt bad, okay?" Nathan said, looking down at them.

"We promise," they said together.

"Why don't you two chase Ares some more. He's been sleeping most of the day," Nathan suggested. They both jumped out of his lap to find Ares, only to find him waiting to pounce. Holding them down, Ares licked their faces and took off running. They ran after him, screaming with laughter.

It was almost five and Nathan was dreading the sun going down because everyone was leaving at dark. They weren't going to use the headlights so they wouldn't attract attention. He'd figured that would be the safest for everyone.

As he was lost in thought, well, day dreaming since Nathan hadn't taken his Adderall, he heard a truck pull up. He jumped up and looked out in the parking lot. It was a big flatbed farm truck with a deputy behind the wheel. The deputy stopped the truck and jumped out, straightening his uniform. Nathan smirked and was having a hard time trying not to laugh. The deputy might have been twenty-five and was about five and a half feet tall, but was thin as a rail. Barney Fife came to Nathan's mind as he walked to the diner door.

Renee walked over to the door. "Neil, what are you doing here?" she snapped in a harsh tone.

"My job!" Neal shouted back.

"We're safe, go away!" she barked at him.

"You will open this door because I'm the law," he told her.

"Get your skinny ass or I should say, no ass out of here. Mark will be here in a minute. We don't need you," Renee said, crossing her arms and scowling at him.

Neil's face turned red. "I know Mark's coming here, that's why I'm here," he said.

"Mark better have a real good reason for sending you here, Neil," Renee said, throwing the lock and opening the door.

Neil strutted in with a smile on his narrow face. The reflective sunglasses he was wearing made him look like a giant insect as he looked around at the group of people. When he saw Nathan, he stopped scanning the group and his smile turned into a grin.

"You," Neil said, pointing at Nathan. "Place your hands on your head and turn around." He tried to make his voice deep but it kept cracking.

"What are you doing?" Renee screamed.

"I'm arresting a killer. I'll be a hero," he said, looking at Nathan.

"It was ruled justified!" Renee shouted.

"I haven't heard that and quit yelling at me. I can still arrest you," Neil snapped.

"Oh, I'd like to see your stupid ass try," she challenged with her hand dropping to her pistol.

"Mister, I'm not going to tell you again, put your hands up!" Neil shouted.

"Ah, no," Nathan replied. Neil moved for his pistol and before his hand touched it, he was looking down the barrel of Nathan's pistol.

"Move and you're a dead man," Nathan told him.

Neil stood, petrified. He'd never seen anyone move that fast. This was not going like he'd dreamed. Even if the shooting was justified, he would've been seen as bringing in a killer even the sergeant hadn't brought in. "You won't shoot a fellow cop," Neil said, trying to smile.

Chuckling, Nathan said, "Oh yes I would, but you aren't a cop, just trash wearing a uniform."

Neil started gauging how fast he could get to his pistol.

"Even if he doesn't, I will," Renee said, aiming her pistol at his head.

"I get to shoot a dirty cop!" Andy yelled, aiming at Neil. Neil looked around the room and noticed the only ones not pointing a gun at him were two blond kids. But they were holding a big ass dog by the collar that was growling at him.

Nathan walked over and put the barrel of his pistol on Neil's forehead then undid Neil's belt and suspenders, letting his rig hit the ground. Frisking Neil, Nathan found a pistol in the small of his back and laughed, throwing it down. Pulling out Neil's pockets next, Nathan threw down a spring assist knife and Neil's wallet. Ripping Neil's shirt open, Nathan pulled it off then undid the bulletproof vest and threw that on the floor.

"Take your boots off," Nathan commanded.

"No!" Neil shouted.

"Then I'll cut your balls off and shove them in your mouth, watch you choke to death on them, and I'll take them off myself," Nathan threatened.

Neil quickly bent down and took off his boots. Nathan kicked the boots over to the other supplies. "This was just a lesson. Now sit your ass down on the floor with your back against the door and cross your ankles. Twitch and I'll shoot you and throw you in the field," Nathan told him. Neil slunk down to the floor, doing what Nathan had told him and wanting to cry.

"I was going to be a hero. You're supposed to be a cop," Neil whined.

"Oh I am, but I also want to live. I'm not taking the chance you wouldn't just shoot me. You'll never be a hero; you don't have it in you. You want to pick on someone and intimidate them. That's not being a hero. I can never explain it to something like you. To me you're worthless and I'll kill you if I ever see you again," Nathan told him. Neil just pursed his lips together, his face turning red. "See, you can let words get to you. I rest my case," Nathan said, walking over to the pile.

He picked up the duty belt and took out the Glock 19, nodding then noticed three triple-magazine holders. "What the hell. You have nine magazines on your duty rig? That's almost two hundred rounds plus fifteen in the well. If you need that many you need a better gun or you need to shoot better," Nathan said.

They heard a vehicle pull up. Everyone looked outside and saw it was Mark. He got out of his Cherokee, eyeballed Neil's truck, and walked to the door where he saw Neil sitting against one of the doors. Pushing the other door open, he walked in and looked down. "Neil, what the hell are you doing here?" he shouted.

"Trying to arrest a murderer and everyone pulled a gun on me," Neil said, looking down.

"It was ruled justified," Mark snapped.

"I was still bringing in a killer," Neil answered.

"Get up," Mark said. When Neil stood up, Mark opened the door. "Get to the station. I'm having you removed from duty," Mark told him.

Moving toward his gear on the floor, Neil looked up at Nathan who was shaking his head, a hand on his pistol. Dejectedly, Neil walked out empty handed and headed to his truck. Mark stood in the door, holding it open, watching him. Then Mark turned around.

"I'm sorry about that Nathan," he said and saw Nathan's arm blur and suddenly he was aiming his pistol at him.

"Pull it out and you will die!" Nathan yelled.

"Nathan, I'm not reaching for anything. It's me, Mark!" Mark said in complete shock.

"Your boy is trying to pull a shotgun from the truck," Nathan said with his arm holding the pistol rock steady.

Mark looked at Nathan carefully; he realized the pistol was aimed right under the arm that was holding the door open. Turning his head to look behind him, Mark saw Neil frozen halfway out of the truck with his right hand on the stock of a shotgun. Mark spun around and pulled out his new pistol and aimed at Neal's face.

For the first time Neal was more scared of someone else than Nathan. Mark walked over, raised his right foot and flat kicked Neil in the chest. Neil sailed back ten feet through the air before hitting the ground and rolling end over end. Lying there and trying to get air in his lungs, Neil felt someone grab his arms and his wrist suddenly hurt.

"You're under arrest, Neil," Mark said sternly.

"You can't do that to me," Neil moaned.

"Yes I can, and you're going into the cell block. You've heard there will be no trials until this is over," Mark said, picking him up by the arm. Hauling Neil to the front door, Mark walked inside and looked at the three brothers. "Guys, the sheriff wants you as deputies. If you still want the job I will be out tomorrow to swear you in. One of you will ride with me and the other is to stay with the sheriff. Only two of you will be on at any time, but one of you will be with the sheriff every day. If your brothers want to join later they can," Mark told them. "Want the job?"

The brothers started jumping up and down yelling. Everyone ran over to hug and congratulate them. When they saw Mark waiting for an answer they all yelled, "YES!"

Mark smiled. "Grab some rope and hog tie Neil and throw him in the back of my ride," he said, and the brothers started fighting to get outside. Everyone laughed as Fred and Billy actually got stuck shoulder to shoulder in the doorway but then Andy hit both of them, knocking them out of the door.

Nathan walked over to the pile of Neil's stuff. "This is mine, so don't think about it," he said, pointing at the pile.

"Won't fit me," Mark said, smiling.

Nathan held up the duty belt to Abigail. "You have a Glock," he said. She skipped over and took the belt and put it on. Everyone noticed she was bigger than Neil as she buckled the belt and suspenders on. "Give the Sig to Jessie," Nathan told her, bending down and picking up the vest. He looked at Renee and held it out.

"Ah no, I'm not wearing anything Neal's had on," Renee told him, crossing her arms.

"Renee, as a sergeant, Mark is a target. That means you're a target that can be used against him. Take it or I'll strip ya and put it on ya," Nathan said firmly.

Stomping her foot and looking at Mark, she said, "You're going to let him talk to me like that?"

"I'll help him," Mark told her, crossing his arms.

She stomped over and took the vest. "Thank you," she replied furiously as she put the vest on.

Nathan looked at the truck Neil was driving, "What's in there is mine too," he said, walking to the door.

"That stuff is the department's," Mark said as Nathan walked past him.

"Not my fault Neil lost it somewhere," Nathan said, pulling out the shotgun and Mark nodded in agreement. Reaching in, Nathan moved the front seat forward, grabbed a rifle bag from behind it and pulled it out. Not seeing anything else, he let the seat fall back and looked in the truck's cab to see several clip boards and two plastic ammo cans on the floor. He grabbed them and headed back inside. He knew from talking to everyone that there were only two people who didn't have long guns.

He walked over to Abigail, holding out the shotgun. "Here you go, a big gun," he said.

"Thank you," she said, smiling and taking the shotgun. "We watched the prepper shows all the time and have three shotguns just like this one. Brad even bought an AR-15. Granted, he had to get the stupid limited-capacity magazines," she said, racking the slide and ejecting the eight shells. Then she picked them up and reloaded the shotgun.

Nathan handed Brad the rifle bag. "This should replace yours then," he said, and Brad reached in and pulled out an AR-15.

Running his hands over it, he leaned over and hugged Nathan. Then he kissed Nathan on each cheek. "I don't care if you hit me. Now we can really fight back if we need to, and you don't even ask for anything," he said. "Thank you."

In shock, Nathan just looked straight ahead. "You're the only man pretty enough I would allow to kiss me," he said, making everyone laugh and shaking him out of his shock. "Jessie, pull this truck around and let's get it loaded with stuff. One of the brothers can drive it back tomorrow after they become deputies. With it we should be able to get a lot of shit," Nathan said as Jessie moved to the door.

After he pulled the truck around, the group had it loaded to capacity in thirty minutes. Nathan gave the pump he'd rigged up to Mark to pump gas; Mark was very happy with it. Then they moved to the diner.

"Jessie, do you know where Mitch lives?" Nathan asked.

"Yeah, about ten miles from me," he said.

"Without them knowing it, I want you and the brothers to go over once a day to see if they're still there. If you see no one there two days in a row, get the stuff they have," he said.

"They might just have gone somewhere," Jessie said.

"They are going to be driving around selling booze. You told me when they drove up here that was everyone in his family," Nathan said.

"It was," Jessie replied.

"They are going to die driving around selling booze. Those are just the people that will kill them for nothing. They only had one weapon: a pistol. If you get booze from them, don't trade it to people, trade it to a place or the same will happen to you," Nathan told Jessie but was looking around at everyone to make sure they understood.

"He's right. We've had a lot of murders at bars," Mark said.

"Guys, with Mark here the trucks can take off. Fred, Billy, and Andy, I don't think anyone will mess with you seeing how you're bigger than your rides," Nathan said.

"Trying to get rid of us?" Renee demanded.

"No, you have a lot of stuff to unpack. Then you and Mark have to go to your house and get your stuff. I really want you guys done before dawn," Nathan told her.

"Hey, we can ride over with them and help them move," Billy said, and everyone agreed.

"Sounds like a plan to me. I'll be here tonight in case you have to run back or need a safe haven. Please be careful and remember what I've said and read what I gave you," Nathan told them.

"Read?" Mark asked.

"Yeah, they need a laptop. I let them download a ton of information on how to survive," Nathan said.

"That's simple, I have two in the Jeep," Mark told him and everyone just looked at him. "What? The sheriff told us to be on the lookout for laptops that work. I've found six so far, I've just haven't turned in these two," he said, smiling. "Guess I can forget about them if you let me read this stuff too," he added.

"You're part of our group, aren't you?" Brad asked.

Renee ran over and jumped up several feet in the air. Mark caught her in his arms. "Most definitely," he said, kissing her resoundingly.

Everyone made a round to make sure they had everything including the stuff Nathan had bought them. Not finding anything, they all hugged Nathan goodbye and headed to the vehicles.

Nathan walked back to the diner and grabbed his M-4. Hearing footsteps behind him, he turned around and saw Abigail running toward him. She stopped in front of Nathan and pushed some pictures in his hand. Then, reaching up, she pulled Nathan's head down and kissed him passionately. After she let him go, Nathan was still leaned over, kissing the air with his eyes closed.

"Thank you more than you will ever know. I liked bringing your flip flops and see, Brad thought it was cool," she said, breaking the spell.

"My pleasure," Nathan replied with a goofy grin.

"Don't forget your flip flops. Those pictures are just for you and the originals are on your computer," Abigail said, grinning.

"I'll never look at flip flops the same again," Nathan promised. "Ever," he added, making her laugh. He looked down at the pictures and gasped, "Good goobidee goo!" Nathan shouted, shoving the pictures in his pocket. Abigail laughed, clapping her hands as Nathan grabbed her and hugged her then let her go.

"Check your purse tonight," Nathan told her, leading her outside.

Brad was in the driver's seat of Neil's truck with the kids beside him. Nathan walked over and leaned in and hugged the kids. Then he picked up Abigail and put her in the truck and closed the door and went to the driver's side. He opened the door and hugged Brad. Brad returned the hug.

"You can come with us, you know," Brad said.

"I know, but I have to go. I would invite you but it's going to be bad," Nathan said, looking at Ashlee and Raymond.

"I've thought about it but these two are my life," Brad said, noticing Nathan was looking at the kids.

"Keep your promise to me about them," Nathan said, closing the door.

"We love you!" Brad, Abigail, Ashlee, and Raymond yelled. "Bye Ares, we love you too," Ashlee and Raymond yelled. Ares barked as Mark pulled out and the two trucks followed. Then a moped and two riding lawn mowers pulling trailers drove past him, the brothers waving.

The group drove off with everyone crying, except Neil. Even the lone man still standing in front of the store had tears rolling down his cheeks as he watched them disappear from sight. It felt like they had been together for a year instead of mere days.

Ares threw his head up and let out a long mournful howl and Nathan wanted to join him.

CHAPTER 10

It was almost six when Nathan headed back into the store. The first thing he did was walk around and lock all the doors. Then he went to the office and pulled his stuff out to the casino area. They had left him a cot even though Nathan had told them to take it. Dropping his stuff beside it, he went back to the office and grabbed the last of his stuff. Throwing it on the cot, Nathan walked the store and was glad to see so much gone now, even though there was still a lot of shit there.

With what was in the freezer and on the shelves, he could eat for two months easy. Walking over to the camping aisle, Nathan just browsed and saw another hand pump water filter. It wasn't as good as his, but water would be a determining factor so he grabbed it. Ares could carry it. Grabbing a bag of dog food that Ares loved, Nathan carried it over to the casino and poured him a bowl then got him a bowl of water.

Ares looked up at him then at the bowls. Then he looked back up at Nathan like, Are you kidding? "Hey, Lenore isn't here to cook for you, buddy," Nathan told him. Ares pushed against him with his nose. "Forget it, I'm cooking for me," Nathan said, grabbing Ares' backpack. Grabbing packs of dog food, he divided it up in zip lock bags. He put two big bags on each side, figuring it was close to ten pounds per side.

Picking up his rifle, Nathan looked over at Ares. "Let's go have a walk around. I'm going through our stuff one more time, and then we're going to bed. We start for home at first light," he told Ares as he headed out the door.

Ares wasn't sure what he said but he knew what going to the door meant and took off running. Nathan propped the door open as Ares ran around the parking lot. Nathan wasn't worried about getting locked out;

there was still a key to the store under the floor mat in his ride. In truth, he just wanted to let some fresh air in. It was hot and humid as only March can be in the South.

Thinking about his truck, Nathan looked to the north, towards the Interstate, and saw it just sitting there. "I would already be home," Nathan said out loud, looking at it. Hearing gunfire from the north, he stepped back toward the building. It sounded like it was over a mile away, but it was a lot of gunfire, and as he listened he narrowed it down as coming more from the northeast.

Then it suddenly stopped and all that could be heard was the buzzing of insects. Nathan was guessing it had been about twenty to thirty rounds from at least two different caliber guns. How many of each caliber there was no way to know, unless he went to see, and that wasn't happening. "Hurry up and do your business, Ares. Let's get back inside," he said and looked down. Ares was standing rock steady, looking behind him.

Nathan spun around, crouching down and bringing up his rifle. "What?" he asked Ares. Ares let out a low "oof" with his eyes locked on the tree line on the south side of the store parking lot. "If you go after a rabbit, I'm cutting your blanket up," Nathan threatened scanning the trees and brush sixty yards away.

"I don't see shit, what is it?" he asked, and Ares remained rigid, looking at the tree line straight ahead. "I'm not kidding about the rabbit," Nathan said, flipping his selector to burst. "Ares lead, slow," he commanded Ares.

When Ares was five feet away, Nathan crouched over, following him with his rifle held low. Looking and studying the tree line, Nathan thought he saw something move in the bushes. "Ares, if you lead me into an ambush I'm kicking your ass," Nathan whispered. Ares ignored him and crossed the parking lot. When they were twenty yards away, Nathan spotted a bush move beside a tree.

"I know you're there. Come out slowly. I'm a cop so don't try anything," Nathan said, aiming his rifle at the spot. "I'm not kidding, I don't want to send the dog in." The bush moved and a kid stepped out. At least Nathan thought it was a kid. Its hair was going everywhere with mud, twigs and leaves in it.

"Is that it, Ares?" Nathan asked and Ares started panting, letting his tongue hang out. "You could've told me it was a kid." Nathan lowered his rifle but kept it ready. He walked closer and saw the kid back up, getting ready to bolt.

"Hey, it's okay. I'm a cop, see," Nathan said pointing at his badge and the kid stopped. "I'm not going to hurt you," he said. "If I tried, Ares would bite me," he added and the kid relaxed. Easing closer, he thought the kid was a girl when he was ten feet away but still wasn't sure. The arms and legs were covered in scratches and from the neck down was just mud.

The kid was skinny. Not from lack of food, just skinny. Nathan figured the kid was about five foot and just over eighty pounds, if you threw in the mud. Looking at the kid, Nathan still couldn't make out if it was a boy or girl. All he knew was the kid was nowhere near puberty. Where there wasn't dirt on the face there were scratches, and the lower lip was busted with the left eye swollen. Even the clothes didn't help. At onetime the shirt 'might' have been blue but now it was more tie-dyed. Nathan knew the shorts were blue jeans but that still didn't help.

"My name is Nathan and this is Ares," he said. "What's your name?"

The kid just stared at him; not really at him, more through him.

"Hey, if I can't tell Ares your name he can't be your friend," Nathan told the kid.

The kid looked up at Nathan's eyes and mouthed something he couldn't hear.

"Little one, I didn't hear you," Nathan said, moving close enough to touch the kid.

In a dry, whispering voice, the kid said, "Amanda."

"Ares, this is Amanda and a friend," Nathan said, looking at Ares. Ares walked over and started licking her hand then nuzzled his head into her belly till she petted him. Then Nathan saw her smile weakly.

"Amanda, you look thirsty and hungry. You want something to eat and drink?" he asked, and she nodded her head.

"Okay, I'll fix you some food and something to drink. Are your parents around here?" he asked. Amanda shook her head and looked down. "Okay, let's go eat," Nathan said, turning around and heading back to the store. Looking down at his side, he didn't see Amanda or Ares. He stopped and looked back to see her still standing in the same spot with Ares beside her.

He walked back to her and reached down and gently grabbed her hand. "Come with me so we can eat," he said, stepping toward the store.

When her arm was straight out she took a step and let him lead her. He opened the door and led her inside, making sure the door closed and locked.

Leading her to a table, Nathan sat her down in a chair and was fixing to find some water but she wouldn't let go of his hand. "Amanda, I have to get you some water and food. Ares will be here with you; don't worry," Nathan told her and removed her hand from his.

He walked over to the cooler and grabbed several bottles of water and came back to see her petting Ares. Smiling, Nathan sat down and opened a bottle, putting it in front of her. He sat staring at her, waiting on her to drink. After five minutes he gave up and scooted his chair over beside her. Grabbing the bottle, Nathan put it to her lips and slowly poured it in her mouth. The water ran out of the side of her mouth until she started to drink. Slowly at first; then she started taking gulps. With half the bottle down, Nathan took it away from her mouth, watching her lick her lips.

"How old are you, Amanda?" he asked and she just looked straight ahead. "Sweetie, you have to tell me how old you are so I know what to fix you. You have to be over ten for hot dogs and under fifteen for onion rings," he told her.

"Thirteen," she whispered.

"You want a hamburger or a hot dog?" Nathan asked and she just nodded her head. "Okay, French fries or onion rings?" he asked and again she just nodded her head.

"Okay," Nathan said. "Are you hurt?" he asked and she nodded her head. "Where at?" he asked and she just stared ahead, but tears started spilling down her cheeks. "Everywhere?" he asked and she nodded. "Amanda, look at me please," he said, and she slowly turned her head till she was looking at him. "I'm a cop but I'm also a nurse. I need to clean you off to see where you are hurt, okay?" She just gazed at him. "I'm taking that for an okay," he told her, standing up, and she quickly grabbed his arm and held on.

He looked at her and saw the fear in her face. "Amanda, no one is going to hurt you while I'm around. If they can get through me, they sure can't get through Ares. You're safe with us but I'll make Ares stay beside you till I get back, okay?" he told her and she let go and nodded as she lowered her hands and started petting Ares.

He came back from the kitchen carrying a big bowl of water and towels and rags over his shoulder. Picking up her bottle, Nathan made her drink some more then put it down, noting she'd never stopped petting Ares. Wetting a rag, he started on her face. He didn't really get it clean, just knocked the chucks of mud off but the water turned filthy. Grabbing the bowl, Nathan went and dumped it, refilled it, and sat back down.

Gently grabbing an arm, he wiped it down from the shoulder to her hand. Her arm was covered in scratches but her hand was covered in cuts and a few small punctures. None deep enough for stitches, but he stopped counting at a dozen and they were filled with dirt. "Sweetie, did you get your shots for school?" Nathan asked and she nodded her head. "Well at least you had your tetanus shot," he said and looked at her legs.

"Sweetie you need to bathe. You have too many cuts and scratches for me to clean you up with a bowel of water," he told her. She didn't acknowledge him, just stared off into space. Opening another bottle of water, he held it as she drank half of it. Putting it down, he picked up her hand and pulled her up gently and led her to the back. Grabbing a lantern, Nathan lit it and led her into the shower room. Getting some towels and rags, he moved to a shower and turned on the water. "A girl used this one today so it has shampoo and stuff in there. Ares is going to stay in here with you while you shower and I'll fix some food, okay?" he said and she nodded.

He walked out and went to the kitchen. Taking out some hamburger patties, hot dogs, and a steak, he grabbed a pot, filled it with water and put it on the stove. Getting out the bread and some other stuff, he laid it out, then started getting his cooking supplies and set them up. He turned on the grease vat and turned it to auto, then headed back to check on Amanda. He knocked on the door.

"Amanda, are you done?" Nathan called out. Not hearing her, Nathan stepped in to find her in the same spot he'd left her at.

He walked over to her and kneeled down. "Amanda, you have to get clean so I can treat your cuts. Then we can eat," he told her and she nodded her head. "You want to get clean and eat so I can make your cuts better?" he asked and she nodded her head. "You want to jump off a building?" he asked and she shook her head no slowly.

"I had to make sure you could do more than nod," he told her and she nodded. "Why didn't you bathe her? I've bathed you enough," Nathan said, looking at Ares. Ares was sitting down, looking up at Nathan and just cocked his head sideways. 'You want me to wash her but I don't like to get washed,' the look said. "Wait here," Nathan told Amanda and Ares.

He walked over to the store and grabbed a pair of swimming trunks. He had bathed kids at work many times. Just remembering how some of them came in made Nathan cringe. Walking back in the shower room, Nathan walked to the back and took off his vest and set it and the rifle on the floor then stripped down. He put on the shorts and headed back to Amanda.

Kneeling down in front of her, he asked, "You ready to shower?" and she nodded. "Raise your arm," he said and she slowly did. He eased her shirt off to see bruises and scrapes on her belly and chest. He spun her around and clear as day saw a complete boot print on her back. Nathan calmed his breathing and slowly stripped her down. He discovered she was wearing sandals, after he'd dug through the dirt to get to them.

"Ares, guard," he said, leading Amanda into the shower. Nathan scrubbed her down three times to her knees before he saw her skin. Nathan had no false hopes; he knew from the knees down was going to be some work. He scrubbed her head gently, searching with his fingers for bumps or cuts. All he found was a shit load of mud, leaves, and twigs. Satisfied, he finished scrubbing her head and rinsed it off. Then he did it three more times, finally lathering her hair in conditioner.

He looked down at her feet and they were still black and brown from dirt. They had been in the shower for forty minutes and that dirt wasn't going without a fight. "Hold on," Nathan said, opening the door and walking out. He grabbed a plastic lawn chair and brought it in the shower. He sat her in it and he sat down on the floor. Grabbing rags and soap, he went to work and twenty minutes later he could see her feet; granted, they were stained brown but he could see them. What made it so bad was that her feet were covered in cuts and blisters. For another twenty minutes he cleaned them out and got most of the brown stain off. Not one time did Amanda move or say anything.

Finally finished, Nathan stood up and washed off; that much dirt made him feel dirty. Finished, he turned the water off and stepped out and threw a towel on the floor. Going back to the shower, Nathan picked up Amanda and stood her on the towel. He dried her off and wrapped a towel around her head and another around her body. He walked back and grabbed his rifle, slinging it across his back. Then he just picked her up, noticing two bloody footprints on the towel.

Shaking his head, he carried her to the diner and sat her on a barstool. He walked over and closed the blinds, not wanting anyone to see the fire on the stove. He cooked them some food and carried it to the casino where he put it on a table and dared Ares to touch it. Going back to the diner, he picked up Amanda and his rifle, carrying them to the casino and setting both down at the table.

Closing the door, he walked back to the shower and grabbed the lantern. When he came back, he saw Amanda petting Ares. Ares had his head in her lap. Glancing at the floor, Nathan noticed blood dripping off her feet and pooling on the floor. Grabbing some towels, he wrapped them around her feet and sat down beside her. Not even asking, Nathan halved her burger and stuck it in front of her mouth. She took a bite and he held up a glass with a straw and she drank. After she ate the burger and fries, he went to the store to get supplies.

Coming back, he sat down on the floor and started on her feet, using the towel from her feet to wipe up the blood on the floor. At first he tried to put some antibiotic ointment on each cut after making sure it was cleaned out. Giving up, Nathan just coated both her feet and wrapped them in gauze. Then he moved up, putting ointment on cuts and scrapes. He looked at her hands and shook his head. He just coated them and wrapped them up. Two tubes of ointment and a shit load of gauze later and he was done.

He looked at his watch, seeing it was almost eleven. "That took almost four hours, Ares. You could've helped," Nathan said, looking down at Ares with his head in Amanda's lap.

"He was protecting me while you made me better," Amanda whispered.

Nathan smiled and touched her cheek. "Yes he was, Amanda," he said gently.

"Thank you," she said, staring straight ahead.

"Amanda, will you do something for me?" Nathan asked and she nodded her head. "When you talk to me, look at me please. Ares does but I don't know what he says," Nathan said.

Amanda turned to look at him and the corners of her mouth briefly turned up. "Thank you," she repeated in a small voice.

"You're very welcome," he said. "You're much easier to give a bath to than Ares. He tries to eat the soap so I have to stop the bath." Her face lightened into a real smile. "Do you know your address?" he asked.

"Yes sir," she whispered.

"What is it?" he asked.

"210 Jacobs Circle, Atlanta, Georgia," she told him and looked down. Knowing he was pushing too fast, Nathan stopped.

"You still hungry?" he asked and she nodded her head.

"It hurts to move your hands, huh?" he asked.

"Yes sir," she told him, looking down.

"Look at me, okay," Nathan reminded her.

She lifted her head and looked at him. "Yes sir," she repeated.

He pulled a chair over and sat down. "I'm going to feed you, Ares and myself," Nathan said, getting her another burger, Ares one, and pulling his steak over. Forming an assembly line, Nathan fed all of them, making Ares work for his food. When he made Ares stand and walk for the last bite, Amanda uttered a tiny little laugh.

When Nathan had finished his steak, he could see Amanda's little eyes getting heavy. He picked her up and laid her on the cot and moved away. Her hand shot out and tried to grab him but there was a lot of gauze on it. He took her hand and held it in his as he leaned over, looking at her. "I'm going to check the doors. Ares is here with you. Amanda, he is a trained attack dog. If anything gets by me, it won't get by him. I'll be right back but I'll never be far. You can call for me and I'll come running, okay," he said, smiling.

"Promise you won't leave?" she asked.

"Yes Amanda, I promise with all my heart," he told her, caressing her face. She smiled at him and closed her eyes. "Ares, guard Amanda," Nathan said as he stood up, and Ares moved over by the cot. Nathan grabbed his poncho liner and covered Amanda up. Amanda reached out a wrapped hand and put it on Ares' back.

Nathan put his clothes and gear back on and walked around the store. Looking out to the north window, he saw a small campfire burning by the Interstate. He walked back to the casino and heard Amanda snoring softly; Ares was sitting by her cot, watching the room. Nathan reached down and grabbed the last backpack he had bought and a hydration bladder.

With the pack in hand, he went through the store, grabbing food and supplies and laying them on the counter. Seeing the lighter display, he grabbed two and put them on the counter with the other stuff. Opening the electronic cabinet, he found a small LED flashlight and dug through the closet till he found batteries. He wasn't using his yet as they were all taped up. He tested the flashlight to make sure it worked then nodded in satisfaction and added it to the pile.

He realized the electronic cabinet was metal, he was sure for security reasons, and the shelves were covered in velvet. Grabbing another flashlight, he dug out more batteries. Then he noticed several handheld radios in the back of the cabinet. Spotting some Motorolas, Nathan grabbed them. Then he started breaking everything down and bagging or taping it up. When he was finished, the bag weighed somewhere around thirty pounds and could feed Amanda for a week. The bag held everything but clothes and weapons. She wasn't getting any weapons, and clothes were slim pickings.

He found her a few t-shirts, a pair of shorts, two packs of panties and two packs of socks. He walked over to a display rack that had tennis shoes in clear plastic bags. Nathan grabbed Amanda's size and looked at them. If Nathan's parents had ever bought these for him, he would've run away from home. The sandals weren't an option, however, as the only thing holding them together was the dirt.

Sighing, he walked toward the counter and noticed Neil's shirt and boots. He picked up the boots; they weren't very old and were small in size. He looked in the boot for the size and scoffed, seeing W-6. "Yeah, right these are six wide. Maybe for a midget," Nathan said, and then started laughing. "Neal, you had to buy girl boots for your feet, you little twerp," he said.

"Maybe a little over a size too big but she can wear socks," Nathan muttered to himself, carrying the boots to the counter. He poured some powder in so Amanda couldn't get Neil cooties. Grabbing a shine kit, Nathan polished them up and put the kit in her bag. Walking the aisles again, Nathan picked up a large can of coffee. He only had few pounds so he grabbed it and some powdered cream.

Walking over to the rack of sunglasses, Nathan grabbed her two pairs then went and looked at the mechanic gloves but none were even close to her size. He grabbed two packs of Playtex gloves and a watch. Putting the watch on one of the straps of her pack, Nathan finished loading her pack. Putting her undies and socks in bags beside her hygiene supplies, he walked over to the vitamin aisle and grabbed several bottles of Gummi vitamins and put them in a bag.

When he was done, he looked down at his watch seeing it was almost two a.m. "Time for bed," he said, walking into the casino. "Ares, guard the house," he said, sprawling out on the floor as Ares trotted out. With his head on Amanda's pack, Nathan was asleep almost instantly.

CHAPTER 11

Day 4

Dreaming someone was pressing down on his back and butt, Nathan slowly came awake. Then he realized the discomfort was real. He tried to sit up but his left arm wouldn't move. He looked down and saw Amanda curled up at his side. He tried to slowly pull out his arm without waking her but she lifted her head and looked at him.

"Morning," he said, and she just smiled as she sat up. He was really envious with how fast she sat up. His body was throwing a raging temper tantrum. Hearing panting by his right ear, he looked over and saw Ares. "Dude, your breath stinks," Nathan told Ares, and Ares licked his face. Amanda laughed as Nathan made faces, wiping dog slobber off his face. Ares walked out of the casino room and Nathan stood up. With her Q-tip-like hands, Amanda grabbed at him.

"Don't leave, please," she begged.

"I'm not, sweetie. I have to let Ares go use the bathroom but you can come with me," he told her. Reaching down, he lifted her up to her feet as she held on to her towel, trying to tuck it in. He moved her hands and tucked the towel in so it stayed wrapped around her. She grimaced as she took a step. Nathan looked down and saw the dressing on her feet had bloody spots on it with yellowish tint. He bent down and picked her up, carrying her in the bend of his arm.

Ares was waiting on them at the door, dancing in a circle. True to form, when the door cracked open, Ares shot out which made Amanda laugh. Propping the door open, Nathan saw Ares jump out of the ditch after his business was done and start running back and forth, making Amanda laugh even more. Nathan observed her closely. She had deep green eyes with wavy light ash brown hair. Her face was still swollen around the cuts, and her bottom lip and eye was still swollen. She was as tall as a thirteen-year-old, but man, was she skinny. His first instinct was to feed her, but since he once used to be a skinny kid, Nathan didn't try to force feed her. At least Amanda was just skinny and not bony, he thought, turning to watch Ares.

He was just running around chasing a butterfly and the butterfly was winning. Nathan smiled, watching him; then Ares stopped and ran back to Nathan and stood beside him, looking toward the north at the road with the bristles on his back standing up. Turning to look, Nathan saw three men running down the road; they were almost to the parking lot entrance.

"Amanda, get behind me. If anything happens, call Ares inside. If anyone tries to get in, point at them and tell Ares to 'kill.' Understand?" he said, putting her feet on the ground and standing back up. Amanda hid behind him as he brought his rifle around to the front of his body, his left hand on the fore grip and his right grasping the grip, finger outside the trigger housing as he flipped the safety off.

When they were fifty yards away, Nathan yelled, "That's far enough friends!" and pointed his rifle in their direction. "The store is closed and the merchandise is gone. I'm guarding the building," he told them in a loud voice.

"Hey man, give us some food," one yelled out; another man was mumbling to him, edging the speaker on.

"Don't have any to spare," Nathan told him.

"Bullshit, man, I know there's food in there," the first one said. Nathan pegged him for the leader.

"I don't care what you know, you're trespassing. This is your last warning. I'm in a good mood today and not in the mood to drag more bodies to join the stack in the cooler." Nathan told them a little lie.

"Man, I told you the people at the shelter said he killed people. Let's go," the quiet one finally spoke.

"He ain't going to kill a man trying to get some food," the leader said and Nathan brought the rifle up to his shoulder, sighting in on the man's chest. He wanted to just send Ares out, but if things went bad Ares was going to have to protect Amanda.

"You're fixing to die!" Nathan shouted.

"I'm with ya, Junior, let's just take the shit!" the second man shouted. The leader reached behind his back as Nathan squeezed the trigger, feeling the rifle stutter. *Phhhta-Phhhta-Phhhta*. The M-4 spit out three suppressed shots, all three striking the leader in the chest and dropping him with his hand still behind his back.

Swinging his point of aim, Nathan centered on the other one who'd been edging the leader on. He was just staring at his fallen buddy in shock. "You were with him to take the shit," Nathan said, squeezing the trigger and watching three impacts on the man's chest as he fell down screaming. Moving his aim to the quiet one, he held the crosshairs on the man's chest.

The man held up his hands in a pleading motion. "Please sir, I didn't come at ya," he begged.

"Lay your weapons on the ground and don't say you don't have any or I'll just kill you. Then empty your pockets of everything. When you're done, hold your hands up and turn away from me so I can frisk you. If I find more on you I'll kill you. Even a pair of fingernail clippers. And your pockets better be empty. The only thing you better have on you are your clothes," Nathan said grimly.

The man lifted up his white hoodie with a bloody fist print on it and threw down a gun and some magazines. Then he threw down stuff from his pockets and patted his body and turned around, looking away from Nathan.

"Amanda, go inside and take Ares with you. Only open the door for me," Nathan told her.

"Ares, come here, boy," she said, but Ares stayed where he was.

"Ares, go with her and listen," Nathan told him. Ares turned around and went inside with Amanda. Keeping his rifle aimed at the last man, Nathan walked across the parking lot. Getting closer, he saw both downed men were still alive. The leader was choking on his blood and his helper was grunting in pain. Nathan saw his hands move and swung down, sighting in on his head and squeezed. *Phhhta-Phhhta-Phhhta*. The rifle spit and the man's head disappeared.

Swinging his rifle back up and aiming at the quiet one, Nathan continued walking toward him. Dropping the rifle, Nathan let it dangle across his chest on the single-point sling then pulled his pistol and put it to the back of the quiet one's head. "Don't move," Nathan said as he frisked him and didn't find anything. "Why'd you come here?" Nathan asked.

"We wanted some food, man," he whined.

"Lie again and you'll die. I'll shoot you in the gut so you can live your last days in pain," Nathan told him, pressing his pistol in the quiet one's back.

"We heard from some folks that some trucks left here yesterday and we was just checking it out," he whimpered.

"You're testing my patience. I already have to move two bodies; a third won't make much of a difference," Nathan told him. "You knew someone was guarding this building," he said.

"Yeah, we was going to pop ya," he said meekly, and Nathan raised up his pistol, putting it to the back of the quiet one's head. "Hey, you wanted the truth," he cried out.

"Yes I did. What was the shooting about last night?" Nathan asked.

"Another crew came down from Atlanta and we chased 'em off," he said.

Nathan turned around to look at the two he'd shot, and for the first time noticed the leader was white and the helper was black. They were both dressed like gangsters. He looked at the quiet one and noticed his pants were at his knees. "Keep your hands up and turn around," Nathan told him and he complied.

"I should kill you but I'm going to give you the benefit of the doubt. If I ever see you again I'll kill you. Do you understand?" Nathan asked, and the quiet one nodded.

"Kilo's going to be mad you killed his brother," he told Nathan.

"Well I suggest you run the opposite way Kilo is," Nathan said. "There's nothing inside worth your life. Even if you took it just for the building, the cops would take it back. You're too close to town." Nathan studied the man. He was a black kid around nineteen. "Now go, and remember if I see you I will kill you," Nathan told him as he started backing away. "That means run," he added and the quiet one took off.

When he was a hundred yards away, Nathan looked down at what he'd dropped: a large bag of weed, a wad of cash, a Taurus 9mm and a magazine. Grabbing the cash, gun, and magazines, Nathan moved over to the other two. Helper had a cheap .380 piece of crap and a few hundred dollars. Taking the pistol apart, Nathan threw it in separate directions. Then he moved to Leader and rolled him over, pulling up his shirt.

"Oh my," Nathan said, reaching down and pulling out an HK Mk 23. It had a suppressor on it with a laser. "What the hell are you doing with this?" Nathan asked the corpse. When he didn't answer, Nathan laid the pistol down and frisked the body and felt something on his thigh underneath the six-sizes-too-big pants. Grabbing the pants legs, Nathan pulled the pants off. On the leader's naked thigh was a tactical holster for the Mk 23, attached to his waist with a regular belt.

"You have no concept of tactical. Deception yeah, but not tactical," Nathan said, undoing the holster and seeing it had two magazines and another dual pouch on the belt. Throwing them down with the gun, he continued frisking the body and found a bag of what looked like crack. Rolling Leader on his back, Nathan looked at the gold necklaces. "Dude, they're fake," he said, standing up and kicking the body.

Grabbing the pistol and its supplies, he left the drugs and bodies where they lay. Stepping up to the door, he tapped it. "Amanda, it's Nathan, can Ares play today?" he called out. He saw her peek out from behind the counter. "Hey, I see you, open the door please," he told her.

She smiled, limped over to the door and let him in. "You did very well, young lady," he told her, making her smile bigger as he locked the door. "You hungry?" he asked and she nodded her head. He carried her over to the diner and sat her on the stool and fixed them breakfast.

"It didn't bother you to kill them?" Amanda asked Nathan as he cooked.

"No, I would rather them be dead than us," Nathan answered truthfully.

Amanda looked down at her lap. "You don't feel bad?" she asked.

Turning around, Nathan reached over and lifted her face up. "No I don't," he answered.

"You've done that before?" Amanda asked, just a little scared.

Nathan hopped up and sat on the counter, looking at Amanda. "Yes I have. I have been in several shootouts as a cop. When I killed my first man I was terrified I would be haunted about it, but an old cop came up to me and told me, 'Boy, if you feel bad about killing someone who wants to kill you then you don't need to be livin' anyway. They made the choice'," Nathan told her. "So that's how you look at it."

"Has Ares killed before?" Amanda asked as Ares stood up, putting his front paws on the counter.

"Not a person but several dogs, a deer, and a skunk that wouldn't leave his dog bowl alone," Nathan told her, and Amanda giggled. "Hey, don't laugh. Ares had to have a bath that lasted a whole day." Amanda looked at Nathan and smiled.

Nathan took a deep breath. "Amanda, I only fight to protect, not to rule. I hope you understand," Nathan told her with a serious face.

Amanda thought about it for a few minutes then looked away. "I do," she said then looked at Nathan. "Thank you."

"You're welcome, little lady," Nathan said, trying to impersonate John Wayne, but not pulling it off. Amanda didn't know who John Wayne was, but Nathan sounded funny saying it so she laughed. "Well let me get to cookin' us some groceries," Nathan said, sliding off the counter.

When the food was put out, Nathan watched her eat four eggs, nine pieces of bacon, five pancakes and three biscuits till she didn't ask for more. He undid the bandages on her feet and hands, relieved that they looked better and not worse. Coating her feet and hands with ointment, he rewrapped them then moved up and down her body, putting on ointment and using another two tubes.

Carrying Amanda to the casino room, he sat her on the cot and put socks over the bandages on her feet. Then Nathan grabbed one of the shirts he'd found for her. "It's a little big but it'll have to do," he told her. "Arms up," he said, putting the shirt on her over the towel. Grabbing a pair of undies, he handed them to her and watched her try to use her wrapped up fingers and hands. Taking the undies, Nathan held them open and she stepped in them as he pulled them up.

She took off the towel since the shirt came to her thighs. He grabbed the shorts and put them on her. Next, Nathan grabbed the boots and put them on her, not wanting her to get dirt on her bandaged feet after all the work he'd done. Telling her to follow him, he led her to the store and grabbed a hairbrush and comb set, a toothbrush and toothpaste then led her to the shower room and he brushed their teeth. Then Amanda laughed as Nathan held down Ares and brushed his.

When they were done, she followed him to the diner. He sat her up on a stool and started brushing out her hair. Halfway through, he knew he should've wet her hair first. "Amanda, I need to ask you some questions, okay. They are going to make you remember stuff you don't want to, but I have to know the answers please. I need to know if someone is looking for you," he told her gently.

"No sir, nobody's looking for me," she said.

He spun her around on the stool to face him. "Are you my friend, because I'm yours," he told her and she nodded. "Then don't call me sir. It makes me feel really old," he said and she grinned.

"Okay Nathan," she told him.

"What happened to your mom and dad?" he asked.

"They died," she told him in a low voice.

"Do you remember the day the power went off?" he asked.

"Yes," she said softly.

"I want you to tell me what happened from then to now. Can you do that?" he asked.

"I don't remember some," she admitted.

"Tell me what you do," he said and started to brush her hair again.

"I was at school in math when the lights went out. The teacher kept going until we heard a loud screeching noise; then a loud boom made the ground shake and blew the windows in on us. The water started shooting out of the ceiling and the fire alarm went off. That's when I saw outside was nothing but fire. I moved with my class into the hall and heard another boom that shook the ground. Then the hallway in front of us just came down on top of a bunch of people and there was fire. Everyone turned and ran down the hall but I could see fire through the windows so I ran across the hall to another room. Looking out the window, I didn't see fire but lots of smoke. I opened the window and crawled out. My brother's high school was right beside my school so I ran to it.

"I ran around calling for him, hearing lots of screaming. He always told me to meet him at the flag pole so I stayed there. I don't know how long but it was hurting to breath in all that smoke when I felt someone grab me and take off running. I was fixing to hit them when I saw it was my brother Johnny. He ran with me to my dad's office which was a long way away. The entire time we were running loud bombs kept going off in those gray metal cans on the telephone poles, throwing fire out."

"At my dad's office, we found him and my mom. Fire was everywhere so my Dad said to follow him. His car wouldn't start so he started walking us home. Some mean men jumped out with guns and told my dad to be quiet. He tried to give them money and they shot him. Johnny ran at them and they shot him. Momma picked me up and they dragged us to a building," she said, stopping to wipe tears off her face.

"They started being mean to Momma and one was holding me. She bit one really hard somewhere and wouldn't let go. The man holding me let go and Mama yelled for me to run. I turned and ran, hearing her scream and then shooting. I heard yelling as I reached the door and more shooting," Amanda stopped and wiped her face and Nathan gave her some water which she gulped down.

"I ran back to my house and went to my best friend Casey's house. When I got there I saw a big piece of a plane in the middle of my street and all the houses were on fire. I saw the girl next door, Paula, laying in her yard on fire, yelling. Someone grabbed me and started pulling me but I got away and just ran. It was dark when I stopped running so I walked till I came to a playground. It had a water fountain and I drank till my stomach hurt but I wanted more.

"I heard guns shooting so I ran into the woods. I kept falling but I got up and ran. It was day when I quit running and I saw the highway out there and stayed beside it. At one of the places you get off I saw a picnic table, laid down on it and went to sleep. I don't know when but a woman came out and I jumped off and was fixing to run away till she said food. She went into the house by the picnic table and I sat down. I hurt so much but Momma said run.

"The lady came out and I jumped off the table and she put down a bottle of water and a sandwich. I don't even remember eating it or drinking the water. She came over to me but I wanted to run but she said more food so I stayed. She came back with a bag and sat it on the table. She wanted me to come with her but I heard shooting so I grabbed the bag and ran. The sun was going down when I stopped by a bridge and opened the bag to see two sandwiches and a bottle of water. I drank the water when a man came up pushing a shopping cart," she said, tears rolling down her cheeks again.

"He was wearing a green coat and had a white dog in the cart. I walked over to pet the dog and the man hit me in the face really hard. I don't know how long I was on the ground but when I sat up he was eating my sandwiches. I held out my hand and said please and he hit me again. He told the dog to bite me and when I tried to push it back it bit my hands. He laughed till I kicked the dog. I tried to run but he caught me, picked me up and threw me down and stepped on my back. When he got off I ran. He told his dog to bite me and it did on my feet till I ran into the mud beside the road. I looked behind me and saw the dog was stuck and I had to swim out of the mud.

"When I got out the other side the mean man was holding up my teddy bear necklace my Momma got me, saying thank you. I turned and ran through the woods. I fell down and went to sleep. I woke up and started running but I couldn't go fast anymore and I kept falling down no matter how hard I tried. I came to a place where you get on and off the highway and saw a school with a whole bunch of people. I went under the bridge and saw trucks leaving here. I ran around the building and hid, watching it. Then you came out," she told him.

Nathan took the story in and smiled at Amanda. "You want me to braid your hair?" he asked.

"Yeah, like the French kind," she said with a smile.

"I can do that," he told her and started French braiding her hair. "Amanda, what did the men that shot your family look like?" he asked.

"Like the ones you shot out front," she answered.

"You watched?" he asked as he stopped braiding her hair.

"Yes, I wanted to make sure they didn't hurt you. I was going to tell Ares to get them," she told him.

He spun her around to look at him. "If something happens to me, you take Ares and leave. To make him listen you say his name then a command. Watch," he said. "Ares, here," he told Ares. Ares came over and sat down beside him. "Ares, beg," he said and Ares did. Nathan petted him and rubbed his belly.

"He knows how to guard a person or place. To guard a building like this, you tell him 'house'," he told her. "If you want him mean looking and growling at people, tell him it's 'time to work.' When you want him to guard someone that you don't want to get away, tell him to 'watch them.' If you trust someone, introduce them by calling his name and say 'friend.' When you want him to just attack, say 'get 'em,' and if you want him to kill, say 'kill.' He is trained to kill dogs and people," Nathan told her. "Remember, the first command is his name then the action," he added.

"You mean he will do that for anyone he thinks is a friend?" Amanda asked.

"No," Nathan answered. "Ares only listens to some people. He will listen to Tim and Sherry; they live on my land. There was a girl here yesterday that he listened to, her name was Renee," he told her. "It's only someone special he listens to. He knew you were my friend before I did and he really likes you," Nathan told her.

She looked up at him, smiling. "He's a good dog, and he's so fluffy," Amanda said.

"Where's the rest of your family?" he asked.

"I have a grandmother that lives in New York but I've only seen her once. I have an uncle that lives in Miami that we visited a few years ago," she told him.

"Anyone else?" he asked.

"No."

"If I take you to some people I trust, will you stay with them?" he asked.

"Are you staying?" she asked.

Nathan thought about it then said, "No, but if I make Ares stay with you would you?" he asked, feeling his heart break just thinking about leaving Ares.

Amanda looked at Ares then at Nathan. "I don't want to," she told him.

"Okay. How about I take you to someone that can get you to your uncle?" he asked.

"He's mean and stinks. I want to stay with you," Amanda said firmly.

"Sweetie, I'm going over two thousand miles to get home. You can't go that far," he told her.

"Yes I can. You shot the men that got Momma, Daddy, and Johnny," Amanda said with confidence.

Nathan just pursed his lips up. "They were gang members but we don't know if they were the same gang. Hell, I don't even know what gang they're in," he told her.

"Then they were their friends," she told him.

"Okay," he told her and she smiled. Nathan figured she would change her mind or he would do it for her. "Let me show you your backpack," he told her, helping her down.

"Want me to braid your hair?" she asked.

"Ah no, I'll wear a ponytail but no braiding," he told her, leading her to the casino room. He picked up the pack and handed it to her. When she grabbed it she almost let it fall.

"It's heavy," she said.

"Yes it is and you'll have to carry it. I can't. I have my own bag and it weighs more than you," he said, pointing to his pack and she gasped. "Even Ares has a pack," he told her, pointing to it. "You sure you want to come? The people I'll take you to will take care of you and they have kids to play with," he told her.

"If you stay, I'll stay," she replied in a tone that told Nathan leaving her wasn't an option.

Giving up, he sat her down on the cot. "I want you to go through your pack to learn where everything is. Food is on top, next is hygiene then clothes," he told her.

"Hygiene?" she asked.

"Oh, bathroom stuff," he said. "The outer pockets are for small, frequently used items. Lighters, forks, spoons, eating kits and stuff like that," he said as she opened up her pack. "We've got to find you some pants."

"It's hot outside," she said.

"Yeah, and pants will keep you from getting burned and the sun from cooking the water out of you," he told her. He helped her pull everything out and put it back. No easy feat for Amanda, with the bandages on her hands looking and acting like boxing gloves, but she did it. "When we camp at night, always repack your bag in case we have to leave fast," Nathan told her when they were done. "Come on, let's eat."

She followed him to the diner and he fixed them lunch. Nathan wondered why a deputy hadn't stopped to ask about the bodies. After all, that's why he'd left the damn things there. When Mitch came tomorrow he would get him to give him a ride out to Jessie's. He would stay there for a few days and convince Amanda to stay. It would add a lot of days but he didn't have much choice. Nathan went to his bag and started

Amanda on antibiotics since she had been bitten by a dog. Rabies wasn't that prevalent down South compared to home, but the wounds had been packed with dirt.

That afternoon he showed her his .38 revolver after he set up the foldable solar panel to charge the radios he had taken. Nathan figured he would run across someone to travel with, just not a little girl, and the radios would come in handy.

After Amanda showed him for an hour that she could work the pistol safely, Nathan took her outside and let her shoot it. After getting her hands unwrapped, Amanda squeezed the trigger and the small pistol let out a loud *Bang*. She looked back at him. "It's really loud," she said.

"Yes it is, but that's normal," he said.

"Your big gun didn't sound like that," she informed him.

"It has a suppressor; what most people call a silencer," he told her.

"I didn't make it silent," she pointed out.

"Did it hurt your ears when it went off?" he asked.

"No," she answered.

"Then it did its job," he told her.

They went inside and she played with Ares while Nathan looked at a map of Atlanta. From her story, Nathan traced her route to him. Amanda had run almost sixty miles through hell, in three days. He had to admit she was tough. He watched her play with Ares, noticing she wasn't limping anymore but she wasn't really running either; just sort of trotting.

He took out the pistol he'd gotten off Leader and broke it down then cleaned it. He was surprised to find it was in excellent shape. There was no way that punk could get an approval for a suppressor. Taking off his vest, Nathan mounted the holster for the pistol with the suppressor attached on his left side, with the drop platform holding his six magazines for his M-4.

Amanda came over and sat down beside him, watching what he was doing. "Why is the barrel so long?" she asked.

"This is a suppressor that screws onto the barrel like the one on my rifle," he said, showing her.

"I want one for my gun," she demanded.

He looked at her and started laughing. "Let's get you gun-wise first," he told her. He stood up and took off his concealable ballistic vest. "Stand up," he told her and he put the vest on her. Looking at her, he was sure he could fit two and a half of her in it. Taking the vest off, he took out the front and back plates. Then he put it back on her; he took the straps from the right to lock on the left then did the same for the other side.

Spinning her around and checking out the fit, he shook his head. She still had inches of slack inside. "Wait here," he said, walking over to the store. He came back with a roll of Velcro. Putting Velcro across the back of the vest, he pulled the straps around, sticking them on. The front panel almost met at her spine and the back did the same on her chest. She was almost wearing two level-three vests.

"What's this?" she asked, looking down at it.

"Bullet-resistant vest," he told her, nodding in approval.

"I'm a kid. Why do I have to wear this?" Amanda asked.

"Kids get shot too and it will take a hit, or a kick, really well," he told her. He picked up the plates. "These are rifle plates to stop a rifle bullet," he told her.

"I have to wear it?" she asked, motioning to the vest.

"If you come with me you do," he told her, walking to the casino room and putting the plates in her pack. "Now at least your pack can stop a rifle round," he said.

"You need this more than me," she pointed out.

"My vest with all the stuff on it is a bullet-resistant vest, just bigger. That one's to be worn under clothes to hide it," he told her.

"Okay," she said, sitting down and holding out her feet and wiggling the boots. "I didn't think I would like them but I do," she said, admiring them.

"I'll try to find some that fit better," Nathan promised.

"What happened, Nathan? Were we attacked by aliens?" Amanda asked.

He was fixing to laugh but he could see how she could think that. Sitting down beside her, he explained a CME and an EMP, using simple terms. He was by no means an expert, but he explained the basics. When he finished, she looked down at her lap. "It's always going to be different, isn't it?" she asked.

"Yes Amanda it is. It's going to get a lot worse and a lot of people are going to die," he answered. He didn't believe he had the right to lie to her.

"I was going to be in a play next week," she told him.

"What play?" he asked.

"The Wizard of Oz," she said sadly.

"I was in that when I was in school. I was the scarecrow," he told her.

"I was going to be the Good Witch of the North," she said, smiling.

He put his arm around her and she laid her head on his chest. "We are a lot alike, Amanda. I lost my parents when I was young too," he told her.

"What happened?" she asked, never thinking he might not want to tell her.

He took a deep breath. "It was April and I was a senior in high school. My parents had traveled to Spokane. They told me it was to be alone but I found out later it was because they had gone to buy me a truck for a graduation/birthday present. On the way home, a man crossed over into their lane, hitting them head on. They died instantly but he lived. He was drunk. He was four times the legal limit and already had three DWIs," he said, remembering it like it was yesterday.

"I have no other family. Both my parents were only children. They had appointed a guardian for me in their will but they wrote the will when I was twelve. I turned eighteen two days before graduation and the judge let me live alone until then. I found out on my birthday why they went to Spokane, when the truck was delivered to the house with a bow on it," he said with a zoned-out stare.

"Where did you live? Daddy always told us it took him and Momma to pay for the house and stuff," she asked.

"The insurance paid off the farm and funerals. Mom was a nurse and I got her retirement. My Dad retired from the military when I was ten and I received that for a while. The estate lawyer had to fight to get it but I got it," he answered.

"You were alone?" she asked.

"The whole school cheered when I got my diploma, but yeah," Nathan said. "When I got my nursing degree, no one was there, but when I got my degree in criminal justice, I had Billy, Aidan, and Rusty there," he said, smiling as he remembered them and their wives yelling and jumping up and down cheering as he walked across the stage.

"Who are Tim and Sherry?" she asked. He gave a startled jump, snapping back to the present. "You said they live on your land and Ares listens to them," she reminded him.

Laughing, he said, "You have a good memory. I met Tim when he was training to become an officer at the academy. I was one of the instructors and liked him right away. I got to know him and his new wife for over a year and they started hanging around with me, Rusty, Billy, Aidan, and their families. They lived in some real crappy apartments and I lived on a fifty-acre farm with a huge house and a guest house, just me and my animals. So I offered them the guest house rent free if they helped on the farm," he told her.

"What happened to the man who killed your parents?" she asked.

"Oh, he got five years' probation and had to do some community service," Nathan told her with scorn in his voice.

"That's not fair," she said. "You know where he is?" she asked.

Nathan nodded. "He lives forty-three miles southeast of Spokane in a double-wide trailer on a farm. He is now fifty-nine and has four grandkids. He would've retired next year," he said.

"You know where he lives?" she almost shouted.

"Oh yes, I check up on him every few months. He got one more DWI after my parents' deaths then said he got sober and got religion," he told her.

"I'm sorry, Nathan," she said, putting her head back on his chest.

"I'm sorry you lost your family, Amanda," he told her, patting her head. "Let's fix some food and check our gear. I want you to be able to leave in five minutes," he said, standing up.

"Can I have some chicken tenders?" she asked.

"You bet," he told her, picking her up and carrying her to the diner. Ares was jumping up and down, trying to tell Nathan that Amanda was his toy, not Nathan's. Nathan laughed down at him, promising that he'd get to play with her later.

After they ate, Nathan redressed her hands and feet, seeing they were looking much better. While they were packing up, he took out one of his old ACU jackets and boonie hat and gave them to her. It took some work to make the hat small enough to fit her, but they did it with safety pins.

When she was loading her pack, Nathan noted she had added several items. Among the items was a notebook and two teen magazines from the rack. On the cover of one was a teen boy; he couldn't remember the name but knew of him and it sent loathing down Nathan's spine just looking at him. He wasn't going to tell Amanda she couldn't take them. If she wanted to carry them she could.

They ate dinner then played go fish and checkers. She beat him two to three in each game. Letting Ares outside, they walked around the building and then Nathan headed over to his truck, willing it to start. He even went so far as to turn the key one last time; letting out a sigh, he emptied the glove box of all personal information. Then he checked the Suburban, front to back, making sure he hadn't forgotten anything. The only thing he found was a picture of him with the guys and their families at one of Billy's kid's birthday parties. He took it. Walking back inside, he grabbed his cellphone and some lighter fluid then headed out back.

Grabbing some wood, Nathan threw it in a burn barrel, soaked it with fluid and set it on fire. Then, one by one, he threw the pieces of paper in: his insurance, title, maintenance records and such. Then he pulled out the memory card after downloading everything off the phone, broke the phone in two parts then threw it in. It was only seven o'clock but it felt much later as he watched the fire.

"Why did you do that?" Amanda asked.

"The papers had my name and address on them. The phone has a lot of information I don't want other people knowing," he told her, throwing more wood in.

"That's smart," she admitted. "Hey, there's a ladder going up to the roof from inside. Can we go up it please?" Amanda begged.

"Sure," he said as she jumped up, clapping. She called Ares as she trotted to the front door. On the way to the ladder in the storeroom, Nathan grabbed his binoculars. Ares was a little pissed off that he couldn't go, and he let them know as he barked at them. "Ares, quiet," Nathan said, looking down the roof access door. Nathan was almost positive that Ares gave him a 'go to hell look.'

"Man, you can see a long ways up here," he heard Amanda say behind him.

Turning around and looking, Nathan had to agree. He walked over to stand beside her on the north side, looking toward the Interstate. Up here he could see over the trees and across the road all the way to the Interstate. He looked through the binoculars and saw a lot of people walking on the Interstate heading each way. On the exit bridge he saw a large group of people at what looked like a shanty town.

"That's a lot of people," Amanda said.

"Yeah, it's about an hour till dark and that's hundreds of people traveling," he said, handing her the binoculars.

"Cool," she said, taking them. "Can we leave tomorrow?" she asked, looking out at the Interstate.

"Don't you want to let your wounds heal first?" he asked.

"They barely hurt anymore and they aren't bleeding," she said with the binoculars to her face.

"What's the hurry?" he asked her.

Lowering the binoculars, she looked up at him. "That group of people on the bridge wasn't there when I came through. They're going to come down here and you can't kill them all. You said you only have six hundred bullets for the big gun," she told him. "And more gang friends are going to come. They know I got away," she added, looking down.

He put his arm around her. "Amanda, even if that was the same gang, they could care less about you. I killed two of them," he told her.

"I know. They will want to kill you now too," she told him in a whisper.

Reaching down, he lifted her face up by her chin to look at him. "I may not be able to kill them all but we can outrun them," he said. "If they follow, I'll just leave them lying out like those down there," he added, nodding his head toward the bodies.

"We can leave tomorrow?" she asked, smiling.

"Let's go make sure we're ready first," he told her, and she handed him the binoculars and took off running to the ladder. Ares started barking when he saw her, telling her to hurry and get down.

Amanda went to the store and found her some little binoculars and a small tote bag for a laptop. She wanted the bag when she saw Nathan was taking his messenger bag. Nathan sure wasn't leaving it; it was another fifteen hundred cubic inches he could use.

Nathan opened the case of MREs he had bought and showed her how to break them down, throwing out the utensils and other useless stuff and leaving only the food. It was only around three ounces per pack but twelve packs added up to three pounds saved. He grabbed some more bandages and the last of the ointment, putting it in his bag.

They put on their equipment and packs then stepped on the scale in the shower room. Nathan was carrying one hundred and thirty-seven pounds of stuff; Amanda was carrying thirty-four pounds; and Ares was carrying twenty-nine pounds. Ares wasn't leaving his blanket. Seeing they were packing, he kept grabbing it and pulling it over to his pack, just to let them know.

Nathan was real tempted to leave his old pair of boots but decided not to. You just don't throw away good boots, especially on a trip of this magnitude. Amanda made one last run to the store and came back with another ziplock bag full of water-flavoring packs. Nathan smiled at her as she put it in her tote bag; he already had two bags full just like it. He joined her in her run, getting a ThermaCELL and all the refills on the shelf. He had one and now she had one; he also grabbed more bug repellant. They had mosquitos at home but here the damn things could throw you down and rape you.

They went outside to let Ares go to the bathroom and Nathan took down the recharging station for the batteries. Going back inside, Nathan watched as Amanda locked the doors and checked all the others as he followed. Getting back to the casino room, Nathan put the solar panel and batteries in his pack.

It wasn't even nine o'clock when they went to bed. Nathan put her on the cot and he lay down on the floor. He really didn't want to leave early and was unsure if he should start out on his journey or head to Jessie's.

CHAPTER 12

Day 5

Something kept tapping his chest and he was dreaming it was a woodpecker. Struggling to open his eyes, he lifted his head and saw Ares sitting at his feet. "How did you tap my chest from down there?" he asked Ares in a groggy voice.

"I did. He needs to pee," Amanda told him.

He looked over and saw her sitting there. Then he realized she had been sleeping on the floor beside him with the blankets he had given her. "I gave you the cot," he said.

"I had a bad dream," she whispered, looking down at the floor.

He sat up and rubbed her head. "That's okay. You're better to have next to me than Ares. He chases rabbits in his sleep and scratches me with his claws," he told her, making her laugh. He looked at his watch. He had put on the good one from his pack. It wasn't even five a.m. yet. "Ares, you better be quick," he said, standing up.

Nathan put on his vest and started the routine of buckling up then grabbed his rifle. He turned to see Amanda already dressed and ready. She had on her little hat and his coat, with shorts and combat boots. He wanted to chuckle but controlled himself.

They stepped out of the casino room. Amanda was fixing to run for the door but Nathan grabbed her arm. "Some people are on the road," he told her as he looked out the window.

Amanda looked out the same window but it was still dark. "How can you tell?" she whispered.

"Shadows moving on the road," he told her.

"Is it the gang's friends?" she asked with a worried tone.

Nathan shook his head. "Not unless they have toddlers in the gang," he told her.

"There's kids out there?" she asked.

"Yes, there are kids out there but also adults. They are walking down the road that way," he said, pointing south. "Three adults, a kid, and a toddler," he added. He pulled her to him and kneeled down beside her. "Look at the background of the shopping center across the street but don't focus on it and you will see shadows moving," he told her, pointing.

Looking where he was pointing, she did what he said and suddenly five shadows popped in her vision. "I see them," she said kind of loud.

"Not too loud," he said. "They can't see us but they might hear us."

"Sorry," she whispered, watching the people walk down the road. "Ares has to pee. What are we going to do?" she asked.

"Let's take him out the back," he told her.

"There are no windows back there; we can't see outside. Somebody could be waiting," she told him.

Nathan nodded and pulled her close, hugging her to his side. "Good girl. You saw the danger, but have we used those doors?" he asked and she shook her head. "They would go for the doors we use and there are two doors out the back not counting the bay doors. We will just open the door and stand beside it and let Ares out to do his business," he said.

"He could run off and chase somebody," she said.

"Not unless you tell him to," Nathan said, turning around and going back into the casino room. He stopped at his pack and pulled out the hand-held night vision scope. They went through the shop to the south door and Nathan cracked it open. As he held the scope to his eye, night was suddenly green-tinted day. He saw over a dozen deer in field and a raccoon in the dumpster but nothing else.

"Ares, go," he whispered and Ares took off. The raccoon saw Ares and stood up, chirping. Ares froze and let out a low growl. The raccoon jumped in the air and scurried off.

"What is that?" Amanda asked, pointing at the scope. He passed it to her, putting her wrapped fingers through the nylon handle and pulling it to her eye. Looking through the eyepiece, she took a sharp breath.

"Woo," she exhaled. In the green light spilling across her face he could see her smiling from ear to ear.

Ares ran back inside but she was still looking around. "Come on, let's get some food started," Nathan said.

She lowered the scope. "I want one of these," she said as he closed the door.

"Ah, that one is a cheap one. My other one mounts on a bracket and hangs over your left eye. It has much better definition," he told her, leading her through the shop.

"Kind of makes it hard to see after though," she said, blinking her eyes. Her left eye could see fine but her right was blind. "How much did this one cost?" she asked out of curiosity.

"Two hundred," he told her.

"And what did the expensive one cost?" she asked.

"Three thousand," he replied.

"Dollars!" she shouted this time.

He turned around, laughing. "Yes, volume," he warned.

She threw a hand over her mouth. "Sorry," she mumbled.

Putting a hand on her back, he pushed her forward and followed her into the diner. After he closed the blinds, he laid his rifle on the counter. The skylights let in more than enough light to see by. "There were scopes just like that one; two of them in the electronic cabinet here, but Jessie took them," he told her.

"I so want one," she said, climbing up on a stool. He took out the food and started setting everything up. "Can I help today?" she asked.

"Well I guess so," he told her, and she jumped down and ran behind the counter.

She turned the oven on and grabbed a pan for the biscuits. "I cooked breakfast at home," she told him, greasing the pan. He shook his head, marveling at her resiliency.

After they ate, he eased over to the window and peeked out but didn't see anyone. The sky was starting to lighten up and he turned around to see her fixing more biscuits.

"Still hungry?" he asked.

"No, but you cooked a thousand pounds of bacon," she told him. "I'm just making some biscuits to take with us to eat with the bacon," she added, putting the pan in the oven.

"Pack your stuff," he said, grabbing his rifle.

"We're leaving now?" she asked, almost jumping up and down.

"No, but we need to get in the habit of waking up, eating, and repacking. In other words, always be ready to run," he told her, heading to the casino. With only the blankets out it didn't take long; true to form, Ares grabbed up his woobie in his mouth and pulled it over to his pack. "I'm not going to forget it," Nathan told him, reaching over and folding it up and tying it to his pack. "I worry about you. I should've called you Linus," he told Ares, rubbing his head.

"Who's Linus?" Amanda asked.

Nathan shook his head. "A cartoon I used to watch," he told her. "I'm going to the roof. Want to come?" he asked.

"I will when the biscuits are done," she said. He smiled, grabbed his binoculars and headed to the roof.

He walked around the roof, scanning the area and noticing the deer that had been in the field had left as soon as the daylight started coming up on the horizon. Moving to the north side, he noticed the shanty town was bigger than yesterday. Of course he was only guessing, but he was putting the number at or close to a thousand. Continuing to scan the Interstate, he noticed a large group coming from the east about a mile from the exit.

Even from two miles away, he could see they were holding their pants up and the flash of jewelry around their necks. Lowering the binoculars, he wondered if it was the same gang as yesterday. And why were they following the road? If they just walked across the field and through the patch of trees they could save a mile.

It's probably not them, Nathan thought as he raised the binoculars back up to watch them. He noticed other people were moving out of the group's way and some were running. Still not able to get a count, he could see some holding their arms like they were carrying weapons. He lowered the binoculars and ran over to the ladder. "Amanda, can you hear me?" he called down.

A few seconds later she was looking up at him. "Yeah," she said.

"Get your pack on and put Ares' pack on then stand by that door," he said, pointing to the south door.

"They're here?" she exclaimed with fright on her face.

"I don't know. The group I'm watching is over a mile away on the Interstate, but just in case get ready," he told her.

"Okay," she said and disappeared.

He ran back over to the north corner and watched the group; they were about a half a mile from the exit. Looking at the shanty town, he saw people moving west from it. Letting the binoculars hang, he shouldered his rifle, aiming down the road to the north. With the exception of a few phone poles, he had a clear field of fire. He saw a caution sign he was putting at two hundred yard in his scope. Turning up the power, he relaxed and sighted in on the center of the sign. Flipping the selector to single, he squeezed the trigger and saw a hole pop about an inch from where he was aiming.

"Just a tad over two hundred," he said, kneeling down and raising up the binoculars. The group was now on the exit ramp and heading down to the road in front of the store. "Well, there's still a chance," he said, watching them closely.

Now he could tell most were carrying rifles and counted thirty-three of them. He wanted to laugh as he watched them try to carry a rifle and hold up their pants at the same time. Continuing down the ramp, they turned toward the store. He trotted over to the ladder, fixing to call Amanda, only to see her standing there looking up at him.

"Good, you got your pack on. If you hear shooting getting close and Ares starts growling, run out the door to the trees and wait five minutes. If I'm not there by then, run," he told her.

"Just come on," she begged.

"It's okay for now. Do what I said." He trotted back to his corner. Kneeling down, he brought up his rifle and watched the group coming at him through the scope. Lowering the rifle, he looked through the binoculars. He put the group around eight hundred yards out. Zooming in with the focus, he saw three men leading the pack. On the right he saw a man wearing a white sweatshirt with a bloody fist. "Quiet man, you came back," Nathan said out loud.

Feeling his heart start to beat fast, Nathan lowered the binoculars and took several deep breaths, letting them out slowly to calm down. Bringing up the rifle, he pulled it tight into his shoulder and looked through the scope, settling the crosshairs on the quiet man's chest. The anticipation was trying to get to him like he was fixing to play a college prank on them instead of killing them, or at least some of them.

When they were at four hundred yards, Nathan wanted to yell at them to hurry up. To his surprise, they just kept strutting down the middle of the road, holding up their pants and trying to carry their rifles. Now he could tell most of the rifles were AKs and SKSs with at least one AR and a deer rifle. As they just gaggled down the road like a flock of geese, it dawned on Nathan that he'd shot those two yesterday later than this.

"I bet they want to surround the store before I let the dog out," he mumbled to himself.

"I have a promise to keep to Quiet Man anyway," he said, grinning. The entire group was now spread out across the road about ten yards deep. Nathan ticked the distance down till he saw Quiet Man and the other two with him at the caution sign. Letting them a little closer, he saw Quiet Man pointing ahead toward the building.

Looking back, Nathan saw the last one pass the sign and rested the crosshairs on Quiet Man again. Taking a deep breath and letting half out slowly as he flipped to burst, Nathan gently squeezed the trigger, feeling the rifle shudder. Three red splotches appeared on Quiet Man's chest as he fell back with his mouth open.

Not stopping to watch, Nathan shifted and squeezed at the next one, seeing him jerk. Shifting to number three, he squeezed, seeing two hit his chest and the man's left arm fall off. Moving back to the pack, Nathan saw everyone just drop to the pavement and could hear yelling off in the distance.

Aiming at one, Nathan squeezed the trigger and watched half his head evaporate in a mist. Swinging to another one that was lying prone across the road, he squeezed and watched him roll when the bullets ripped into his side. Shifting, he shot two more then noticed the group crawling to the sides of the road. Seeing someone trying to pull Quiet Man to safety, Nathan shifted to them and squeezed before the crosshairs settled, shooting them in the pelvis. Noticing two were trying to pull one of the first three away to the ditch, Nathan rested the sight and squeezed on the first, watching him jerk and fall down. Moving to the next one he squeezed and only felt the rifle shudder twice. The man he was aiming at doubled over, grabbing his lower chest.

Dropping the empty magazine, Nathan grabbed another magazine and settled back down. He could see eleven on this side of the road and only heads popping up on the other side. Everyone was orientated head first in his direction. He moved his crosshairs to the furthest man in the ditch and saw he was crawling away. Putting the sight between his shoulder blades, Nathan squeezed and watched him quiver with the impacts. Moving his sight to the next one in line, he squeezed, watching the man jump.

Quickly but steadily, Nathan moved the crosshairs to the next one; as the man lifted up and looked behind him, three bullets struck him in the head and the top of his chest. Dropping his sights down to the next man, Nathan watched him lift up his rifle and aim at him on the roof; Nathan squeezed the trigger. Two bullets hit the man's face and Nathan couldn't tell where the third one went as he lowered his aim to the next one. Nathan squeezed the trigger and watched the man roll over, yelling.

He heard several shots and moved his crosshairs to the next one, only to see him shooting out in the field beside them. Nathan squeezed the trigger, letting him know that he wasn't out there. More shots were sounding off now as Nathan sighted on another one, hitting him in the back. It was chaos in the ditch as men scrambled and dove for cover. Hearing a bullet hit the cinderblocks around him, Nathan squeezed off two more bursts, hitting two more men. Then Nathan spotted one running toward the store and fired the last burst. The man did a flip as Nathan grabbed his empty magazine and quickly duckwalked back to the ladder.

Throwing his leg over the side, Nathan heard, "It's about damn time," from below him. Grabbing the side of the ladder with his hands and scissor grabbing with his feet, Nathan did a fireman slide down. Landing beside Amanda, Nathan spun around, running for his gear.

"Get ready by the door. We are leaving now," he said, grabbing his pack and throwing it on then snapping the belt. He grabbed his bag, throwing it on over his head then glanced around to make sure everything was packed. Satisfied, Nathan ran back to Amanda. He pulled out the empty magazine, handing it to her, "Hold this," he said, pulling out another one and ramming it home. Chambering a round, he opened the door. "Stay close," he ordered, moving across the parking lot at a quick pace. "Ares, heel." The dog followed closely behind them.

Down the road the gunfire had intensified to a steady stream. They hit the tree line around the parking lot, hearing the front glass windows shatter from gunfire. It was starting to sound like a war zone. Moving quickly, they continued on another hundred yards to where the field ended at the woods. Behind them they could still hear shooting but it was now just a shot every few seconds.

"Boy did you piss them off," Amanda said, breathing hard.

"Yes I did, didn't I," Nathan said, grinning, and moved south deeper into the woods.

"Hey, the Interstate is that way," she said, pointing west.

He stopped and looked at the tree line at the edge of the field. "Okay, let's get started," he said, turning west and keeping the field in sight. They moved through the woods at a rapid pace.

Six hours later, Steven pulled into the parking lot and noticed the front door busted open and several windows blown out. His son and one of the men that worked at the farm were in the box truck with him. Mitch had told Steven about Nathan's warning, but he hadn't believed him. He jumped out of the truck and ran to the door. Seeing the gang inside, Steven started yelling for them to get out.

An hour later, Mitch pulled in with the rest of the family and help. Seeing the front door busted, he stopped and was fixing to back out. Then Mitch noticed the box truck parked beside the building. Shrugging his shoulders, he pulled up to it. When the nine other family members got out of their vehicles, they were looking at a dozen men aiming weapons at them.

When they pulled them inside, Mitch saw Steven naked and spread-eagled across a table. He was bleeding from too many places to see which spot was the worst. Then Mitch noticed his grandson naked and dead on the floor.

For the next two hours, Mitch had to listen to his family get tortured, raped, and killed. His last thought before he died was that Steven would burn in hell for leading the family into a slaughter.

The gang didn't have long to celebrate their victory. The sheriff showed up that afternoon with Mark and Fred's entire family: all five brothers, two sisters, their husbands, their dad, and four kids over sixteen. They threw in tear gas and sixteen men came out coughing. Two died when they didn't drop their weapons. Seeing none of them were Nathan, Mark yelled 'Open fire,' killing those that had kneeled down.

The group moved inside and found what was left of Mitch's family and nineteen dead gang members, two already starting to bloat up. The brothers and Mark looked around but couldn't find any of Nathan's stuff, but they did find some pictures of a teenage boy pop singer pinned up in the casino. They all cheered, knowing Nathan had gotten away, although they wondered why he liked the teen boy singer.

Fred and his brothers walked the area around the parking lot and found Nathan's bootprints on the north side of the property. They followed them till they turned west behind the field, which told them that Nathan was heading to the Interstate and not Jessie's. Fred found Mark and told him what they'd found, and Mark sighed with relief. Then Fred told him they'd seen another set of bootprints alongside Nathan's.

"What?" Mark said.

"Yeah, another pair, and the thing is, I know whose boots those are. I've seen 'em before; they're Neil's boots. He tried to follow me last year saying I was bootleggin'. You know I don't bootleg. I was poachin' deer though," Fred admitted. "Anyway, Neil left his prints everywhere. He wears a girl's combat boot and the left heel is more worn than the right."

"Fred, Neil is in jail; you know that. You helped me carry him in," Mark told him.

"I'm just sayin'."

"Neil's boots were here; anyone could've taken them," Mark pointed out.

"Yeah, but who?" Fred asked, and Mark shrugged his shoulders. Fred walked out and got the family as the sheriff and Mark got the scene locked down.

The brothers grabbed Mitch's vehicles and their family followed them to Mitch's house. The rest of the 'store group' showed up and loaded up the stuff there. It took them two days but they moved all the stuff over, along with a working tractor and fuel. The group, now at forty-six adults, blocked off the deadend road leading to their farms after the brothers moved Mark's new trailer over. Monica's granddad had the first house on the deadend road and became the lookout as they worked to survive. They all spent time reading the information they'd downloaded from Nathan.

Abigail opened her purse that night in the room Jessie had given to them. It was the first time since leaving the store she'd had any time, since they'd spent all day putting away all the supplies they had gathered. Inside her purse, she found two black t-shirts with 'Sheriff' in big white letters across the front, two pictures of Nathan and Ares standing beside a horse, two pictures of Ares and Nathan playing, and a flash drive with a note. Grabbing the note, she read:

Abigail, the shirts are for you and Brad. Wear them and remember me. I really wanted to stay but—. The picture of me with Ares and the horse is for you and Brad, the one of us playing is for Ashlee and Raymond. I wrote a letter to you and Brad on the flash drive and I have to say I feel honored knowing both of you and calling you friends. I hope 'this' calms down soon because I want all of you to come up here. Who knows, you may like it and stay. I have room. I will do everything in my power to see all of you again.

Love and will always miss all of you (I just have to say WOW)
Nathan Owens
P.S. I have my flip flops

Abigail smiled.

CHAPTER 13

It only took an hour for Nathan and Amanda to reach the Interstate. It was around eight a.m. They dropped their packs and caught their breath. Looking back to the east, they could see the exit to the store and the shanty town but nothing else. Nathan reloaded his magazines he had used as they ate the biscuits, cheese, and bacon Amanda had put in a bag before Nathan started gunning down bangers.

Amanda took a bottle of water from the side of her pack and took a long drink. As she started to put the top back on, Nathan grabbed it, getting a drink. "Hey, you have your own," she said, pointing at the one-liter bottles on each side of his pack.

He shook the half-empty bottle. "When we drink from bottles, we drink from one. They make a lot of noise sloshing around," he said then took another drink. Kneeling down, Nathan cupped his hand and poured water in it, letting Ares drink.

"At least you didn't let him drink out of the bottle. He licks his butt," Amanda said, patting Ares' head.

"I have my limits," Nathan admitted as Ares finished the bottle off. "Remember to keep your bottle unless you get a new one," he said, handing it back to her.

"I remember," she said, putting the empty bottle away. "There are not as many people today," she said, putting on her pack.

"It's early yet," Nathan replied, getting his pack on and stepping onto the highway. "I want you to hold my left hand and if you see something squeeze it. Every five minutes, look behind us and if you see something behind us squeeze my hand twice. Tell me what you see in a calm low voice." He started walking.

She grabbed his hand. "Why?" she asked.

"I'm the one armed, and if they see me focusing in on them they might just shoot. You're a kid and curious so most will ignore it," he told her.

"That's smart and kind of makes sense," she said, nodding.

"Thank you," he told her, glad she was thinking.

After they had walked a little ways, Amanda turned around, looking behind them. "How many were coming for us?" she asked, looking on each side of the road.

"Thirty-three," he replied.

"Thirty-three!" she yelled, stopping in her tracks.

"Remember your voice we don't want to attract attention," he told her, pulling her to get her walking again. "That reminds me. If someone comes up talking don't say anything to them. I may have to lie and I don't want you to mess it up. Just act afraid of them."

"I have the pistol," she said, motioning to the .38 he'd put on the belly strap of her pack.

"Don't call attention to it and remember, if I catch you playing with it I will spank your butt. It's not a toy and the deal will be off. You could kill yourself, me, or Ares," he told her with a serious tone.

"I don't want it then," she said.

"No, if something happens to me you will need it. Just don't play with it. Only pull it out when you need it, and that means when you or me are about to die. It's a tool just like a hammer. A hammer is dangerous if you don't use it correctly."

"Okay," she said, looking up at him, her hat falling off her head. "How many did you kill?" she asked, grabbing her hat and putting it back on.

"Seventeen," he told her.

"You shot seventeen of them," she said in a normal voice.

"No. I shot nineteen; seventeen were dead by the time we reached the end of the field. The other two I'm sure will die but it might take a while," he told her.

"I wish I would've went up with you," she said.

"I wouldn't have shot them then. We only had that one little hole to the ladder for an exit and then both of us would've had to get packs on then get Ares' pack on. The ones left might've caught us then," Nathan said.

"Wow, that is thinking ahead," Amanda smiled. "I'm glad I stayed down then. They should leave us alone now," she said.

"I'm glad too; these biscuits are good," he said, grinning. "There will be others, Amanda, and I'm afraid many others. People who don't know how to take care of themselves are going to try and take. That's why we don't give anything," he told her.

"I understand. I just wish I could help you more," she said, glancing back.

"You are helping and once you learn you will help more," he assured her as they came up to a car parked on the side of the road. He stopped and looked in the back seat and saw a blue expedition backpack. He took out his window punch and popped the back window, shattering it and hearing a gasp from his side. Pulling a crowbar from the bottom of his pack, Nathan cleared the glass and opened the door.

Pulling the pack over, he undid the top and took out a bra. Throwing it down, he looked at the pack and noticed it was a good one. He looked at Amanda and threw the pack back inside and moved on. It was too big for her.

Half a mile further, he stopped at an SUV and looked in. He saw bags in the back and sandals close to Amanda's size. Taking out his punch, he popped the window and raked out the glass with his crowbar again and put it up. Reaching in the back, he started pulling out bags and noticed three were personal baseball equipment bags. He grabbed one and started going through it.

"This is going to take forever if you have to look in each car," Amanda told him, glancing around nervously.

Nathan never stopped his digging. "I'm shopping. The first car I popped had a Junior High School bumper sticker and this one had a sandal that looks like it would fit you in the floor board," he told her.

"If the sandal is on the floor, why are you digging in the bag?" she asked.

"Someone needs clothes and I'm not saying who," he said, pulling out some pants, holding them up then throwing them over his arm. He pulled out another pair along with a t-shirt and a button-down flannel shirt. Digging in another bag, he pulled out some batting gloves. Holding them up, he shook his head and threw them down and grabbed another one. These gloves he kept and closed the door.

He turned to see Amanda looking behind them with her little binoculars. "There is someone back there at the car we just left and he's looking at me with binoculars," she told Nathan before he looked up.

Nathan unzipped her pack and pushed the stuff in and zipped it up. "That's about half a mile away. What do they look like?" he asked.

"It's a boy," Amanda said with certainty, "and he looks really fat," she finished.

Nathan looked up and saw the person as well. He lifted his binoculars and saw it was a fat kid with some truly gigantic binoculars. The kid waved and Nathan dropped his binoculars, letting them hang on his chest. "That's good. Let's go," he said. Amanda grabbed his hand as he started off.

The highway split ahead with a stand of trees growing in the median. Nathan could see people resting on the ground and some under blankets hung up like tents. Getting closer, he noticed they were camped all throughout the trees and he couldn't see the end of the divide. "Keep an eye out," he said in a low voice.

He saw men in tattered business suits, women in dresses that had seen much better days, men and women in casual attire that was filthy, and one man in a speedo. What made it bad was that Speedo didn't have the body to wear it, being two hundred pounds overweight. Nathan gave a shiver and looked ahead.

When they were past Speedy, Amanda asked, "Why do people wear that when they look like that?"

"They think they look good. I'm mad at the companies that make them in those sizes," Nathan said. "Speedos are like spandex: 'It's a privilege, not a right,'" Nathan added, making her giggle.

"That kid is following us. He's further back than he was," she told him.

"He may just be going this way but keep an eye on him," Nathan said.

Just before ten a.m., they saw a group of five men and three women sitting around a small fire. They all appeared middle-aged and looked like hell. Suddenly, one of the men started at them at a fast pace when they were fifty yards away. Amanda squeezed Nathan's hand and Nathan gently squeezed it back. When the man was thirty yards away, Nathan moved his rifle hanging across his chest toward the man and he stopped upon noticing it.

"Please give us some water and food!" he shouted.

Nathan shook his head. "I'm sorry, don't have any to spare," he said, never slowing.

"We're thirsty and hungry," the man said when they were even with him. Ares gave a growl and bared his teeth, making the man back up to the side of the road.

"I'm sorry," Nathan said, never looking away from the man.

"You have water bottles on your packs. Just give us one," he begged.

"We need them," Nathan told him as they passed by.

"You look like the military or police. You have to help us," the man said, moving toward them again.

Nathan let go of Amanda's hand and walked backwards keeping his rifle, aimed at the man. "I'm sorry sir, but you're wrong. I'm just someone who thinks ahead, and if you advance further I will shoot you and you won't have to worry about being hungry or thirsty. At the exit five miles east is a shelter at the school. I suggest you see if they can help," Nathan told the man and continued to walk backwards till they were fifty yards away.

"How do you walk backwards that long?" Amanda asked, grabbing Nathan's hand when he spun back around.

"Train for it," he told her.

"Okay, why would you train for that?" she asked.

"For one, situations just like that. I had two choices. One, keep him covered till we were a safe distance away or kill him. Then if someone is shooting at you, it's not that smart to turn your back and run. One thing I will admit to you, I don't think I can shoot someone unless I know they are a threat. The only way that man was going to be a threat was if I allowed him to get closer," he told Amanda.

"How close till you consider them a threat?" Amanda asked, thinking about what Nathan said.

Shrugging his shoulders, he said, "Each situation is different, but never let anyone get within twenty feet of you."

"Okay, so how far is twenty feet?" Amanda asked.

Pointing to a mile marker, Nathan said "That sign is twenty-five feet away." Then he dropped his hand back to the pistol grip of the M-4.

"What's a meter?" Amanda asked.

Nathan sighed and started teaching distance to Amanda. They walked for half an hour, draining another bottle of water out of Amanda's pack. He put the bottle back and she looked up at him. "Thank you for getting me out of the bushes. Fixing me up and taking me with you and teaching me," she told him.

"You're welcome, but I really wish you would let me take you to Jessie and Renee," he told her.

"They can't keep me safe till I learn how to do it myself. I know you can," she said, and he liked the answer.

"I can't promise I can either. We are starting a twenty-five-hundred-mile-long journey," he told her.

"Where did the extra five hundred miles come from?" Amanda asked, wondering if the United States was getting bigger.

Nathan shrugged his shoulders. "Giving myself leeway. I expect when this is over it will be closer to three thousand," he told her. She didn't say anything as they continued walking, happy that the land wasn't growing. Seeing another exit ahead, Nathan slowed his pace; he didn't notice anyone in the woods bordering the Interstate. He asked Amanda and she agreed. He saw a few people in the median twenty yards ahead but none on the outside woods.

"Come on, let's take a break," Nathan said, leading her to the side of the road and up into the trees. They walked up an embankment then twenty-five yards into the tree line where he dropped his pack, followed by Amanda. He took off Ares' pack and rummaged around till he pulled out the collapsible water bowl. He pulled out a water bottle and filled the bowl up. Ares started lapping up water as he was pouring it in.

"I could've kept going," Amanda told him.

"I'm sure you could've," Nathan said, sitting and looking down at the Interstate.

"When Ares gets finished, let's go," she told him.

"Amanda, your pace was starting to falter. This is a marathon, not a race," he told her. She stayed standing, looking at the road. "What is it?" he asked.

"I don't want you to leave me behind if I slow you down," she told him. Looking at her, Nathan could see her trembling.

"Hey, get over here," he told her, pointing at the ground beside him. She came over and stood beside him. Then, seeing his face, she dropped on her butt; her feet sent her a silent thank you for sitting down. "Didn't I say you're my friend?" he asked.

"Yes," she mumbled.

"That means I won't leave you behind unless you want me to," he told her.

"You wanted me to leave you if you got shot this morning," she whimpered.

Nathan grabbed her face and turned her to look at him. "You couldn't have saved me. There is a big difference," he told her.

She wiped tears off her face, "I know you can go faster without me. I've seen you slow down for me. I promise I will keep walking till I fall down then I'll crawl," she moaned.

"You damn well better not," he snapped, making her jerk back. "If you run yourself down like that it will take a lot of time to get you better to move. I would stay with you and do it but I would be disappointed that you didn't say something," Nathan told her.

"Okay," she said, giving a weak smile and feeling relieved.

"That was a crappy smile," Nathan told her, making Amanda smile bigger. "How much biscuits, cheese, and bacon do we have?" he asked.

"A lot," she said, digging it out of her tote bag.

He lifted up his binoculars and looked at the group on the other side of the highway. It was two men, a woman, and two kids. They were only sixty yards away so he could see them real well. Studying them for a minute, Nathan let the binoculars drop as Amanda handed him some food. They sat eating, drinking, and just relaxing.

"When the woman comes up with the kids, don't say anything," Nathan reminded her as he leaned back on his pack. Ares groaned and lay down and rolled on his back, holding his paws in the air. "Oh, you aren't tired so don't even start," Nathan told him. Ares just snorted at him.

Amanda sat and watched the woman arguing with one of the men through her binoculars and was fixing to ask what Nathan was talking about when the woman walked away from the man. Two kids ran over and followed her across the road. "They're coming," Amanda said, putting down her binoculars.

"I see 'em. Good girl," Nathan said, pulling his rifle across his chest. The woman led the kids up the embankment to them and stopped when she was twenty yards away. *She's smart*, Nathan thought.

"Hello, can we come closer please?" she asked.

"Come on, just keep your hands where we can see them," Nathan called out. She walked toward them at a casual pace and the kids held their hands over their head. *I wonder where they saw that*, Nathan thought as the woman stopped ten feet from them. He looked at the kids. Both were boys, one looked about six, the other eight. "You can put your hands down, boys," Nathan said and they did.

"Sir, my name is—" she started and he held up his hand.

"I don't care what your name is and you don't care what ours are, so let's just dispense with introductions," Nathan interrupted.

"Yes sir," she said. "I wanted to ask you for some food and water. The kids haven't eaten in two days and the last of the water was yesterday," she said. He looked at the mother, putting her around twenty-five; she looked like she had been rode hard and put away wet. Looking at the kids, he saw they didn't look much better. They weren't starving but he could see their eyes were getting a sunken look to them from dehydration.

"What did you and the father fight about before coming up here?" Nathan asked and he saw the shock hit her face; then she regained her composure.

"He wanted me to ask for food and I didn't want to," she told him.

"You're lying," Nathan told her.

"No sir, I'm not," she answered quickly.

Nathan smiled at her. "He wants you to use the kids to get him some food," he told her. "Don't lie again," he said.

She gawked at him in astonishment. "You can read lips?" she asked with her mouth hanging open.

"No, just body language," he said. "He has eaten recently; my guess is this morning. Don't lie again. The evidence is on his shirt," Nathan told her.

The mother looked down. "Yes sir. A man gave me a can of stew and some crackers and Stan ate them," she told him.

"Thank you for being honest. You and the kids, please sit down," Nathan said and she sat down and pulled the kids down next to her. "Amanda, give each one a biscuit with bacon and cheese," Nathan instructed her. "Those are to be eaten here and I mean every last crumb," he said, looking at the mother. With wide eyes, she nodded as she watched Amanda fix the biscuits.

"Where are you coming from?" Nathan asked her.

"Peachtree," she said, watching Amanda's hands with longing.

"Should've stayed," Nathan pointed out. "Where are you going?" he asked.

"Cedar Town. My sister lives there," she answered as Amanda handed over the first biscuit. The mother held out her hands, and as soon as Amanda put it in her hands, the mother gave it to the six year old. Nathan smiled.

He reached back and grabbed his other bottle and held it out. The mother took it and opened it and helped the young one drink. Nathan noted she was being real careful so the young one didn't let it run out the side of his mouth. Amanda fixed the biscuits and laid them out for mother and kids. "Eat and drink slow or it will just come back up," Nathan told them. He looked at Amanda. "Boots off," he told her and turned back to the three.

The mother was pulling the biscuit back from each child, telling them to chew what they had in their mouths. "Boys, listen to your mother and neither one of you get another one till you drink half that bottle in small sips," Nathan told them, leaning his head back. "Ma'am, take a drink," he told the mother.

"Thank you, sir, I'll give mine to the kids," she said, making the kids take small sips.

"That wasn't a request, ma'am," Nathan told her, and she looked up at him and then took a small sip. He saw her gasp when the water hit her parched throat making it hard for her to breathe. "More or you'll get sick, and still in small sips," Nathan said, and she complied. When the bottle was empty, Amanda filled it from her hydration bladder on her pack and gave it back.

Nathan reached in his tote bag and pulled out the small med kit. "Hands," he said, and Amanda moved over and sat down beside him, putting them on his leg. He undid the dressing and noted the cuts were scabbed over but a little red. He cleaned her hands off and put ointment on. "They don't need to be bandaged anymore," he told her and she sighed with relief. "Wear the batting gloves from now on," Nathan said.

He looked at her sitting beside him and noted her boot laces were undone but the boots were still on. "Boots off and let me see your feet," Nathan told her. Amanda let out a long breath and gently pulled her boots off, trying not to cringe. Nathan looked down at her socks that were red with blood; not soaked, but red nonetheless. "Hurt a little, huh," he said to her. Giving a half-smile, Amanda shrugged her shoulders as she extended one foot toward Nathan.

Taking the sock off, Nathan found the dressing was soaked. Shaking his head, he undid the dressing to find all the cuts were open and bleeding. He held her foot under his drinking tube and rinsed her foot off then cleaned it up. Covering her foot in ointment, he put on a new dressing, much tighter this time, and taped it down. Then he repeated the process for the other foot.

"Put on clean socks and pack the dirty ones up. Get your boots back on and lace them tight," he told her and turned back to the mom and kids. Seeing the water bottle was empty, Nathan refilled it and handed it back. The three passed it around, taking long drinks. Then he saw the food Amanda had laid out for them was gone. He grabbed the bag with the biscuits and stuff and pulled out one more apiece for him and Amanda. Handing the bag to the mom, he said, "Fix you and them another one and eat it here in front of me." She took the bag, smiling gratefully, and fixed the kids more. She ate hers in two bites and made the kids drink the last of the water. He refilled the bottle and watched the kids finish off the food.

"You need to get to where you're going quickly. It's only going to get worse for those that are traveling," Nathan told her.

"Stan wants to wait," she said quietly.

"Leave his ass," Nathan said.

"Sir, it's beyond bad now. We've seen five people shot and I don't know how many women attacked."

"Which one has the gun?" Nathan asked her.

She frowned at the question. "The other man, Doug."

"Do you know how to use the gun Doug has?"

"Yes sir, I bought it. They both have records and can't. My boyfriend in high school taught me how to shoot," she explained.

"If you had that gun would you take off, and if threatened, could you use it?" Nathan asked.

She nodded her head vigorously. "Sir, I would use it on Stan and Doug now. That's why they don't let me near it," she told him.

"Drink," Nathan ordered.

She looked at him pleadingly. "Sir, Simon cut his foot two days ago on a piece of glass. Will you look at it please?"

Nathan nodded and the mom took off the older boy's shoe after pulling him over to Nathan. His foot had a piece of shirt tied around it and Nathan took it off. The cut ran the length of his filthy foot and was packed with dirt. "Simon, this is going to hurt but if you don't let me do this your foot will rot off and you'll die," Nathan told him. Tears welled up in Simon's eyes and he nodded.

Nathan cleaned the foot then pulled out a small metal probe and scraped the dirt out of the wound. Simon twitched and moaned but stayed pretty much still, letting Nathan clean the wound out. The wound was red and Nathan knew it would do no good to stitch it up now. "The wound is infected, but if you clean it two times a day with soap and water it should heal. You have to wrap it tight with a bandage after each washing. If he had his school shots and you keep him fed and hydrated he can make it," Nathan told her.

"Don't you have some medicine?" she asked.

"All I can give you is some antibiotic ointment. The rest is up to you," Nathan told her.

"Stan spent all our money," she told him.

"That's on you, not me. You picked Stan so don't expect me to feel guilty," Nathan said.

"Yes sir," she said, looking down guiltily.

"I will get you that gun. Then the rest is up to you. If you want to live, you will leave them and will have a chance. If not, the kids will be dead in a week, you the week after," Nathan told her and tears ran down her face.

Seeing Amanda putting Ares' pack on, Nathan stood up, grabbed his stuff and put it on. The woman held out the bag of food and the empty bottle. Nathan motioned to Amanda to refill the bottle. "Keep the food and start out after I get you the gun. The rest is up to you," Nathan told her, checking his and Amanda's equipment.

The mother nodded and followed them down to the highway. When they reached the road, the two men were standing in the middle of it waiting on them. When Stan saw the bag of food, he yelled, "Give me that damn food," and advanced on the mother. She cringed back from Stan as he got closer.

Nathan took two steps and lashed out with his right foot, hitting the man in the chest and sending him crashing to the pavement, striking his head hard. Nathan spun around, aiming at Doug's chest with his rifle. "Hands up buddy and you might see tomorrow," he told him. Doug trembled as he raised his hands. "With your left hand, grab the pistol and lay it on the road and take four steps back. You know what happens if you try to act stupid," Nathan said. Doug did as Nathan said and stepped back.

"Get the pistol. It's all on you now," Nathan told the mom. She stepped over Stan, who was rolling around on the road, holding his head. Bending over, she picked up the pistol and aimed it at Doug.

"NO!" he screamed as she pulled the trigger. A loud boom erupted as the bullet hit Doug in the chest, sending him to the ground screaming. She turned and walked over to Stan and aimed at his chest as he raised his hands. Another loud boom shattered the quiet as she shot him. He screamed as he rolled on the road. Mom walked over and pulled a wallet from his back pocket and did the same to Doug. Motioning for the kids to follow her, she walked over to the campsite and pulled on a duffel bag and reloaded the pistol. The kids put on backpacks and they stepped up on the road.

"Thank you," she said, looking at Nathan.

"What's your name?" he asked.

"Catherine."

"Catherine, I'm Nathan. You need to hold what you have and don't share unless you have enough. This won't be the last time you're going to have to kill, so just be ready and take care of you and yours. I wish you luck," he told her.

She smiled. "Thank you Nathan, I will," she said, and turned, telling the boys to follow her. Nathan watched them walk away as the two men moaned. Catherine would have many hard trials but she would remember what Nathan had told her. She and her boys would have a chance.

As Catherine and the boys disappeared around a curve, Stan tried to stand and move towards Nathan and Amanda.

"Dude, your best bet is to lay there and die. If I shoot you it's going to be in the legs so the wild dogs can tear you apart," Nathan told him, turning away as Stan fell down. Doug was coughing up blood as they walked past him. Up ahead, a hundred yards from them, a kid was sitting on a blue backpack beside the road.

"That's the kid that was following us," Amanda said, grabbing Nathan's hand.

"It sure looks like it," Nathan said as they walked toward the kid and he put on the pack. "Seems he was waiting on us," Nathan said to himself. As they got closer, Nathan saw it was indeed a kid who was, for lack of a better word, round. Looking at his eyes, Nathan knew he was a teenager, but with the amount of flesh on him that was all Nathan could determine.

When they got closer, the kid held up his hands. "Sir, can I follow you and the girl?" he asked.

Nathan stopped and saw the kid was covered in sweat; it was literally raining off of him in sheets. "We are going that direction and you can follow but not with us," Nathan told him.

"Mister please, I can keep up," he begged Nathan.

"Nice pack," Nathan told him.

"Yes sir, I found it in the car you opened up. Seen you get some stuff out of another one and did what you did," the round kid answered with a chubby smile.

Nathan nodded with approval. "How did you get by all those people back there that wanted food? I want the truth," Nathan told him.

The boy looked down at his feet. "I told them you was my dad and had all the food to make me keep up and wouldn't let me carry any," he said.

Nathan smiled and chuckled. "Now that is thinking, boy, good job," he said with approval.

"Thank you, sir," the boy said, his face lighting up with the compliment.

"Tell you what, you can move with us for a while. If you work out you can stay. If not, you go your merry way," Nathan told him, impressed with the boy's quick thinking and guts. "You do what I say when I say it. That means stop to rest or eat. You do nothing without me telling you," Nathan instructed him.

"Yes sir," he said, smiling and letting out a sigh of relief.

"What's your name?" Nathan asked.

"John," he answered.

"John, this is Amanda. I'm Nathan and the dog is Ares. Don't get near him yet; he doesn't know you," Nathan told him. "I hope you have food."

"Oh yes sir, I have a lot of food for us," John said.

"It's for you. We have our own but you still don't eat until I say and only how much I say, is that clear?" Nathan asked.

"Yes sir," John replied, smiling.

"You will walk on my right side a few feet behind me. If you see something, don't yell, just cough to get my attention and every ten minutes take a look behind us with those huge binoculars," Nathan told him. John nodded and took two steps back, falling into his position.

Nathan smiled and started walking. In the background they could hear the faint moans of the two in the road. When they were a mile away, Amanda doing her look-behind asked, "Are they going to die?"

"Doug is probably already dead. Stan will more than likely die. If he had someone to care for him he might live. It's a lot harder to kill someone than you think," Nathan told her.

She looked up at him with a serious expression on her face. "On TV they shoot them and they die," she said.

"Better storyline. Unless you're the hero you get shot a bunch and end up in the hospital," Nathan said as they continued on. After an hour, he led the two to a spot under some trees to rest. He told John to eat, but just a small snack. Nathan watched John pull out a can of Vienna sausage and a handful of crackers then start eating. Getting up from the rest break, Nathan looked at the map, noting they were just over three miles from the state line.

Motioning for the two to get up, he turned, bringing up his binoculars. Up ahead was a bridge over the Interstate. It wasn't an exit, just an overpass of some little county road. He noted movement under it and something on the shoulder of the road too small to be a car.

Thinking about a car, he looked around on the road, seeing them frozen in their last movements. Some were in the middle of the road but most were pulled over on the shoulder. They had seen so many, the cars just blended into the background now like trees.

When the two came up to him, Ares bounded over, taking the lead. They all laughed as Ares trotted down the road with his tongue hanging out. They fell in behind Ares at a steady pace. When they were four hundred yards from the bridge, Nathan brought up his binoculars, never slowing his pace. Seeing what was ahead, he dropped the binoculars to his chest.

"Amanda, you will not show any fear. Is that understood?" Nathan said sternly.

"What?" she asked with a hint of nervousness in her voice.

"You heard me. If you show fear there is nothing I can do for you," he told Amanda.

"I promise," she replied.

"What color was the shopping cart the man had?" Nathan asked.

"Blue," Amanda answered immediately.

"What color was the dog?" he asked.

"Black and white," she responded.

"There's a blue cart under that bridge and a dog running around that's black and white. If it's him, show no sign of fear or that you know him until I ask, is that clear? But you will not be afraid no matter what," he demanded.

She raised her little binoculars up and gasped, her steps faltering. "It looks like the dog," she said.

"Keep up, you're with me now and answer my question," he said.

"Yes sir, I understand," she said with a quivering voice.

"John don't say or do anything," Nathan commanded over his shoulder. John didn't say anything, wondering what he'd gotten himself into. Nathan walked over to Ares and unclipped his pack and handed it to John, who grunted with the weight, "Carry this," Nathan told him. Nathan reached up and pulled the Velcro tab, uncovering his badge.

When they walked under the bridge, Nathan stopped in the shade. "This is our spot. Go get your own!" a man shouted from next to the abutment under the bridge.

"Taking a break, boy, so shut your fucking mouth!" Nathan shouted, seeing three men sitting under the bridge. He stepped over to the cart, acting like he was looking inside, but was watching the men.

One of them stood up and walked down the easement. "Get the hell away from my cart and get those kids out of here. You can't do nothin', cop," the man sneered. Nathan lifted up his face, looking at the speaker. He was around fifty, wearing an old Army olive-drab field coat; he was around 5'10", a hundred and sixty pounds and filthy as hell.

"Watch your tone with me, boy," Nathan told him as a dog ran down and stood beside the man, barking at Nathan. It was an Australian Shepherd and a nice-sized one. He understood why Amanda would want to pet it; it looked cute but they were not good with strangers.

"I said git," the man said as Nathan circled the buggy, acting like he was looking in it. When the man was four feet away, Nathan jumped forward, lifting his right foot and planting it in his chest. The man shot back from the impact as his dog ran at Nathan; Ares let out a loud series of barks that stopped the dog in its tracks.

Nathan turned to the dog, looking at Ares, and punted it. The dog let out a sharp yelp as it flew through the air. Spinning around, Nathan walked over to the man on the ground; he was holding his chest with one hand as the other hand held him up on his knees. Bringing up his left leg, Nathan stomped the man's face, driving his head into the concrete.

The two men up top stood up and ran down the easement. One pulled a knife; the other pulled out a pipe. Nathan swung up his rifle, sending two bursts and hitting Knife Man in the gut and Mr. Pipe in the left hip. They both fell, screaming and clutching their wounds, and rolled down the slope, stopping at the bottom.

The man's dog had gotten up and was standing about ten feet from Nathan, barking and growling as Nathan squatted down and rolled Green Jacket over, going through his pockets. Lifting his jacket, Nathan pulled out a revolver and threw it over by Amanda, who picked it up and put it in her bag.

Nathan stood back up as the man groaned and put his hand underneath him and pushed up, raising his upper body off the ground. Lifting his foot, Nathan stomped on the man's right humerus, snapping it. The man dropped down on his face screaming. Jumping in the air, Nathan brought one foot down on the man's back, feeling several ribs crack. The man's dog lunged at Nathan and he kicked at it, barely catching it in the chest. The dog yelped and backed off, barking.

"Scooter, get 'em," the man groaned at the dog. The dog came at Nathan and he kicked at it and missed, but Scooter backed away. Nathan stepped back and motioned Amanda and John over.

"Doesn't feel good when someone jumps on your back, does it boy?" Nathan asked the man lying on the ground.

"I ain't hurt you," the man groaned.

"Yes you did, but you didn't know it at the time," Nathan said, and the other two men quieted down, not wanting to draw attention to themselves. "I beg to differ. You recognize the young lady by the big dog?" Nathan asked, and the man looked at Amanda.

"I ain't never seen her before," he coughed, holding his broken arm gingerly as he rolled over and sat up. His nose was crushed and he had to keep spitting out blood. Scooter came over beside him and growled at Nathan.

"I'm sure she looked different when you last saw her. Trying to kill her, taking her food, and making your dog bite her," Nathan said.

"I ain't done no such thing, mister," he spit out with a lot of blood.

"Amanda, describe the necklace the man took from you," Nathan said.

"It was a teddy bear on a gold chain and the teddy bear had diamonds around him with two for his eyes," she said.

"Your crime speaks through your pockets," Nathan said, holding up and displaying the necklace she'd just described.

The man coughed and his eyes got wide. "She was trying to get my stuff; it's mine, I found it," he said.

"So this cart is yours, everything you own?" Nathan asked with sincerity.

"Yes sir," the man said, smiling with blood running down his face.

Looking down in the cart, Nathan saw a pack, clothes, some food and assorted crap. "You hurt a little girl and stole from her for this worthless shit?" Nathan asked.

"It's not worthless, it's all Scooter and I have!" he shouted.

"Oh I'm sorry, sir," Nathan said. Reaching behind him to a pocket on the side of his pack, Nathan pulled out a small bottle of lighter fluid. Flipping the top open, he squirted the liquid over the contents.

"No please, don't! You have her stuff and you hurt me bad. Please just leave," the man begged.

Reaching into his pocket, Nathan pulled out his Zippo. "A little girl asked you the same thing and you sent your dog after her. It bit her and she fought it off and you hurt her again. She ran and you could've stopped again but sent your dog after her again. So please sir, tell me why I should stop?" Nathan asked, striking the lighter across his thigh and holding up the flame. Turning to the cart, he touched the flame to it, setting its contents on fire.

"No!" the man screamed, trying to stand up. Nathan shouldered the rifle and shot the man in his left ankle. He fell down screaming, holding his ankle and writhing around in pain. Nathan looked around and could see people off in the distance watching; the closest was a hundred and fifty yards away.

Turning back to the man, Nathan saw him tying a dirty bandana around his ankle, even using his broken arm. "Pretty good," Nathan said, nodding with approval.

When the man was finished, he looked back at Nathan, crying. Snot was running down his face, mingling with the blood. "Please don't," he begged.

For an instant, Nathan didn't see the man with the green coat. "You could've stayed at the bar; you didn't have to drive home," he said and shook his head and snapped his fingers. Ares trotted over to stand beside him. "Do you like your treatment?" Nathan asked.

"I know I done wrong," the man said.

"But you were laughing, weren't you?" Nathan asked with ice in his voice.

"Yes, but I was wrong!" the man shouted.

Nathan lifted up his hand. "Ares, kill the dog," he snapped, pointing at Scooter.

"NO!" the man screamed as Ares lunged through the air. Scooter may have been big for an Aussie dog at fifty pounds, but Ares was one hundred and twenty pounds of trained muscle.

Scooter, seeing the massive dog flying through the air, tucked his stub of a tail and tried the submissive approach. It didn't matter; the command had been given and Ares put Scooter's entire head in his mouth and clamped down. Scooter yelped as Ares swung his head back and forth, swinging Scooter like a rag until his neck popped.

Ares opened his mouth and dropped Scooter on the ground. He walked back to Nathan and sat down, panting, as the man crawled over to his dog, weeping. "See what doing unkind things to others has cost you?" Nathan asked.

"Damn you to hell, I hope you die!" the man yelled, reaching out and stroking his dead dog.

Amanda walked over to stand beside Ares. "I would've shared my food with you. I just wanted to see your dog. Now look at your stupid dog," she said.

The man rolled over and looked her. "I should've killed you!" he shouted.

"You're right, you should've, but I got away. I have a dog now and it's better than your stupid dog. You've seen Ares knows how to kill, but he can do something else," Amanda said. The man's eyes got wide as she raised her arm. "Ares, get 'em'!" she shouted and Ares leapt forward.

The man raised his hands, seeing nothing but an open mouth with big white teeth coming at him. Ares latched onto his broken arm and started to violently shake his head back and forth, dragging the man around.

"Ares, here!" Amanda yelled out in her tiny voice and Ares let the man go and went and stood beside her.

Amanda stroked Ares' back while looking at the crying man. "Look at me!" she yelled and the man looked up. "I'm not scared of you. My name is Amanda. Amanda Sterling, and I'm not running away from you this time. I choose to leave while you die." She turned around. "Ares, come," she said and walked off.

Nathan smiled at her then walked over to the man and kneeled down. "Your choice led you here. You're not in danger of dying now," Nathan told him, seeing the relief grow on the man's face. Nathan grabbed his pistol and rammed it into the man's gut and pulled the trigger. The muffled shot startled Amanda, causing her to turn around.

Nathan stood up. "Now you will die but it should take a while," he said, turning away.

One of the men who'd been shot called out, "If we'd known he did that to the girl we wouldn't have helped him," he said.

"Guess in the next life you need to choose your friends a little wiser," Nathan said. "You're just like some judges I know; letting killers walk and wondering why people want to attack you," Nathan said as he left. John stared at the men groaning and then trotted off after Nathan and Amanda.

When John came up beside Nathan, Nathan reached down and grabbed Ares' pack. "Still want to stay with us?" he asked.

"Are you kidding? Tell me what I have to do to stay," John almost shouted as they caught up to Amanda. She was walking with her hand on Ares' back, still petting him with a broad smile on her face.

They walked for an hour, passing the Georgia welcoming center as they came to the state line. Leaving Georgia behind, Nathan adjusted his watch and looked around at all the people on the road in the eastbound lane. There were not many people behind them; most had stopped, letting the three get ahead of them after seeing what was happening under the bridge.

They had not even walked a thousand yards into Alabama when Nathan turned north off the Interstate where a small creek ran under it. "Come on, we aren't walking the Interstate anymore," he said as he crossed the ditch.

"You said we had to go ten miles into Alabama before we got off the Interstate," Amanda said, following him into the woods.

"I don't have the ammo to stay on the Interstate," Nathan admitted to her. He followed the creek through the woods. At a little clearing beside the creek, he stopped and looked around at the forest; after a moment, he dropped Ares' pack and then his.

Amanda and John saw Nathan drop his pack and did the same as Nathan pulled out his computer and turned it on. "We are about half a mile from the Interstate so we should be okay," he said.

"We're camping here?" Amanda asked.

"Yes," Nathan said.

"That means we only went like twelve and a half miles," she said. Then she looked at her watch. "We still have like four or five hours till dark."

"Amanda, take your blankets out and get your boots off," Nathan ordered and she whined but did as he said.

Nathan walked over to the creek and saw a small sand bar that led down to the water. There were a shit load of animal tracks showing this was a crossing spot. He looked at John, who was sitting down, leaning back against his pack. "John, let me see your pack," Nathan said, kneeling down.

John carried the pack over and sat it down, then kneeled down beside Nathan. Opening the pack, Nathan saw several plastic bags full of food. *Those weren't there when I first looked in it*, he thought, taking them out, impressed with the weight. "Where did you get the food?" Nathan asked.

"I got most from the first center I was at. Then I stopped at every place I could and most had shelters set up, so I got more," he told Nathan.

"You haven't eaten a lot," Nathan said, more to himself than John.

"No sir, I've only been eating three things a day; small meals," John told him.

"Where's your family?" Nathan asked.

"My mom's dead and my sister is off at college in California. I haven't seen my dad since I was three," John answered.

"You sure your mother is dead?" Nathan asked gently.

"I ran home from school to find the house on fire. My neighbor said my mom had run in to bring out more stuff. He tried to stop me but I ran inside and found her on the floor in the living room on fire. I couldn't get close and the neighbor pulled me back. I saw in the yard some stuff she had pulled out. Nothing but crap like chairs and the TV," John said, wiping his eyes.

"Any other family close?" Nathan asked, feeling very sorry for the kid.

"No sir, we moved here from Cleveland four years ago and that's where the rest of the family is at," he answered.

"We will get you to a rescue center and get you sent to them," Nathan said, pulling out more stuff.

"No thank you, sir," John said. "I went to one the first night and it was okay but the second day some mean people started showing up. I saw a few guys stabbed and two women that were being held down and having guys do stuff to them. One of the guys looked at me and said I had a nice butt so I grabbed my bag and headed to the kitchen. I grabbed some stuff and a man saw me. I told him I was going to a cousin's house in the country but it was fifty miles away. He helped me fill my bag and wished me luck."

"And you wanted to send me to one of those places?" Amanda shot at Nathan.

"Drop it," Nathan said over his shoulder. "What about the rest of your family? Don't you want to see them?" Nathan asked.

"Maybe my sister, but sir, I'm not stupid. I was just outside of Atlanta and I know Cleveland is a thousand times worse. My best bet is stay with you two and hope in a few years I can find my sister," he told Nathan.

Nathan nodded; the boy had a plan. "Okay, here is what you have to do now," Nathan said, handing him a pile of stuff. "Go to the creek and bathe. Then wash your clothes, and I mean scrub them. Wrap the towel around you so I can inspect you. Just to let you know I'm also a nurse." Nathan looked back down at the stuff he'd pulled out.

"You mean in that water?" John said, pointing at the creek.

"Unless you see another way to bathe, yes," Nathan said. "Did you even check this pack before putting it on?" he asked.

"No sir, I figured I could do that later. I didn't want you to get too far ahead of me," he answered.

"You were carrying ten pounds of female clothes for no reason," Nathan said, holding up a pair of black lace skimpy panties and a bra. "These will not fit you," Nathan told John with a tight little grin.

"I can wear them," Amanda snapped.

"Amanda, you are a little girl. You saying that sends shivers down my spine and puts images I don't want in my mind," Nathan told her.

"I'm thirteen and a girl," she popped off.

"Check the attitude," Nathan warned her. Amanda stuck her nose in the air and snorted at him, crossing her arms over her chest. "John, go do what I said," Nathan said, and reluctantly John stood up and headed to the creek. When he peeled off his gray sweatpants, Nathan noted the discoloration on his lower legs. He looked at Amanda. "Turn your head," he told her quietly; John was twenty yards away.

She turned around on her blanket. "What's wrong with his legs?" she whispered.

"That's from poor blood flow from being overweight," Nathan told her.

"Is he going to be okay?" she asked.

"It all depends on him," Nathan told her, still digging through the stuff in John's pack. He held up some feminine supplies. "Have you started your cycles?" Nathan asked Amanda.

"Cycles of what?" she asked, clueless.

"Never mind. They'll make good bandages," Nathan, said throwing them down. Then he held up a real camp stove with a high pressure bottle. "This is totally unnecessary," he said.

"That's a stove!" Amanda said, looking at it.

"Yeah, one made for high altitude hiking. I still prefer my fuel tabs. If I have to carry the oxygen to burn, I'm not going that high up," Nathan said throwing the stove down.

"What's that?" she asked pointing at a large silver bag.

"It's a camping shower," he told her.

"Cool," Amanda said as Ares came over to her. She wrapped her arms around his neck. "I love you, Ares," she said, squeezing him tight. Ares looked at her and started licking her face. "Eww," she said, trying to move away. Ares pushed her down and started licking everywhere and nibbling on her neck. "Help, Nathan!" Amanda cried out, giggling, curling up in a ball.

"Nah, that one is on you," Nathan said laughing. Ares looked up at him with his tongue hanging out, panting. "What? You try that on me and I'll throw away the woobie," Nathan threatened.

"No he won't," Amanda said, raising her head up. Ares started on her again.

Nathan got up and strung up a clothes line as John walked over to him, carrying his wet stuff. Nathan hung it up and looked over John. The skin folds around his body were red and inflamed. The ones under his pecs were the worst. Nathan walked over to his pack then John's pack and came back.

"John, those red areas in your skin folds is a yeast infection and a bad one. You will bathe every day, and during the day wipe them out. You want to keep them dry. Here is some antifungal cream. Just a little dab on each area at night; this is all we have so use it sparingly," Nathan told him. "This is foot powder. I want you to put it in all the places it's red. If you do what I tell you, it will go away. If not, it will get infected and move into your body and kill you." Nathan handed over the supplies.

"Yes sir," John said with quivering lips.

"Grab that blanket on your pack to wrap around you and move over to my pack," Nathan said, then walked over and sat down on his poncho liner. John came over and Amanda saw Nathan motioning her to join them. She walked over with her hair sticking up in spikes and covered in dog slobber.

Nathan held up his rifle. "This is an M-4. It has a fourteen-inch barrel and a collapsible stock," he said, pointing them out. "This is how it works," he said, taking it apart.

As Nathan sat and taught them about the M-4, he realized they had a lot to learn in the days to come and it was his responsibility. Watching the two study his hands as he took the M-4 apart, Nathan smiled. They had the intelligence, heart and will; he only hoped they had the strength to live and survive in this new world.

ABOUT THE AUTHOR

Thomas A. Watson lives in Northwestern Montana, but grew up in Doyline, Louisiana and Grenada, Mississippi. He moved to Shreveport, Louisiana to start a family. He graduated from Northwestern University with a Bachelors in Science. Watson's love of reading, which was instilled in him at a young age by his parents, inspired him to begin his writing career.

Working currently as an RN in an emergency room in Missoula, Watson loves the outdoors and taking time off of work.

ACKNOWLEDGMENTS

Thank you to my readers. To all those who provided support, read, wrote and offered comments. I would not be where I am today without all of you.

To my family: Thank you all for giving me the courage and strength to pursue my dreams. I love you very much. Nick, Khristian, and Phillip, you three make my days brighter.

To Monique Happy: Thank you. You have been a pleasure to work with, and your work is amazing. Thanks for the recommendation, Shawn Chesser, she truly is the best.

And finally to my wife, Tina. Thank you for putting up with me and keeping my side of the bed warm on the long nights I was clicking away at the keyboard, for all your insightful input, and for just being there for me. I would have never made it this far without all your help and encouragement.

The Worlds of Thomas A. Watson

Thomas A. Watson has created an exciting and often terrifying array of worlds, including *The Blue Plague* series and *Dark Titan: Journey,* both available from Winlock Press.

The Blue Plague series

The Fall
Survival
Sacrifice
Rage
Decisions
War

The Dark Titan: Journey series

Sanctioned Catastrophe
Wilderness Travel
Finally Home

. . .and you can stay in touch with Thomas and all his work on
Facebook at www.Facebook.com/ThomasAWatson
and
Twitter @1BluePlague

PERMUTED PRESS

needs **you** to help

SPREAD (THE) INFECTION

FOLLOW US!

f | Facebook.com/PermutedPress

🐦 | Twitter.com/PermutedPress

REVIEW US!

Wherever you buy our book, they can be reviewed! We want to know what you like!

GET INFECTED!

Sign up for our mailing list at PermutedPress.com

PERMUTED
PRESS

14

Peter Clines

Padlocked doors.
Strange light fixtures. Mutant
cockroaches.

There are some odd things about
Nate's new apartment. Every
room in this old brownstone has
a mystery. Mysteries that stretch
back over a hundred years.
Some of them are in plain sight.
Some are behind locked doors.
And all together these mysteries
could mean the end of Nate and
his friends.

Or the end of everything...

PERMUTED
PRESS

THE JOURNAL SERIES
by Deborah D. Moore

After a major crisis rocks the nation, all supply lines are shut down. In the remote Upper Peninsula of Michigan, the small town of Moose Creek and its residents are devastated when they lose power in the middle of a brutal winter, and must struggle alone with one calamity after another.

The Journal series takes the reader head first into the fury that only Mother Nature can dish out.

Michael Clary
THE GUARDIAN | THE REGULATORS | BROKEN

When the dead rise up and take over the city, the Government is forced to close off the borders and abandon the remaining survivors. Fortunately for them, a hero is about to be chosen...a Guardian that will rise up from the ashes to fight against the dead. The series continues with Book Four: *Scratch*.

Emily Goodwin
CONTAGIOUS | DEATHLY CONTAGIOUS

During the Second Great Depression, twenty-four-year-old Orissa Penwell is forced to drop out of college when she is no longer able to pay for classes. Down on her luck, Orissa doesn't think she can sink any lower. She couldn't be more wrong. A virus breaks out across the country, leaving those that are infected crazed, aggressive and very hungry. `

The saga continues in Book Three: *Contagious Chaos* and Book Four: *The Truth is Contagious*.

PERMUTED
PRESS

A PREPPER'S COOKBOOK

20 Years of Cooking in the Woods

by Deborah D. Moore

In the event of a disaster, it isn't enough to have food. You also have to know what to do with it.

Deborah D. Moore, author of *The Journal* series and a passionate Prepper for over twenty years, gives you step-by-step instructions on making delicious meals from the emergency pantry.

PERMUTED
PRESS